From "the dirty" I didn't write those. Rob

PALM AVENUE

Rob Neighbors

"There is a need for aloneness, which I don't think most people realize for an actor. It's almost having certain kinds of secrets for yourself that you'll let the whole world in on only for a moment when you're acting. But everybody is always tugging at you. They'd all like sort of a chunk of you" – **Marilyn Monroe**

One

Three attractive young ladies sat in plush velvet chairs in the lobby area of a darkened five star restaurant high on the infamous Sunset Strip. It was two hours before the dinner rush. Afternoon sunlight spilled in through the blinds and created prisms of light across the floor. The elaborate granite bar sat vacant of customers but its shelves were stocked with the finest top shelf liquor. Two men sat at a large burgundy colored velvet booth in the back of the restaurant interviewing a forth young lady.

One of the women, a pretty African American, wore a blonde wig and squinted as she tried to fill out a job application on a clipboard. A tall leggy brunette wearing a mini skirt and thigh high boots talked into her cell phone. The third young lady, Ashley Duncan sat quietly clutching her resume and job application.

There was something different about Ashley from the other two. She was blonde, strikingly attractive, but in an all American girl next door kind of way. She looked eager, anxious, yet hopeful and optimistic. She wore a navy blue skirt, matching top with panty hose and had her hair pulled back into a ponytail and wore little makeup, unlike the other two girls.

"Don't tell me you went home with that dude? Isn't he a coke dealer?" the leggy brunette with artificially plumped lips said into her cell phone, giggling and glancing at Ashley and the other girl, who looked up from her application.

"Are you going out tonight? I hear that the Avalon is off the hook on Tuesdays," the brunette said into her phone.

The black girl looked over at Ashley.

"Where did you park? I gotta' go put more money in the meter if we have to wait much longer," the black girl said.

"I walked here. I live just down the street on Palm Avenue," Ashley said.

"Sweet. How long you lived there?" the black girl asked.

"I just moved here a couple of weeks ago from Kansas. I'm still settling in. I heard about this job and I thought it would be perfect since I live so close," Ashley said in her perky Kansas voice.

"Kansas, huh? You a long ways from home," the black girl said giggling, looking Ashley up and down, and judging every inch of her. Ashley fidgeted a little, but smiled politely.

"Hey, I'll call you later. I'm at this new club, Kraven trying to a get job. Bye," the slender brunette said into her phone and then put it away. She looked at Ashley and couldn't contain a jaded grin.

"Did I hear you say you are from Kansas?" the brunette asked.

"Yes," Ashley answered.

"And I suppose you are an actress?" the brunette said.

"I'm trying," Ashley answered a bit defensively. The brunette and black girl both shared a laugh. Ashley's face turned a little pink.

The girl who was being interviewed walked past the other three women. She was a little overweight, wore a tight skirt and had full sleeve tattoos on both arms. She shot the other three girls a haughty look as she walked by and out the front door into the glaring sunlight of Sunset Boulevard.

"*Baby's got back*," the black girl said, prompting a cold laugh from the brunette.

One of the men conducting the interviews was a quintessential California blonde sliding into his thirties, and wore a white shirt unbuttoned one button down too far. He walked into the lobby area and looked at a sign-in sheet.

"Tonisha?" the guy called out.

The black girl stood quickly, dropping her phone from her lap, and she then scrambled to scoop it up off of the floor. She recovered and followed the guy back to the booth where the other man was sitting smoking a cigarette. The brunette rolled her eyes.

As soon as the black girl was out of earshot, the brunette leaned toward Ashley.

"She doesn't stand a chance," the brunette said.

"Why?" Ashley asked.

"C'mon. They don't hire black chicks. Not like her. Even her name is Ghetto. You want a job like this in Hollywood - you had better look like Beyonce. This is the hottest club in Hollywood right now. They only hire the cream of the crop. Most girls would kill someone or suck the manager's cock to get a job here. You'll find out soon enough," the brunette said to Ashley.

Ashley contemplated it a moment, and then stood. "Excuse me," she said, and then walked toward the restroom. The brunette took out her phone and started dialing a number, as if she couldn't stand one moment with her own thoughts.

Ashley stepped into the dark restroom and turned on the light. It was the most ornate restroom she had ever seen. Purple velvet curtains hung over the stalls. The sinks and floors were covered with polished burgundy colored granite. Ashley stepped in front of the huge gold trimmed mirror and looked at herself. She realized that she *was* a long way from home. She almost had to pinch herself to see if she wasn't dreaming: That she was actually in Hollywood, at the Sunset Strip's hottest nightclub Du Jour, applying for her first job in Los Angeles. What the brunette said had rattled her, and she suddenly realized that she would have to take a different approach to make it in the big city. She took a long look at herself in the mirror, and then she reached back and undid her pony tail, letting her blond locks fall down onto her shoulders. She took out some lip stick from her purse and brightened her lips. She smiled to herself admiring her perfect white teeth and then she did one last thing – she unbuttoned the top button of her blouse and let a little cleavage show. If one word could be used to describe her, it would be "wow". It was a subtle, yet immediate transformation.

When Ashley walked out of the restroom, Tonisha, the African American girl was on her way out the front door. Another new girl was sitting next to the brunette. The blonde guy was staring at the sign-in sheet.

"Ashley?" he said. Ashley smiled at him and followed him back to the booth where the other man was seated.

The brunette noticed that Ashley had let her hair down and it occurred to her that she might actually have some competition. The new girl sitting next to the brunette was a bleached blond with huge fake tits and crooked teeth. "What is she wearing? She looks like she's on her way to Church," the blonde whispered to the brunette. They both shared a laugh.

"She's from Nebraska or somewhere," the brunette said.

Ashley walked back to the booth where the general manager, Jean Pierre, a wiry middle aged French man sat smoking a cigarette. He stood quickly upon seeing Ashley and took her hand.

"Hello, I am Jean Pierre, the general manager of Kraven, and this is Kurt, my bar manager," he said in a thick French accent and motioned Ashley to sit. Ashley took a seat and Kurt took a seat next to Jean Pierre across from her. Ashley handed him her resume and he sucked on his cigarette looking at it. Smoke billowed around his head.

"You're from Kansas?" Jean Pierre said glancing at her.

"Yes, I have been in town two weeks," Ashley said.

"Two weeks! So, you are fresh off of the boat, as they say" Jean Pierre said laughing and Kurt laughed with him. Ashley let out a little laugh.

"Yes, I guess you could say that. "I'm not in Kansas anymore", Ashley said in a falsetto voice mimicking Dorothy and they all shared a laugh.

"So, you are an actress?" Jean Pierre asked.

"I'm going to give it my best shot," Ashley answered.

Jean Pierre glanced at Kurt and grinned, then took a sip from a glass of Chardonnay.

"We have many celebrities; VIP's who come in here. You have to be discreet. You have to have tact, shall we say. You can't be ogling them asking for their autographs like some giddy tourist. Do you understand what I'm saying? You can't go running to the tabloids with information about what goes on in here" Jean Pierre said.

"Oh, of course not," Ashley said.

"Tonight for instance, Jack Wrangler is coming in here with his whole entourage and he doesn't like to be bothered by gawkers, do you understand what I'm saying?" Jean Pierre said.

"He's a major dick," Kurt chimed in. Jean Pierre shot Kurt an irritated glance.

"I understand exactly what you are saying, sir." Ashley said.

"You are a very pretty girl. You must know that right?" Jean Pierre said, placing his hand on top of Ashley's.

"Thank you, I appreciate that" Ashley said, with a little twinkle in her eye. Jean Pierre removed his hand.

"We just need to teach you how to dress," Jean Pierre said.

Ashley suddenly felt hot with embarrassment and realized that she didn't know how to dress for a job like this and didn't have many other nice clothes to choose from. She suddenly felt like the biggest hayseed in Hollywood.

"So, tell me why, Dorothy, I mean Ashley, should I hire you at Kraven? Why you from hundreds of other beautiful girls who have way more experience at nightclubs?" Jean Pierre said and then stared at her, stone faced. Kurt sat with his arms folded, also scrutinizing her.

Ashley now sweating, was flustered from the remark about her choice of clothes, but she wasn't about to give in and accept defeat. This was her very first "audition" in Hollywood and she had to nail it. This was her first big moment. She drew a deep breath, and then sat taller in her seat, looking Jean Pierre directly in the eye.

"Well, sir. I'm a hard worker. I grew up on a farm and have worked hard my whole life. I know the value of a dollar. I'm honest and loyal to a fault. I'm friendly and very good with people. I think well on my feet and I show up on time - early even. I live just around the corner on Palm Avenue within walking distance. I don't call in sick and I'm not a drama queen. I'm here in Los Angeles to be an actress its true, but when I'm here I'll be a hostess. I promise you that if you give me this opportunity, I will be the best damn hostess you have ever had," Ashley said.

There was a long moment of silence as Jean Pierre and Kurt sat studying Ashley. Ashley did not lose her composure.

"These qualities – honesty, loyalty – shall we say they might not be your best assets here in Hollywood, Ashley, but I like your style. There is something refreshing, something, something alluring about you. I can't put my finger on it," Jean Pierre said and then let out a big laugh. Kurt also let out a nervous laugh and Ashley smiled, knowing that she had them.

Jean Pierre took a long drag off his cigarette and stared at Ashley, looking straight into her eyes.

"Can you start tonight?" he asked.

Ashley smiled a broad smile. "Yes, sir," she said.

Both the brunette and the blonde were talking on their cell phones when Kurt walked back into the lobby area. Both girls quickly put their phones away when they saw Kurt standing there.

"You can go. The position has been filled," Kurt said, relishing the slight bit of power he was exercising over them.

"What?" the brunette stammered, looking towards Ashley who was still in the back with Jean Pierre.

"I said you can go. The job's been filled," Kurt said again, waving his hand dismissively.

The blonde stood looking defeated. The brunette stood, stunned that she was being kicked out without even an interview. The brunette was craning her neck back toward Ashley as she walked out.

"Fuck me," the brunette mumbled as she stepped out into the bright sunlight glaring off of Sunset Boulevard.

Two

A walk-in closet was packed to capacity with designer gowns, coats, shoe boxes and a collection of shoes and boots that would rival any in Beverly Hills. Designer names and logos populating the boxes and purses the closet spoke volumes – Chistian Louboutin, Kate spade, Michael Kors, Burberry, Louis Vuitton, Gucci, among others.

Jillian was standing in the middle of the closet wearing only panties and a bra. She was a tall, pasty skinned former fashion model with long strawberry blonde hair. She was 37 years old and she had traded on her looks her entire life. She had once been strikingly attractive, but recent years had not been good to her. Her face looked gaunt and dark circles formed under her eyes. She was abnormally thin, and out of shape and soft in all the wrong places.

She lingered in the closet, looking through her rack of clothes, pulling the dry cleaner's plastic back to get a better look at a Vera Wang gown. She wondered how much money she could get for it on Ebay. She wondered how to post things for sale on Ebay. It pained her to think about it, because she had no idea, and barely even knew how to send out an email. Somebody had told her that was what she should do – sell things on Ebay. The internet technology age had been going on for nearly fifteen years and Jillian was not yet with the program.

Inside she was churning with terror. She had traveled the world for a time living the glamorous, decadent life of a model. That short period of time when she was a model created an expectation in her mind that was not very much in tune with reality. She had developed a sense of entitlement that was far beyond what her value in the world actually rated. She was really just another long legged beautiful girl that was a commodity to be bought, sold, traded, and discarded. When she finally understood that, it killed her a little bit inside. It was certainly killing her now as each new line formed on her face.

Jillian wanted to blame someone for her discontent and she guessed it was men. Men ran the fashion and advertising industry. Jillian hated them for "using" her the way they did. So she set out to use and destroy as many men as she could, and she had been successful many times. Trading on her looks, she roped in millionaire after millionaire. Benefactors for her champagne dreams and caviar wishes. She had to trade sex for these goodies, but she was a master of keeping men on a string, and gave them the least sex possible in trade for their financial support. She wondered if she had ever really been in love and she decided she hadn't. Maybe once, ages ago…

She continued looking through the clothes. She knew she had paid in flesh for each item in that closet. It killed her that she should have to sell anything. She started yanking various items off the rack and throwing them on the floor. She tried to remember where she had bought each item – and who had bought them for her: The Vera Wang gown, the Gucci Dress, the coat from Michael Kors.

She kicked a pair of Christian Louboutin stiletto heels on the floor and she choked back her tears. She continued her temper tantrum and kicked all of the shoes at the bottom of the closet from their neatly arranged spaces. She had never been so desperate. She was furious that she should have to sell any of her prized possessions. What would she get for them – pennies on the dollar? She began yanking boxes from the top shelf and throwing them against the wall of the closet. Soon the space looked like a hurricane had gone through it.

She came upon the box she was looking for - a box from the gun manufacturer, Smith and Wesson. The tears finally came. She was sobbing when she opened the box and saw the Smith and Wesson Model 442 Lady snubnose revolver with pink grips. One of her ex boyfriends had bought it for her and she had fired it once out in the desert. She took it out of its box and fumbled with it trying to open its cylinder. It finally popped open and exposed five shells inside it. Jillian's tears fell down upon the revolver as she snapped it shut.

She slumped on the floor among the mess of designer clothes she had created. She clutched the gun and sobbed. Suicide seemed like a real option frequently to her lately. She could just point the gun at her heart and pull the trigger. That way she would not have to sell one thing on Ebay. She would not have to fuck one more man that she didn't want to fuck. She was 60 days behind on her rent, and just as many on her car payments. Credit card bills were piling up every day. The only knight in shining armor on the horizon was a 55 year old classless contractor she was supposed to meet later that night.

She pointed the gun beneath her breast and closed her eyes tightly. She started applying pressure on the trigger when her phone began ringing in the other room. She opened her eyes and listened as the phone kept ringing. She suddenly shot up and out of the closet and hurried to answer the phone, still clutching the revolver.

She ran out into her cluttered bedroom and grabbed the phone on the fifth ring. "Hello," Jillian said breathlessly with the revolver hanging loosely in her free hand.

"What are you doing?" said the voice on the other end. It was Chloe, Jillian's best friend, to the extent she was capable of having a friend. Chloe was calling from her car driving down Melrose Boulevard. Jillian sank disappointed into a chair in front of her vanity mirror. "Nothing," Jillian finally answered, staring down at the gun, then to her face puffy from crying in the mirror. She could see her unmade bed behind her in the reflection and the collection of empty wine bottles on the nightstand.

"Are we still meeting at Kraven later?" Chloe asked.

"Oh, yeah. Yes. Fuck... I'm supposed to meet some douche there," Jillian said.

"The contractor?"

"Yeah. I think he's worth *something*. He belongs to the Riviera Country Club, you know" Jillian said, rubbing the barrel of the gun down her bare thigh.

"What about the bartender? What's his name – Kurt?" Chloe asked.

"What about him? He's not paying my bills." Jillian said with a hint of irritation.

"Well, it's just kind of awkward, I mean, if we're going there, and the bartender is working…" Chloe said.

"He knows what the deal with me is," Jillian said, cutting her off.

"Cool. I'll meet you there, say ninenish? Fucking asshole, get out of the way!" Chloe laid on her horn and swerved around a beat up pickup truck full of landscaping equipment.

Jillian looked at herself in her vanity mirror and pointed the gun at her own reflection squinting. "I gotta' go. See you later, ok?" Jillian said

"Are you all right? You seem distracted." Chloe said.

"I'm ok. I'm fine," Jillian said. They said their goodbyes and Jillian hung the phone up. After a moment, she walked back into the walk-in closet with the revolver dangling in her fingertips.

  Chloe continued driving her BMW in heavy traffic westbound on Melrose. She was an ambitious pharmaceutical representative, and was the epitome of a successful self made woman. She was a closeted lesbian and was slightly butch, but attractive and feminine enough to turn men's heads. She was petite with dirty blonde, short cropped hair, a shapely little ass and sexy green eyes that all the doctors that she called on noticed.

She wondered why she even bothered maintaining the friendship with Jillian. Chloe knew what had attracted her to Jillian in the beginning. Jillian was certainly her type: Tall, leggy, beautiful and straight. But Jillian was a hard person to like. She was self absorbed to the tenth degree and everything was about *her*.

Chloe detested most lesbians, however, especially the bull dykes. She loved the thrill of the chase, and that meant chasing straight women. Chloe and Jillian had started out as friends, but Chloe eventually ended up seducing her. They had sex only once and it had been volcanic, but Jillian was disgusted with herself for it. Not because she had any moral qualms, but more because she had been momentarily vulnerable with another woman. They continued on with their friendship after the incident and neither of them ever mentioned it again.

Chloe knew she was one of the few women that Jillian had ever befriended. Probably because she wasn't threatened by her, as she was not competing against her for men. Chloe wondered if the "friendship" had run its course. Jillian certainly wasn't giving it much effort.

Chloe stopped at a stoplight, watched an attractive teenage girl walking across the street. She smiled at the girl and the girl gave her a little smile back. Chloe checked out the girl's ass until someone behind her honked. She shot the person the finger and zoomed off.

Three

A young man quickly pulled clothing items out of a drawer in his room in a rented house just off campus in Lawrence, Kansas, at the University of Kansas. A snowy landscape was visible outside the window in mid November. The young college student, Brady Anderson, handsome, athletic, and all American stuffed the clothes into a large suitcase he had laid out on top of the bed. He stuffed the suitcase and struggled to zip the bulging bag. He looked at a photo on top of the dresser. It was of he and Ashley at a ski resort, smiling for the camera with bright sunlight in their faces. Brady stared at the photo a moment, then grabbed it and stuffed it into a side pocket of the suitcase.

He looked around the room, and checked the closet. He put on a winter coat and then yanked the suitcase off of the bed, extended its pull along handle and started out of the room. He hurried into the cluttered living room he shared with two other students. He was in a hurry to get out of the house before they came home. He took one look around the room and walked out locking the door behind him.

There were two inches of fresh snow on the ground from the night before and steam rose off of the sidewalk that was wet with melted snow. He threw the suitcase into the back of the pickup parked in the driveway. Just as he was doing that, a car pulled into the driveway. It was his roommate, Dave. Dave stared at him through the window a moment, and then got out of the car.

Brady looked like he had been caught doing something. Dave looked at the suitcase in the back of the truck.

"Hey, Brady. What's up?" Dave said.

"Not much," said Brady, obviously irritated.

"Going somewhere?" Dave asked.

"Yeah. I'm going to be gone awhile," Brady answered.

"In the middle of the semester? Where are you going?" Dave asked.

"LA," Brady said.

Dave shook his head in disbelief.

"You've got to be shitting me," Dave said.

"I don't expect you to get it, Dave," Brady said.

"Are you coming back?" Dave asked.

"I don't know. I've gotta' go now or I'll miss my flight," Brady said.

"Jesus," Dave said.

Brady jumped into his truck and backed out of the driveway as Dave watched him.

Brady drove toward the University where he could catch a shuttle to the airport. He was a third year pre-veterinary student at the university, and he was leaving in the middle of the semester to go after his high school sweetheart, Ashley Duncan. She had recently broken up with him when she left to Los Angeles to pursue her Hollywood dream.

Brady was sick about it and hadn't been able to sleep for over two weeks. He had lost his appetite, and was extremely heart broken. Like Ashley, he was born and raised in the small town of Colby, Kansas. They had gone to school together and been the homecoming king and queen. His dad, Henry was the much loved town veterinarian, who had taken care of people's pets and farm animals for the last 30 years. Brady worshiped his father and naturally wanted to take over his veterinary practice.

Brady was now running away from all of that. It was a spur of the moment decision. His family, his friends, or his instructors at the University didn't know that Brady was on his way to Los Angeles. Brady knew it was such a crazy idea that nobody he knew would understand. His dad would surely be upset when he found out. His mom would be devastated and worried. His friends, like his roommate Dave, would think he was a fool.

When Ashley broke up with him and left for LA, they all had told him to let her go. They all said terrible things about her – how she was selfish and delusional. She was never going to make it out there. Her own dad was so mad at Ashley for leaving that he wasn't speaking to her. Brady was mad at her too, more hurt than mad, for her abandoning him, but he didn't follow everybody else's line of thinking. He actually believed that she *was* doing the right thing by following her dream in Hollywood, and that she *did* have what it took to be a movie star.

Brady drove into the University shuttle parking lot and parked his truck, not knowing when he would be back for it. He grabbed his suitcase from the back of the truck and climbed into a waiting shuttle with two other students enroute to the Kansas City International airport to catch a flight to Los Angeles.

The shuttle finally departed and Brady watched hordes of students walking toward the snowy university carrying their books as the shuttle bus was moving in the opposite direction. The students were all bundled up and Brady could see their breath in the frigid air, and knew that within hours he would be in sunny Los Angeles, which seemed like a million miles away from where he sat. He knew one thing - he loved Ashley more than oxygen and he would follow her to the end of the earth if he had to. If she wanted to live in Los Angeles, he would learn to like it there. The shuttle bus rattled across the Kansas River out of Lawrence onto the I-70 heading toward Kansas City and the airport. Brady watched the University town disappear into the background.

The driver played a tinny sounding Am radio as the shuttle moved past the snow covered farmland of Eastern Kansas. Brady stared out the window lost in a day dream about Ashley. He loved every inch of her. If ever there was a finer specimen of women, he had never seen one. He loved her silky hair that was the color of straw, her perfect inquisitive blue eyes, soft unblemished skin that turned bronze in the sun, her giggle and even the scar on her knee she got when she was doing gymnastics in high school.

He loved her perky natural breasts and her supple red lips and her exquisite flat stomach and that trail of fine blonde hair that went from her belly button down to her pussy... He was the first man who had tasted it and smelled it who had felt the creamy inner walls inside of it. He had taken her virginity on prom night in the backseat of his dad's 92' Cadillac Sedan Deville. She was not his first, but he was hers. He had slipped his fingers in and went down on her, and he almost came doing that – he would have crawled completely up inside of her if he could. He would eat her whole body if he could, she was that delicious. He came almost immediately after he penetrated her, it was awkward and she cried afterwards. He had fallen instantly in love with Ashley on that prom night, and his desire for her never wavered one iota since. Brady snapped out of his day dream as the shuttle bus entered the Kansas City International airport.

After waiting in line for what seemed like an eternity, Brady paid $385 for a one way ticket to Los Angeles at the United Airlines counter. With little time to catch the flight, he hustled through security and within minutes he was sitting on the plane at a window seat, looking out at the exhaust rising from other planes taxiing toward the runway.

Brady was queasy with adrenalin. Nauseous, because what he was doing was so reckless and out of character for him. He suspected that Ashley wouldn't be that happy to see him in Los Angeles. That was the risk he was taking. But, maybe she *would* be happy to see him and maybe she missed him as much as he missed her. Brady knew that she was probably busy adjusting to her new life in Los Angeles. He had no idea of what that entailed, and the thought terrified him. He would just have to convince her that he was there for her, to support her in her pursuit of stardom, and let her know he was there for the long run. He knew the odds were against him, but he had to try it.

He would go easy and build her trust that he wasn't trying to coax her back to Kansas. She would feel bad that she had drawn him away from his family and the veterinary practice. Yes, they would all be disappointed. Brady was his own man now and had to follow his heart, and his heart at this moment was drawing him to the West Coast.

The engines of the plane started whirring and flight attendants moved up and down the aisle securing the overhead compartments. Brady's heart was fluttering as he looked at his watch. He pulled out a piece of paper from his pocket and looked at the address he had scribbled down, *980 N. Palm Avenue, #5, West Hollywood.* He would take a cab there and surprise her. An older lady sitting next to him gazed at him and smiled.

"Visiting friends in LA?" she asked.

"Yeah, my girlfriend. She's out there trying to make it as an actress," he answered, trying to sound enthusiastic.

"Oh," the lady said and then patted his hand sympathetically.

The plane started moving backwards as they towed it out of the gate. Brady had to take a deep breath to keep from hyperventilating.

Four

Nine pm and Kraven was filling up. Kurt and another female bartender were sweating behind the bar as they hustled to make drinks for a big crowd packed into the club. The bouncers stood by quietly scanning the crowd for signs of trouble. The restaurant was busy and noisy as waiters and busboys hurried up and down the aisles carrying trays. Some pretentious electro pop/drugster music was playing a few octaves too loud on the sound system. The beautiful and rich dined on Wild Striped Bass, Cote de Beof, and other expensive French entrees, washing them down with Château Du Pap, Opus One, or Barollo.

Among them was movie star, Jack Wrangler and his crew. Drunk as always and abusive, he had been a prick to Ashley when he came in, and it rattled her hard. Wrangler got a lot of pleasure rattling beautiful girl's cages. He knew that was the prelude to having sex with them, and for him it worked nearly 100 percent of the time.

Ashley was still flustered by Wrangler's abusive and aloof act an hour after he came in. Now she was dealing with another kind of abusive and venomous customer: Jillian, very much alive and heavily made up, standing at the hostess stand with Chloe. Ashley was trying hard to find their reservation on the sheet.

"I'm sorry, ma'am, I don't see it," Ashley said, near tears. A line of people was building behind Jillian and Chloe, both dressed to the nines in their expensive designer outfits. Jillian was looking at Chloe rolling her eyes. "Ma'am? Who says that? The name is Jillian Wells. Go get Kurt – he knows us," Jillian said impatiently, looking past Ashley as if she were a speck of dust. Chloe stood just behind her, looking just as jaded, but also quite smitten with the beautiful Ashley and trying not to show it.

Ashley looked back to the bar where Kurt was hustling trying to keep up with drink orders coming in.

"I'm sorry…." Ashley said, now about to break down.

"Sorry? Are you new here? We were supposed to have a fucking booth. Where's the manager? Go get Jean Pierre," Jillian demanded.

Finally Jillian walked away and pushed past some other people and made her way to the bar, where Kurt was pouring drinks for about ten different people.

Chloe stood aside and smiled coyly at Ashley, a bit embarrassed by her friend's behavior. Ashley was thoroughly rattled now, between the abuse of Jack Wrangler and Jillian.

After a few moments, Jillian made her way back to the hostess stand with a sweaty Kurt in tow.

"Can't you get them a booth?" Kurt asked Ashley. Ashley looked back into the packed dining room. There was one empty booth with a reserved sign sitting on top of it.

"What about that one?" Kurt asked, pointing at the empty booth.

"That's reserved for a party of five at 9:30," Ashley said as Jillian stood by shooting daggers with her eyes. Kurt hurried over to the booth, and removed the "reserved" sign.

"Give them that one," he said as he hurried back to the bar.

Ashley was completely exasperated, knowing this would throw her whole night off. She snatched two menus and started walking toward the booth. Jillian smiled, knowing she had gotten to the beautiful youngster. She and Chloe followed the shapely Ashley to the booth, where Ashley dropped the menus down and walked back to the hostess stand without saying anything else.

Chloe watched her walking away.

"That girl is hot. Very hot," said Chloe.

Jillian glanced toward the hostess stand. "She's just another corn fed twat who doesn't know how to dress – I mean look at what she's wearing," Jillian said looking past her for her newest victim.

"It might be fun to help her with a makeover," Chloe said, watching Ashley as she led another group into the restaurant.

"Yeah, I'll bet you want to do a "makeover" on her, that's a hoot!" said Jillian.

At the hostess stand, Ashley was scrambling to find an empty booth to seat the 9:30 group who were waiting in the lobby thoroughly pissed off, after they had given Ashley a "don't you know who we fuckin' are?" tirade.

A busboy signaled Ashley after quickly resetting a booth. Ashley approached the angry fivesome. "We have a table ready now. I don't know how this happened," Ashley told them. The man excoriated Ashley as being stupid and incompetent as he sat down.

Ashley, ready to cry, walked back to the hostess stand past Chloe and Jillian. She avoided looking at them, she was so livid that Jillian had caused her so much heat. She returned to the hostess stand, relieved to see that there was a break in the action. Everyone was seated for the time being. She looked around the noisy restaurant at all the laughing and happy people having fun drinking fine wines and champagne, fancy cocktails, and eating five star foods.

She knew that she would one day be there too, doing what they were doing, and she wouldn't treat the people that served her that way. Why did some of the people have to be so mean? She wasn't use to this kind of abuse – people in Kansas were generally polite and friendly. People in LA seemed to be so uptight, so pretentious, abusive, and coarse.

She looked over toward Jillian's table and saw the two women drinking colored martinis. She wondered if they were actresses, or agents? They dressed and looked so glamorous and beautiful. That tall one was a first class bitch though. Ashley never said the C-word, but this time she felt it – the tall one who called herself Jillian was a cunt with a capital C. Ashley had been abused by other women before because she was deemed a threat. But this Jillian bitch was so cold, and had treated Ashley as if she was no more than a piece of dog shit on the tip of her five hundred dollar shoes. Ashley was going to find out from Kurt later who those two snags were and she would remember them. She smiled to herself knowing that she had the talent and the looks it would take to "make it." She was not going to let anybody, anybody, not Jack Wrangler, washed out drunk and abusive sell-out actor, or this ice queen Jillian (the cunt) get in her way.

"Hi, you must be new," said Chuck Alexander as he approached the hostess stand. Ashley snapped out of her trance and smiled at him. "Yes, I'm Ashley. Tonight is my first night," she said. Alexander was in his fifties, dressed like a swinging middle aged entrepreneur and he had a fresh head of hair plugs. He extended his hand and took hers, not letting go of it.

"Chuck. Pleased to meet you. You are absolutely stunning, honey. I know some people over at Playboy that would love to get a load of you," Alexander said handing her his business card.

Ashley giggled, though flattered. "Oh, I could never do that. Not as long as my Nana is alive."

Alexander looked at her a moment, "Well you call me if you change your mind. Hell, call me anyway. I'll buy you dinner anywhere you want. Hell, I'll take you to Rome and Paris if you want," Alexander said quite seriously.

Ashley blushed, but giggled, liking the positive attention,

"Thank you so much. I'll keep that in mind."

Alexander looked around the restaurant. "I'm meeting someone here, I don't see them. Her name is Jillian Wells? Is she here yet?" The mention of her name cut Ashley like a knife. Who was this woman?

"Yes, follow me," Ashley said and started walking toward the table with Chuck Alexander on her heals. She forced a smile at Jillian and Chloe as she passed Chuck off to them.

"Thank you, "Jillian told Ashley with a fake sincerity, but it surprised Ashley that she had even acknowledged her.

Jillian stood up and hugged Chuck.

"I was beginning to think I'd been stood up," Jillian said laughing a fake laugh.

"I wouldn't do that to you, babe," Chuck said as he kissed her on the cheek.

Ashley walked away thinking to herself what a group of phonies. She could tell that they couldn't really stand each other, but were playing some kind of game.

Brady arrived at LAX, pushed through the crowded terminal and waited at the baggage carousel for his bags to come down. He saw a group of men wearing dark suits ushering a girl who was wearing sunglasses and had her head covered with a hoody out of the terminal. A bunch of photographers and autograph hounds were waiting near the entrance and swarmed the girl as she stepped onto the sidewalk outside. A long black limousine swooped in and whisked her away. Somebody on the sidewalk said it was Brittany Spears, but Brady hadn't recognized her.

Wow, so this is what Hollywood is, Brady thought. This is the glitz and the glamour that Ashley so desperately wanted. Brady wondered if he had anything in common with Ashley at all. Maybe it was just a first love/sex thing. People had told Brady that he should try to get mad at Ashley and that would help him get over her, but he just couldn't bring himself to do it. She was right to want to be a movie star and Brady believed she had the looks and talent to achieve that. He would support her for life – no matter what happened.

Brady finally got his large pull-along suitcase and walked out onto the sidewalk where multiple busses and taxis were jockeying for position. Brady's eyes burned from the exhaust in the air, and the sound of horns honking echoed throughout the structure. Brady talked to an Afghan cab driver and showed him the West Hollywood address. Within moments, Brady was in the cab on his way to his beloved Ashley.

Brady looked out the window of the cab in amazement of the palm trees, the limousines, and the busses pouring out of LAX to their various destinations. Was there a movie star in every limousine? He rolled the window down and enjoyed the warm air. He knew it was frigid back in Kansas. The driver was listening to some kind of Arabic music, and looked straight ahead, sullen, as he swerved in and out of traffic. This was definitely not Kansas anymore.

Brady's cell phone rang and he looked at it and cringed upon seeing his best friend Kevin's name come up. It rang and rang and Brady finally answered it. He saw the driver's dark eyes looking back at him in the mirror.

"Hello," Brady said.

"Please tell me it's not true. Dave is telling everyone you left for LA," Kevin said.

Brady hesitated. "Hey, Kevin. What's going on?"

"No, I asked you. Where the fuck are you?" Kevin said.

"I'm in Los Angeles," Brady said, feeling a rush of heat to his face as he admitted it.

There was a long moment of silence.

"Fuck. That was what I was afraid of," Kevin finally said.

"I don't expect you to understand," Brady said.

The taxi topped the Baldwin Hills area on La Cienega that overlooks the oil fields in the middle of Los Angeles. The lights of Hollywood and downtown Los Angeles to the east were clearly in view.

"Does she at least know you are coming?" Kevin asked.

Again, Brady hesitated before answering. "No."

"Good luck, bro. I wish you would have talked to someone before going out there. Do your folks know?" Kevin asked.

"No," Brady said.

"I guess you gotta' do what you gotta' do," Kevin said.

"Yes, I do. Anything else?" Brady said with irritation.

"You have to let her go, Brady," Kevin said.

"Thanks, Kevin. I'll take that under consideration," Brady said raising his voice, and then he folded his phone shut with a snap.

He leaned forward and stared at the Hollywood sign lit up in the distance and knew he was there, in Hollywood, in the same air space as his soul mate. Fuck all the doubters! Fuck all the negative people that didn't understand true love. This was what all of those hit songs were written about.

As the liquor flowed at Kraven, man after inebriated man made their way over to the hostess stand to talk to Ashley. Each one had a story and business card. Each one knew somebody at an agency or studio. One guy was a photographer and offered to take head shots for free. All of the men told Ashley how beautiful she was, and how well she was going to do in Hollywood. She enjoyed the attention, was friendly and polite but at the same time disgusted with most of the men and their phony witticisms.

She thought that all of the men seemed kind of sleazy, and she had read books to beware of men like these. Even the photographer gave her the creeps. Something about him exuded desperation. Maybe it was the cheap cologne that he reeked of or the alcohol on his breath. The thought of getting free headshots was tempting, but Ashley had read stories about girls who went on photo shoots with "photographers" and were never seen again. Ashley would play it safe and not be a dumb naïve girl from Kansas that they all thought she was.

The photographer handed Ashley his business card and staggered back into the bar area, kind of like a guy does when he gets shot down at the beach, and has to cross the sand in front of everyone who witnessed it. Chloe took her opportunity and wandered up to the hostess stand sipping a flute of champagne.

"Hi, I'm Chloe," she said extending her hand to Ashley. "I want to apologize for the behavior of my friend."

"Oh, it's no problem. It happens all the time in here," Ashley said. Chloe seemed to be undressing Ashley with her eyes and it unnerved her. "I hear you just arrived in Los Angeles, and I thought you might want to go shopping or something, maybe do lunch some time," Chloe said.

"Oh, who told you that?" Ashley wondered aloud.

"The waiter. He said you were from Nebraska or somewhere," Chloe said. "It's nothing to be ashamed of; most of us came from somewhere else. I'm originally from Virginia."

Ashley let her guard down a little upon hearing this. Chloe was probably one of the first women who had been friendly to her in LA.

"I'm from Kansas – I've been here a couple of weeks," Ashley admitted.

"Two weeks! And you already scored a job at Kraven – that's impressive. Do you know how many girls try to get in here?" Chloe said. "Anyway, I'd love to take you shopping. How about tomorrow?" Chloe said touching Ashley's hand.

What was her angle, Ashley wondered?

"I have acting class at 6. I am free during the day, but I really don't have money to spend."

Chloe felt the material on Ashley's blouse touching her breast in the process. Ashley had felt a charge from it and suddenly found herself strangely attracted to Chloe. Women had come onto her before at the university, but they had been the butch types. Chloe was petite and glamorous looking, and Ashley couldn't tell if she was gay or not.

"Let me buy you an outfit. I know how it is when you first come to town and you don't know anybody. Even your clothes give you away," Chloe said as diplomatically as she could.

Ashley felt stupid and embarrassed. Chloe had just confirmed what she already knew – that she might as well have been wearing a big sign that said "hay seed just off the pumpkin truck." Ashley suddenly felt very self conscious and wanted to leave immediately and get out of the clothes that gave her away as a dumb hick. "Let me buy you an outfit – it will be my treat. My welcome gift to you. Welcome to LA," Chloe said, brushing her hand against Ashley's breast again as she tipped her champagne glass to finish it off.

Ashley agreed to meet her for lunch at the clothing store, Fred Segal, and took her card. So this was how it was here? You had to wear the right things and say the right things, and be in the loop to get where you wanted to go. Ashley felt like a fool for not realizing that before, but decided she would go to lunch with Chloe and let her buy an outfit. Maybe just what she needed was a friend who knew how to dress, what to eat and drink, who knew the right clubs and restaurants to be seen in, and who was who. In the meantime, Ashley wanted the night to be over with and shrink into the wall paper so not one more person would see her wearing that blouse from JC Penny back home.

The cab dropped Brady in front of Ashley's Palm Avenue Apartment building in West Hollywood. It was an old, art deco two story building on the hill between Santa Monica and Sunset. Brady paid the cab driver $70 with no tip, and couldn't understand why the driver drove away mad.

Brady stood in front of the building with his suitcase just staring at it. The air was probably 60 degrees warmer than it was back in Kansas, and Brady removed his winter coat and draped it over his shoulder. He felt like a fool, and it was beginning to hit him just how crazy this idea had been. Ashley was likely going to be mad that he had come. He had her phone number but was afraid to call her. He knew that the only way this would work was if she actually saw him in person, otherwise it would be too easy to dismiss him.

Once she saw that he was actually here, she might be pleasantly surprised. Brady kept telling himself that. He would be back in her arms within no time, and they would resume their lives together. He hesitantly walked to the intercom and buzzed her number. It rang and rang with no answer. It was now after 11:30 pm. Brady suddenly panicked a little. What if she was spending the night with some guy? What would he do then, where would he stay? Everything in LA was so expensive and he had to make what money he had last. The $70 cab ride was not something he had planned on. Brady tried to think if he knew anybody else in Los Angeles and could not think of anybody.

Brady sat down on the curb next to his suitcase and listened to the sounds of traffic and nightlife that drifted up from Santa Monica Blvd. and down from Sunset. A police helicopter flew overhead and Brady wondered why Ashley had chosen such a noisy place to live. Brady already hated it: He felt paranoid, boxed in and afraid. This place seemed alien and hostile, dark and threatening, decadent and dangerous. A sinking feeling in his stomach told him that this wasn't going to turn out well. After a few moments, a private security car with police lights on it pulled up in front of the apartment. The driver of the car shined a spotlight on Brady and then got out of his car and approached him. The private cop was very fat, but carried a gun and kept his hand on it.

"What are you doing here?" the private cop asked in a thick foreign accent.

"I'm just waiting for my girlfriend," Brady stood up and answered. The private cop patted his gun subconsciously.

"You can't wait here. Move along," the private cop said as if shooing away a fly.

Brady slowly started moving away, not knowing which way to turn. He decided to walk down the hill toward Santa Monica Blvd. Within moments he was dragging his suitcase in the middle of "Boy's Town" the section of West Hollywood populated by gay nightclubs.

He found himself surrounded by gay males in front of a nightclub where a male go-go dancer was visible through the window dancing on top of a table wearing nothing but a g-string. Brady had never seen anything like this before. Several guys said hello to him and he felt like a vulnerable piece of fresh meat moving down the sidewalk with his suitcase. Now Brady knew what women felt like walking past a construction site.

He saw maybe two females in a block. He wondered what it was like to be gay – they must be having sex all the time because guys are always horny and ready to go. They probably didn't have to play all those games going out to dinner and hoping they were going to get laid. They probably just got right to it. Brady thought of the gay experience he had when he was fourteen. He and a friend who was spending the night had blown each other. The incident eventually ruined their friendship and they always avoided each other after that. Brady had never told anyone about that.

Brady kept walking, not knowing where he was going, but far away from the noisy nightclubs, to a darker section of the boulevard. As he approached the corner he saw a woman who was obviously dressed like a prostitute, but as he got closer Brady realized it was a man dressed in women's clothing. A car pulled to the curb and the "man" leaned into the window, giving Brady a quick side eye as he walked by.

A little further up the street Brady approached a group of teenage boys who were passing around a joint. They were speaking in some foreign language, Russian, Brady thought. They stared at him as he walked by.

"What are you looking at, faggot?" one of the boys said as Brady walked past.

Adrenalin rushed through Brady's body. He kept moving, even though he knew he could have kicked the boy's ass with one hand, but he couldn't beat all five of them. So far, Brady's Hollywood trip was becoming a nightmare. Brady saw a 24 hour diner across the street and turned that direction. As he stepped out into the street he stepped on a used condom and its contents squirted onto his other shoe.

"Goddammit!" Brady yelled as he slammed his bag down on the sidewalk. A homeless man wearing duck tape for shoes was shuffling up the sidewalk towards Brady, and stepped into the street to avoid him.

The two men stared at each other like wild animals as they passed each other.

Chuck Alexander had used every trick in the book trying to get into Jillian's pants, but she was too smart for that. She was the master of the string-along. Chloe got a perverse pleasure watching Jillian operate. Alexander had bought three bottles of Dom Perignon at $550, plus dinner for the three of them. Jillian was the type who will intentionally order the most expensive item on the menu if someone else was paying.

As it was getting close to last call, the dance floor at Kraven was heating up, and the behavior of the occupants became more decadent as the Grey Goose, ecstasy, cocaine, and various other substances took effect. Jack Wrangler was holding court at his table and everyone there seemed to be enamored with him. Ashley could see his face through the crowd and thought about how surreal it was that she was there now in Hollywood, in the same space as the movie stars she had grown up with on television.

Ashley watched from the hostess stand, just waiting to be let go. She really had no interest in the depravity going down. It was only a diversion from her goal, and nothing was going to divert her from that. That was for all of the weak people that came here, the ones that would never make it. The ones that deep down inside *knew* they would never make it.

Jillian was dirty dancing with Chuck, and he was fake humping her from behind. His hand Slipped inside her blouse, but she pushed it away and dodged him, moving onto dance with Chloe, who was now fucked up out of her mind.

Everyone was getting a big thrill out of watching the two women dirty dance to *"Slap Your Bitch Up"*. Chuck stood by like a chump.

Kurt was standing behind the bar watching. He caught Ashley's glance and smiled at her. Jean Pierre arrived at the hostess stand and handed Ashley a wrapped napkin.

"Ok, you can go home. Good job, thank you," Jean Pierre said sipping a glass of Chardonnay. He hugged her quickly and pecked her on the cheek. Ashley noted that his breath was horrible.

Ashley didn't wait for him to say it twice. She grabbed her purse from under the hostess stand, dropped her tip napkin into it, then looked toward the back of the restaurant and saw Jack Wrangler at his table surrounded by people and looking through the crowd at *her*. She smiled to herself. Was he really looking at her?

She said her goodbyes to the doorman and bouncers, walked past some bored paparazzi that were smoking cigarettes on the side of the club. She kept moving up Sunset. A steady stream of traffic was snarled coming up the Strip and she smiled as they looked at the glittering lights up in the hills and she knew that she was in exactly the right place. She turned off of Sunset and started walking down the hill to her apartment building.

Five

Ashley returned to her studio apartment and quickly yanked off her top that she now hated and threw it onto the floor. She pulled her skirt off too and grabbed a beer from the refrigerator. The apartment was a 400 square foot studio built in the 50's with hardwood floors and a window that looked out onto a courtyard. Ashley drew the blinds and walked around in her panties and bra.

A sleeping bag was spread out on the floor with a pillow. A lamp was the only piece of furniture in the room. Ashley's laptop was open and sitting next to the sleeping bag. A few boxes were stacked on the edge of the room, and a picture of Ashley's family – including her mom, dad, and brother was leaning against the wall. Ashley had only brought what she could pack into her 2000 Honda Civic. She had made the trip from Kansas driving straight through in 28 hours.

She sipped her beer and walked to her closet. She scrutinized each piece of clothing hanging there and started throwing items one by one into the pile with her discarded blouse. She had learned a valuable lesson that night. Image is everything in LA and from that point forward, Ashley was going to be image conscious. She would plan every outfit she wore out. She would be conscious of fashion trends and dress accordingly. This was her life now and this was her business – to look good, to look fashionable and hip.

She would not be caught again looking like a hick from Kansas. By the time she was done sorting through her things, nearly everything in her closet was in the discard pile. She would let Chloe buy her one outfit, but she would obviously need more. A lot more. She would have to devout a big portion of her next paycheck to clothes. She was down to $500 in savings after she had put the deposit and first month's rent down for her apartment. She was paying $1075 for her studio apartment. Back in Kansas you could rent a five bedroom house for that amount. Nobody ever said it was going to be easy. Ashley had read all of the books, including "The Actor's Survival Guide: How to Make Your Way in Hollywood," and they told her that it wasn't going to be easy, so she felt that she was somewhat prepared.

Ashley remembered how she first caught the Hollywood bug. She had been probably nine or ten years old. She was at the gas station in Colby with her father. He was gassing up their farm truck when a sleek sports car, a blue Porche, pulled into the station. The most glamorous women Ashley had ever seen got out of the car. It was the actress, Melanie Griffith. Actor, Don Johnson, who was her husband at the time, got out of the driver's side. He wore big sunglasses and looked as handsome and tanned as he did on television. The actress smiled at Ashley as she walked by into the gas station. Ashley's dad stared in awe and mumbled hello as Don Johnson hurried by behind his wife. "Who are those people?" Ashley remembered asking her father. "Movie stars, I think," he answered. That incident had more to do with Ashley's current fate than anything else. Ever since that day, Hollywood had been calling Ashley like a siren.

Ashley put some music on her computer, a Red Hot Chili Peppers CD, and was dancing a little bit as she opened another beer. Her cell phone lit up and she saw Brady's name on it. She looked at it a moment and decided not to answer it. It was now 2am, why was he calling? He had probably been out drinking with friends and she didn't want to deal with it. She hoped he would eventually stop calling and move on. Yes, she had fond feelings and memories of him and sometimes she thought about him, especially when she masturbated, but in her mind she had moved on, why couldn't he? She was in a different time and space now, why couldn't he realize that? Her phone beeped as a voice mail came through and then a moment later the phone started ringing again. She let it ring and ring until it went to voicemail again. She was pissed now. What did he want? He was beginning to act like a little boy and it really irritated her.

She sipped her beer, stewed a moment, and then checked her voicemail. She listened to the first message, "Hi Ashley, you're not going to believe this, but I'm in LA. I wanted to surprise you…..Give me a call when you get this," Brady said sounding desperate and pathetic. She deleted that message and listened to the second one. "Ashley, it's me again. I'm not joking. I'm outside of your apartment building and people are looking at me funny. Please call me back."

"Fuck!" Ashley exclaimed. She yanked a Metallica t-shirt out of her closet and slipped it on, then yanked on some jeans. She punched Brady's number into her phone and started out the door. Brady answered after one ring, "Hello,"

"Brady, you better be kidding. You are not in LA?" Ashley said as she stepped out onto the sidewalk in front of her building looking up and down the street.

After a moment, Brady walked out of the shadows with a sheepish grin on his face and his winter coat draped over his shoulder, pulling his suitcase behind him. Ashley's eyes narrowed upon seeing him. "Jesus Christ," was all she could say.

He approached her and attempted a hug that was very awkward because she didn't reciprocate. She even stiffened up as if he were a stranger.

"You don't seem too happy to see me," Brady said, his voice trailing off.

"What in the world do you think you're doing? Right in the middle of the semester? Are you crazy?"

"I know, I know," Brady mumbled.

"What?" Ashley said, beside herself.

The apartment manager, Larry and his boyfriend walked up the sidewalk and ran into the arguing couple. They heard Ashley's distressed voice and were concerned and prepared for trouble.

"Are you okay?" Larry asked, casting a suspicious glance at Brady.

"Yes, I am fine, thanks, Larry," Ashley said, trying to hide her anger.

Larry and his boyfriend continued into the apartment building, not too convinced that everything was okay.

"Can we go inside and finish this," Brady pleaded.

Ashley nodded, not happy about it and she led the way into the building.

Once inside, Brady looked around the small apartment, scanning quickly for any signs of another man. Ashley was clearly perturbed and she grabbed her beer and sucked on it.

"Have another one of those?" Brady asked.

Ashley opened the refrigerator and grabbed another beer, then dropped it heavily onto the counter.

Brady opened it and stared at her.

"I love, you Ashley…."

She cut him right off. "Brady, we've been through this already. I am following my own path now. Why can't you understand that? I can't believe you just dropped everything to come out here chasing me," Ashley said.

Brady stared at the floor and looked like he might start crying.

"I thought that maybe you missed me too. I can't just fall out of love. You're all I think about. I can't even concentrate on my studies. I've lost 20 pounds. I can't even sleep," Brady confessed as a tear streamed down his cheek.

Ashley now looked like she might cry; she took another gulp of beer.

"I have missed you. I've thought about you - but it's better this way. We have to let it go," she said, now crying also.

"Why? Why? Why do we have to let it go?" Brady asked and he moved to her and wrapped his arms around her. She didn't reciprocate, but leaned her head onto his shoulder.

"I support you. I know you are good enough. I know you will be a big success in the movie business," he told her.

She looked up at him like a vulnerable little girl.

"I can be right here with you while you do it," Brady said, thinking he was getting through to her.

"You don't understand, Brady, I need to do this on my own," she said quietly.

"Why?" Brady asked as he held her more tightly. She pulled away from him and walked into the living room, not facing him.

"You can stay here tonight, but I'm taking you back to the airport tomorrow. You have to go home, do you understand?" she said.

"No, I'm not. You can't make me go back," Brady said, his eyes flashing with anger. He chugged his beer, then grabbed another out of the refrigerator and opened it.

Ashley walked back into the small kitchen and grabbed herself another beer. She looked at Brady a long moment.

"Brady, why don't you just admit that the only thing you really miss is fucking me," Ashley said with a trace of bitterness.

"No! Don't talk to me like that! It's not about that!" Brady protested.

Ashley took her beer and went to her sleeping bag, she sat down on it and sipped her beer, looking away from Brady.

"I can get laid if I want, don't worry about that," Brady said.

Ashley's eyes flashed with jealousy "Go for it then. You deserve someone better than me, Brady. A girl that will have your children and live happily ever after with you back in Kansas. Someone who will help you with your vet practice," Ashley said staring at the wall.

"That's not me, Brady. That's not me," she said softly.

Brady stood there in the small kitchen staring at the floor, torn between anger and grief. Not wanting to let go. He knew this was the risk he had taken. Now, how could he return to Kansas and admit to all of his friends and family that he had made a royal fool out of himself? He could see that Ashley had changed in just the short time she had been here. She seemed harder already. He could see how this place would make a person like that. The seductive weather and palm trees, and flowers and everything masked the underlying darkness, the underlying dog eat dogism that pervaded everything here. He hated her in that moment and just wanted to bash her face in and rape her. The fucking selfish bitch, who did she think she was, the fucking stupid "actress." He stared at her figure, back facing him. Back and shapely delicious ass that he wished he could just make a meal out of.

"It's 2:30. I'm exhausted. There's some blankets over there for you to sleep on," Ashley said pointing to them stacked by the wall.

Brady stomped over and grabbed the blankets and spread them out on the floor on the opposite side of the room from Ashley.

She laid there silently resenting him. He was such a lunkhead jock and small town hay seed. He would never fit in out here, would never understand her plight, and would constantly be jealous of everything she did. The last thing in the world she needed right now was some remnant from her home town to remind her every day what a hick *she* really was. She had rejected all of that and left it behind. She would never return to Kansas except to visit no matter what happened in Hollywood. She did not want children and she did not want a husband to hold her down. She did not want to suffer in silence like her mom had all those years with her controlling, brooding father. Yeah, she liked fucking Brady, but that was about it, and she damn sure wasn't going to give into that urge. Not now, that would just make him dig in deeper.

Brady spread out on the blanket and groaned, trying to get comfortable on the hardwood floor. They both laid there in silence listening to each other breathe.

A couple of miles away in Jillian's Beverly Hills adjacent apartment just north of Olympic, Kurt and Jillian sat in her living room doing lines of cocaine. They did it silently, there together but miles apart internally. Kurt watched her and secretly hated her. Fucking old hag. She had no idea how over it really was for her. He would much rather be with some tasty young slice like that new hostess, Ashley. Kurt had experienced his "golden years" where he sampled all of the best pussy in Southern California and this was what he ended up with now. He looked at the deep lines forming around her eyes and her artificially plumped lips and he just wanted to punch her.

Similar thoughts were running through Jillian's mind. What a pathetic loser. A thirty year old bartender that would always be a bartender. A zero of a man. Not even a man, but a manchild who probably still spent most of his time playing video games. A fucking loser who didn't even smell good. She could smell his acrid body odor as he snorted another line of cocaine.

"You need to take a shower," Jillian told him.

He looked at her and half smiled. "Why don't you join me?"

She leaned down and snorted another line. Her eyes rolled back in her head a little as the coke hit her heart. "Okay," she said.

Chloe brushed her teeth in the bathroom of her swank West Hollywood Apartment on Doheny across from the Four Seasons. She thought of the hostess, Ashley and how hot she was. The girl's eyes sparkled like diamonds and she was so, so, so fresh. Her skin was so perfect, so unblemished and she wasn't yet hardened and cynical like they all were in LA. That wouldn't last long. Chloe knew that Ashley probably wasn't gay, but that was how Chloe liked them. She had persuaded many a curious straight girl to give it a try. They all usually went back to men, stupid men, for one reason or another. Usually financial support.

Chloe would spend some money on the new girl, buy the poor naive thing some new clothes, wine and dine her, seduce her slowly. It might take a week or two, but Chloe would get into her panties eventually. So what if it cost her a few hundred dollars. Chloe had just received a bonus of $8,500, thanks to that new high blood pressure drug she had been pushing. Chloe smiled to herself, knowing she didn't have to rely on any hairy, ugly, stinky man with an ugly, slimy penis to support her like Jillian did.

Jillian was really becoming pathetic and desperate and it was probably about time to cut her off. She was a total bitch to the fine thing, Ashley and almost blew Chloe's chances with her. Yes, Chloe was going to have to reconsider her friendship with Jillian. Been there, done that. Next. Chloe looked into her medicine cabinet where a whole cornucopia of different prescription pills where neatly arranged. She stared into the cabinet a moment, took out a bottle of Ambien, the sleep medication, and popped one into her mouth.

A few moments later she was lying in her bed with headphones on, listening to New Age music as she masturbated thinking about Ashley.

It was the middle of the night and Brady was lying there awake, cold and uncomfortable with one thin blanket on the hardwood floor. What a sour welcome Ashley had given him. He listened to her breathing, asleep across the room. So, this was the life she wanted, to be in one room apartments, surrounded by faggots, working in nightclubs constantly struggling to make the rent. Wanting to go it alone, completely alone. Now, he was starting to understand Ashley: She was all about herself. Completely selfish, she didn't even care about her family and good friends she had left behind. She was a total narcissist, he remembered that term from his psychology class and she fit that definition to a T. Well, he was going to fuck her one last time, and that would give her something to remember him by when she was all alone years from now realizing that life had passed her by and that she had gambled everything and lost. Selfish fucking twat. She was going to be the lonesome loser in the future, not he. He would return to Kansas, finish college, go back home and take over his dad's vet practice, meet some nice Kansas girl and settle down and have a family with her and live happily ever fucking after.

He sat up and stared at the dark breathing figure on the other side of the room. He crawled over and slipped into the sleeping bag with her. She stirred and struggled, but he had already slipped his hand into her panties and was touching her the way he knew she liked. He knew how to get her off better than anyone and had done it hundreds of times. She would never be able to deny that. His hot breath was in her face and he kissed her. She moaned as he slipped his fingers into her pussy. She resisted for a moment, then just relaxed and let him kiss her.

Within moments they were making wild love on top of the sleeping bag.

He thrust into her with fury as if she might be the last fuck he would ever have. She reciprocated and bit his lip and she used every muscle in her vagina to grip his cock with anger. She really needed this as much as he did, but she wasn't going to give him the satisfaction of making her cum first. She would make him blast and she wasn't worried if he came inside her; she was on the pill. She would make him shoot off inside her like a garden hose, and then she would push him off of her and not allow herself to have an orgasm. Then he would win and she couldn't let her high school lunkhead sweetheart win this one no matter what.

He held back he was about to cum but he didn't want it to end this fast. He knew she was trying to get him to cum and maybe he would make her pregnant and maybe that was what she really wanted – to have his baby, to have an excuse to abandon her futile dream. Her pussy was gripping his cock like a vice and he was almost there.

He pushed his finger into her ass just as he was about to cum and she let out a scream as a powerful orgasm shot through her body at the same moment he flooded her vaginal cavity with his hot sperm. He bored his tongue into her neck making a hickey as his dick pulsated deep inside her.

Six

Ashley woke up smothered in Brady's arms. A deep purple hickey was visible on her neck. Brady was sound asleep, lightly snoring as sunlight spilled in through the blinds. Ashley could hear a lawn mower running somewhere. She wiggled out from under Brady, trying not to wake him. He mumbled something, then rolled over and continued his slumber.

Ashley got up and searched for her phone. She looked at it and saw that it was only 8:30. She was supposed to meet Chloe at noon. She looked over at Brady lying under the sleeping bag. She had to get him out. She could not let him stay there one more night. What had happened, happened, but it was not happening again. She gave him his second goodbye fuck and that was it.

His dad would be livid if he knew where Brady was. Probably everyone back home would hate her and blame her for breaking Brady's heart. They expected high school sweethearts to marry and resent each other their entire lives. Become fat and miserable and resigned to their fate of mediocrity and boredom. Bitterly cold winters, stifling hot summers, miles of flat nothingness, corn fields, wheat fields, tornados and violent hail storms and blizzards.

High school football games were the highlight of the year. Stupid yocals having their bake sales at church on Sundays. Singing those stupid antiquated hymms that were so slow that some of the old ladies might die of old age before they were over. And her own father now hated her for leaving home and Brady and the life he had mapped out for her.

He wanted her to marry Brady and be trapped in the small town forever just like her mom was. That's what men ultimately did – wanted to trap and control women for life. This wasn't the Neanderthal age anymore. Ashley wanted to be sophisticated and grow old as a strong independent women like Katherine Hepburn, Diane Keaton, or Faye Dunaway. She would spend summers in France, and winters in St. Barts. She would have an apartment on Park Avenue and a house in the Hollywood Hills. She would eat men up and spit them out, never allowing any of them to control her.

She looked into her refrigerator. There wasn't much in there. One Heineken in the six pack box, a dozen eggs, half a stick of butter, some bread, and a gallon jug of purified water. She poured herself a glass of water and then started tossing the empty beer bottles from the night before into the trash can. They landed with a sharp clink, stirring Brady out of his sleep. His eyes slowly opened and he stared at her. A slight smile came to his face as he remembered what had happened. He loved her again she could see it and it pissed her off.

"What are you smiling about? Get up and get ready to go back home. I'm taking you to the airport," Ashley said.

Brady sat up. "I'm not going back. I don't even have a ticket. I bought a one way ticket."

"Come on, Brady. Cut the shit, okay? I have a meeting with a woman at noon, then acting class at 7:30. I don't have time to hold your hand all day," she said standing there in her bra and panties.

Brady started laughing. "Nice hickey."

"You better not have," she said as she stormed into the bathroom to look at herself in the mirror.

"Oh, you immature little child. I'm not one of your cows to be branded," Ashley screamed from the bathroom.

"Oh fuck, just relax it's no big deal," Brady said standing up, still naked and with a semi hard on.

He walked into the bathroom and pressed his cock against her thigh. "That was hot last night! I really got you off when I stuck my finger up your butt," Brady said.

Ashley pushed him away and dodged him as he tried to grab her, "Get away from me you pig! I'm serious, I'll call the police!" She rushed back into the main room and grabbed her phone as if to start dialing.

Feeling naked and stupid all of a sudden, Brady searched for his underwear and pants.

"I tried to be nice about it, but you wouldn't listen. Now, I want you out. I don't care what you do. You want to hang around LA like a tourist, go ahead. I am done with you, Brady. It's over. Let me get on with my life, okay?" Ashley said with finality.

Brady looked at her a minute as he was putting his pants on. "You really show your true colors now that you're here in this plastic environment. You're a just a selfish bitch. You won't make it here, you're just another small town cheerleader that was a big fish in a small pond. Girls like you are a dime a dozen out here,"

"Get out! Get out of my apartment," Ashley screamed. "You come back here – I'll call the police,"

Brady slipped his shirt on and yanked his suitcase away from the wall.

"You'll end up sucking dicks to pay your rent. Mark my words," Brady said as he walked out, slamming the door behind him.

At Jillian's condo a similar scene was about to play out. Jillian was standing in front of the mirror in her new yoga outfit studying herself. She did not like what she saw – a rapidly aging face with hairline cracks forming around her eyes, sun damage. Lines forming on her neck, and deep frown lines running down from her mouth. Her surgically enhanced breasts stood up nicely but were also sun damaged on the top. Her years of excessive sun bathing were now taking their toll. She had dark circles under her eyes and she felt the lingering effects of the coke and the champagne gnawing at her brain.

She had always been able to party like a rock star and bounce back the next morning, but that seemed to be getting harder. She was supposed to be at yoga class in a half hour and she wondered if she was going to make it. The thoughts of suicide were still with her. She had taken the shells out of the gun and put them in the trunk of her car, but she still had the gun in her closet. There were other ways; she could just step in front of a bus, or the red line train, or she could take a bunch of pills. Well, the thoughts weren't actually turning into action, but she kind of wished it was all over with.

She was tired of the struggle of her meaningless life. She had squandered her youth in hedonism and had never for one moment dreamed that she would get to this point, where her looks couldn't carry her any more. Her phone was not ringing. She had one friend, Chloe, the muff eating drug addict dyke. She suspected Chloe felt superior to her and probably talked about how pathetic she was behind her back. She looked into her mirror over her shoulder; she could see Kurt sacked out in her bed. She felt a bit sicker as she looked at him. Why did she bring him here? Was it to prove to herself that she could still pull younger men? Yes, that had to be it, because there was nothing special about this loser. He couldn't even fuck right, his dick was crooked, and he was a total uninteresting and uneducated bore whose only talent was making martinis.

Then there was Chuck Alexander, the contractor from last night with Binaca breath and hair plugs - the so called millionaire that still dressed like he was in the eighties. Was that who she was going to have to fuck next? The thought of it nauseated her, but that was her only prospect. She *was* sixty days behind on her mortgage. She would be seeing Dr. Davis later in the day and maybe he could break her out of this funk.

She turned and squeezed Kurt's big toe that was poking out of the sheets. "Hey, get up," Jillian said. She poked him again, "Get up, you have to go, I have yoga class."

He didn't stir. She watched him for a long moment to see if he was breathing. Finally she saw that he was and she picked up half a glass of water from the night stand and splashed it in his face.

"Fuck!!!!" he screamed and shot up, "Don't ever fucking do that again!"

"Get up and get out," Jillian said matter-of-factly. Kurt focused on her a moment as the cobwebs in his brain started to break apart.

Jillian began picking up clothes off the floor, folding them and setting them on top of the dresser. After a moment, Kurt laughed coldly to himself.

"Fuckin' bitch. Gladly," he said as he raised himself out of her bed.

He grabbed his clothes and moved past her. She stepped out of the way, bracing herself as if he might hit her, but he didn't. She waited a moment as he dressed and then she heard the door slam as he walked out.

Brady walked down Santa Monica Blvd. dragging his suitcase behind him. He had his winter coat tied around his midriff. The marine layer was still lingering at 9 am but it was a balmy 62 degrees in early November. It was probably 25 degrees back in Kansas. Well, he had taken the risk and been rejected, but he still had been able to get into her panties. That was the key. Brady knew that Ashley wasn't the promiscuous type, that she liked to be with one guy and that she would eventually come around. He would just have to prove to her that he could hang here. That he could adjust and fit in here. It wasn't so bad, he looked at the palm trees and the Hollywood Hills in the distance and smiled to himself. He was here in Hollywood, he had just gotten laid.

Then a troubled thought came to his mind; he had said some incredibly horrible things to Ashley. He didn't really mean them; he felt that she had hit him below the belt, so he responded in kind. Yes, he was on a quest to win back his true love and he would do whatever it took. Wasn't that what all of those hit songs were written about and movies? If you truly love someone you never, never give up. After all, "stalking" was celebrated in popular culture all the time.

In Brady's case it wasn't stalking because he believed that Ashley truly loved him too. That deep down inside she knew she would be back with him, but she was just confused now. Give her some space, let her realize what she is missing and she will come running back into his arms. He just had to be there when that time came. He had to be available. His dad would be angry and heartbroken, but Brady couldn't help that. He had to follow his heart and his heart had brought him *here*.

The gay nightclubs of boy's town were now closed, but the same clientele was now populating coffee shops and sidewalk cafes as Brady walked by dragging his suitcase. Others jogged by him in running gear and gave him quick smiles and glances. Brady kept walking past all of it. A steady stream of traffic kept coming down the boulevard. Brady had no idea where he was going or where he would stay. He had less than five hundred dollars in cash and maybe $300 worth of credit on a card. Asking his family for money now was out of the question. He would have to find a job quickly and a place to live. Maybe he could rent a room somewhere cheap.

He saw a flower shop and went inside. He purchased a dozen red roses and wrote a note:

"Ashley, I'm so sorry for the things I said. I didn't mean them. You are the most beautiful, talented and special person to ever land in Hollywood. I have no doubt you will become a big star and I support you one hundred percent. I love you and will always love you. If you need your space, I respect that. I will leave you alone, but I want you to know that I am not going back to Kansas. I am going to enroll in school here and give it a go. I think I will like it here. The weather is great. I wish you luck with your acting class today, and as they say – break a leg! Yours always, Brady. "

The guy in the flower shop assured Brady that the flowers would be delivered ASAP.

Ashley took a long shower and attempted to wash all remnants of Brady off and out of her. She ended up masturbating in the shower in the process. She knew that whenever she had sex that she became hornier and wanted more and more. Brady was the only man she had really been with. He had taken her virginity; he had given her first orgasm. He had even made her pregnant once when she was only seventeen. She didn't like to think about that. Brady's dad had given them the money for the abortion and they traveled to Denver to get it done. Brady was very sweet with her and had bought her flowers and cookies afterward. They drove back to Colby barely saying a word to each other the whole trip. They didn't see each other for a few weeks after that. They never talked about it again.

There had been a couple of other guys. There was Brady's friend, Kevin. She ended up with him one time when Brady was away on a family vacation. They were drunk at a kegger and she ended up making out with Kevin in his truck. Brady never knew about that, and his friend always had a stupid grin on his face whenever she saw them together. They ended up having sex but she remembered little about it except that Kevin came fast all over her breasts. Then there was the time that she had sex with someone from the theatre department. She suspected the kid, Darren was gay. They were at a party together after the opening of a University play and they had been drinking and Ashley wanted to see if Darren was actually gay. He was so handsome, pretty even, like the statue of David, and she ended up having sex with him. It was awkward and she decided that he was definitely gay, but he had managed to pull it off. Brady didn't know about that one either. So, that was the extent of Ashley's sexual experience. She would have to play the field awhile and get some new experience and she was looking forward to doing that, but was aware that STDs were rampant in Los Angeles. She would have to be careful. She covered the hickey on her neck the best she could with makeup.

Ashley scrutinized all of her clothes and finally decided on jeans and a t-shirt to go meet Chloe. Her phone rang and Ashley saw that it was her mom. She hesitated a moment, then answered it. Ashley ended up spending an hour on the phone with her. She told her about Brady and what had happened. Her mom wasn't very surprised and said that everyone in the town knew that he was heartbroken and couldn't get over her. Ashley complained to her mom and reiterated her whole position on how they should break clean and that she needed to move on with her own life, etc, and Ashley's mom agreed with her. Ashley admitted to having sex with Brady the night before and Ashley's mom clucked, "Oh my. You shouldn't have done that." Ashley agreed.

Ashley finally asked about her dad and her mom told her that he was still mad and hurt about her leaving. Crop prices were down and they were worried about finances for the coming year. When Ashley finally hung up the phone she did not feel any better. Kansas did not want to let her go, as bad as she wanted to let it go.

Ashley fixed herself some eggs and toast for breakfast with instant coffee. She would have to go grocery shopping later and maybe attend some garage sales on Saturday to get some furniture. Start making a home for herself. After breakfast, Ashley called Chloe and agreed to meet her at Fred Segal on Melrose. Chloe seemed very happy to hear from her. Almost too happy. As Ashley was doing the dishes, she heard her buzzer ring. When she answered it was the florist delivering the flowers.

She brought the flowers in and set them on the breakfast nook. They looked gaudy and hideous to her. One dozen red roses. She read Brady's note and it infuriated her. How dare he decide to stay in LA. He was becoming a stalker. She ripped his note up and threw it in the trash. She thought about it a moment, then retrieved it. She might need it later for evidence of some kind. She grabbed the flowers and threw them in the trash – they only reminded her of the abortion.

Brady paid $11.75 for an omelet and cup of coffee at a sidewalk café. He realized that his money was not going to last long at this rate. He looked at a newspaper for places for rent. Everything was over $1000. Rooms for rent were $800 and up and required a first and last month's rent and deposit. Wow, everything was so expensive. The jobs must pay more money than they do back home he thought. Then he looked at the jobs in the paper and saw that most of them paid $10 an hour, even jobs that required college degrees. How was Ashley going to make it here he wondered? He also wondered if she had received the flowers yet. He looked at his phone, thought about calling her, but restrained himself. He had to give her some room. He had to leave her alone now, even if it was for a month or two.

He left the waiter a dollar tip and moved on. As he walked up Santa Monica east of Fairfax he saw a pet store with a HELP WANTED sign in the window. It was a small mom and pop store and he decided to take a look.

The store was small and cramped with merchandise inside and smelled like pet food. He could hear puppies yipping somewhere and could see bird cages, along with a few aquariums on the back wall. An older man sitting behind the counter reading a newspaper with strange, foreign looking print, looked up from his paper and eyed Brady suspiciously.

"Can I help you?" said the man with a thick Russian accent.

"I noticed the help wanted sign as I was walking by," Brady said smiling.

The old Russian man looked Brady up and down. "You want job? I don't pay much money," the man said.

"I just came to town. I'm in veterinary school. I don't know anyone here and I need a job," Brady said. The puppies in the back were making a big racket now.

The man studied Brady a long moment. "Where you come from?"

"Kansas," Brady answered.

"Like I said, I can't afford to pay much money," the man said. Some customers came into the store and the Russian man dismissed Brady and went to help them. Brady stood there for a few minutes waiting, and then finally walked out. He walked up the boulevard and saw a Walgreen's drug store that had a "*Now Taking Applications*," sign in the window. He went inside and went through a run around trying to find somebody to give him an application. An irritated looking assistant manager finally handed him an application and a pen and told him to fill the application out and bring it back. "Are you needing somebody right away?" Brady asked.

The assistant manager looked him up and down as if he could tell Brady was from out of town. "We're always looking for people. Just fill it out and bring it back," the assistant manager said as if he couldn't waste one more minute with Brady. Brady walked out of the store and tossed the application in the trash.

Brady kept walking down the boulevard and he filled out an application at a coffee shop. The manager there was nicer but told him that they were looking for someone who knew how to make all the various fancy coffee drinks. Brady sat and had a mocha latte and called some of the jobs out of the paper. Either the people on the other end seemed irritated by his call, or they seemed too enthusiastic, like they were trying to scam him. He was starting to feel pretty discouraged and thought that maybe he should give up this hair brained scheme and go back to Kansas. He walked back up the boulevard and his feet were hurting and he was getting tired of pulling the suitcase behind him. He felt like people were looking at him as if he were homeless, and Brady guessed that yes, he was homeless. He saw the pet shop again across the street and decided to stop back in.

He walked into the store and the Russian man was sitting behind the counter reading his foreign newspaper again. He looked up from his paper suspiciously. He recognized Brady from earlier. The puppies were yipping in the back ground.

"My name is Brady. I'm a hard worker," he said, extending his hand. The old man stared at Brady through thick glasses, and then finally extended his hand.

The man looked at Brady's suitcase. "Isaac. Where you stay?"

"Uh, I am looking for a place," Brady admitted.

The wheels in the old man's head were turning. An older woman came out of the back carrying a cup of tea for Isaac. He said something to her in Russian and the old woman looked at Brady.

He smiled and she smiled. Isaac and the woman spoke some more in Russian and then she walked away.

Isaac grilled Brady for a few more minutes. What was he doing here? Was he an actor? A thief? Was he reliable? Honest? Was he gay? Could he be trusted with the keys and the money? Isaac showed Brady around the small shop. There were about twenty puppies – high end small dog breeds like Shitzus, and Malteepoos, and there were a few kittens, Persians, etc. Brady stressed his background working with his dad and his hard work ethic and told Isaac just about everything he wanted to hear. He even told Isaac a bit about Ashley and the old man remained poker faced as he talked. Finally, Isaac offered to pay him $300 a week cash, and then offered to let him sleep on a couch in the back until he got on his feet.

Brady looked at the couch in the back store room and couldn't believe his luck. There was a refrigerator back there and a microwave. He could join a gym and shower there. Isaac told him that there had been two break-ins in the past year and that he wanted someone to stay there and also to keep an eye on the puppies. They shook hands on it. "Promise me you won't just quit with no notice," Isaac said.

"Of course not," Brady said.

Seven

Chloe picked up Ashley at her apartment and they drove to Fred Segal on Melrose. The famous store was completely covered with ivy in the front. Chloe pulled her beamer around the back and had it valet parked among the many other luxury cars there.

Ashley realized she was in the big leagues here, as she looked around at all of the beautiful people wearing their expensive sunglasses in the bright noon day sun. It was quintessential LA. Chloe moved around like she owned the place and Ashley was impressed with her almost pushy confidence. People in LA seemed to be brash, and that was a character trait that Ashley lacked. Although she had been told by countless people how beautiful she was, and she inherently knew it, Ashley didn't carry herself that way. She always treated people the way she would want to be treated, and acted politely. That had always worked well for her, but she had a feeling it wouldn't work here. It seemed that people in LA identified kindness as weakness.

They strolled through Fred Segal looking at the $100 t-shirts and the $400 sweaters and the outrageously priced shoes. Chloe would look at items, and then toss them aside as if they were pieces of garbage, and the gay store clerks would have to move after her and refold the items. Ashley smiled at a couple of store clerks who were chatting in the corner. They said hello to her and smiled, but she could tell that they were scrutinizing everything about her, and had probably spotted the hickey. She was furious with Brady for doing that. She was furious that he had sent those hideous flowers. Now, she remembered why she hated flowers and what they reminded her of. She was furious at herself for giving into him, for having sex with him, and now he was wandering around LA somewhere, waiting for his next opportunity to harass her. She hoped he would be beaten by gang members or something. That would teach him. She felt guilty for wishing that, but that *would* teach him.

Chloe pointed to different clothing items, and held them up to see how they would look on Ashley. A particularly obsequious gay store clerk rushed over and complimented Ashley over and over again and exclaimed how "hot" she would look in one mini skirt. Chloe decided against it and tossed it aside with a flick of her wrist. Chloe kept touching Ashley, her arm, her back, her shoulder, even her butt one time. Ashley wasn't completely sure if Chloe was a lesbian, but there was something kind of boyish about her. Maybe it was the short haircut, but it certainly seemed that Chloe was flirting with Ashley, rather than just being friendly.

They finally decided they were hungry and left the store without buying anything for the café in the back. They sat at one of the outside tables. Chloe ordered them two glasses of Pinot Grigio, and they each ordered a seared Ahi salad. "We'll go over to Maxfield and see what they have. That mini skirt would have looked cute on you, but I don't like the attitude of that queen in there," Chloe said.

"Things are so expensive here. I mean, $80 for a t-shirt?" Ashley said.

"Don't worry about the price, honey. I told you, today is my treat," Chloe said lightly stroking Ashley's wrist.

Chloe looked at Ashley's face a long moment, and Ashley was unnerved by her intense gaze."Oh my God! Is that a hickey?" Chloe asked.

"Uh, I was hoping nobody would notice. I have kind of a bad situation on my hands," Ashley said.

The waiter brought the wine and Chloe grabbed hers, fixated on Ashley, waiting for her to divulge the rest of the story.

"Do tell!" Chloe said.

Ashley stared at her wine a moment. Chloe picked up her glass and raised it to toast.

"To new friends!" They knocked their glasses together and Ashley smiled. There was a moment of silence and then Ashley decided to open up about the Brady situation.

"Ok, well here it goes. Last night, when I got home from the club, my ex boyfriend from Kansas was there waiting for me. He flew out here without telling anybody and he even quit his classes at the university," Ashley said.

"Oh no," Chloe said.

"Yeah. We broke up two months ago when I decided to move out here. He can't accept it. I wanted it to be a clean break. I can't believe he has followed me out here," Ashley said.

"So, you let him in?" Chloe asked.

Ashley nodded. "I felt sorry for him I guess. It was 2:30 in the morning."

"So, you had sex with him?" Chloe asked.

"I didn't want to…" Ashley said.

"He raped you?" Chloe said.

"No, not exactly. It just kind of happened. We have a long history together," Ashley said.

"Where is he now?" Chloe asked.

"I don't know. I kicked him out this morning. He said he was not going back to Kansas," Ashley said. She looked vulnerable and worried. Chloe put her hand on top of Ashley's.

"You have to get a restraining order. This guy sounds like stalker material. He is not going to just go away," Chloe said.

"He won't do anything crazy. I know him. He's not like that. He'll run out of money and go home eventually," Ashley said.

"You don't know a man until you have rejected him. They can get really, really crazy. And nasty. Trust me, you need a restraining order. I'll take you to the Weho Sheriff's station after lunch," Chloe said. "Do you want to make the front page of the LA paper – GIRL FOUND HACKED TO PIECES IN HER APARTMENT, EX BOYFRIEND CHARGED?"

Ashley laughed, "That's a bit dramatic." She was already feeling the wine. She never usually drank alcohol this early, but it felt good and she finished her glass. Chloe waived to the waiter and ordered another.

"Dramatic, really? Have you ever heard of the Black Dahlia? It happens about twice a week out here. I'm telling you, you need to take charge of this situation before it spirals out of control. If he quit his classes and came out here, he is probably not going to leave anytime soon. You're a very, very desirable girl, and I can see why he is so nuts about you. I mean, sweat heart, you could be in Playboy magazine, like tomorrow. You don't even know how smoking hot you are! My guess is that he's not going to give up until the police drag him away in handcuffs," Chloe said. "You having sex with him last night just added gasoline to the fire," she added.

Ashley thought about it and wondered what lengths Brady would actually go to. She took another gulp of wine and tried to laugh it off. She hoped that Brady would just give up and go home and she wouldn't have to get the police involved.

Isaac put Brady right to work. His first chore was to clean the puppy cages. He had worked with animals his whole life, but he felt like novice as he tried to handle these expensive puppies. They were certainly cute, but a handful as they would wiggle and slip out of his hands as he tried to move them from cage to cage. A few people came into the store and bought pet food.

Of course, everyone wanted to look at the puppies. A big sign by the cages said NO PETTING. A few Russians came into the store and chatted with Isaac and his wife in their native language. Brady guessed they were Jewish because they were wearing those little round Jewish hats. Brady didn't really know any Jewish people and he guessed that these were probably the first Russians he had ever actually met and talked to. They seemed nice enough, but so serious, and suspicious of him. Well, he was still a stranger and would have to prove himself. This was the big city and people were probably naturally suspicious. Obviously the old man trusted him enough right away to let him stay here.

The puppies gnawed on his fingers and kept shitting and pissing all over the place. He could tell that this was going to be a constant chore. He wondered if Ashley had received the flowers. He smelled his fingers and could still smell her on him, even over the scent of the puppies. He hoped that wasn't the last time he would ever get to be with her. The thought of her with another man drove him crazy. How would he handle it? He thought that he might be capable of killing someone. Just bashing their heads in, pummeling them with his bare fists.

What if she went with a black man? He shuddered to think about it. They would be all over her here, just as the basketball players were at the University. Brady had killed deer, hunting. It was hard at first, but it got easier. He shot one deer in the heart and killed it instantly. Another he had wounded and shot it in the ass. It was limping away and he chased it over a hill and had to shoot it several more times until it finally died, and then he slit its throat for good measure. Yes, Brady decided that he was capable of killing someone. He changed the newspapers that were soaked with puppy urine as the little rascals kept barking and yipping.

Ashley was on her forth glass of wine and definitely buzzed. She picked at her Ahi salad and listened to Chloe talk about how important image was in this town and how everybody judged you by what you wore, how you styled your hair and what you drove. Ashley decided that yes, Chloe was definitely flirting with her and it slightly turned her on. She was already sexually engaged from the encounter with Brady last night and this woman kept touching her and smiling and staring into her eyes.

Ashley wondered what it would be like to have sex with Chloe, and her vagina tingled and she wondered if she was going to have an orgasm just sitting there. A well dressed businessman sitting at another table smiled at her and raised his glass. Ashley decided that she needed to pee and that was why her vagina was tingling, not because she was getting aroused by another woman. She excused herself to go to the bathroom. About the same time, Chloe's phone rang.

"Hi, we're here at Fred Segal having a bite and a glass of wine. Why don't you join us?" Chloe said. "Yes, I'm here with Ashley, the hostess from Kraven."

Ashley walked past the businessman who had smiled at her and she smiled broadly. The man must be at least fifty, but he was handsome and stylishly dressed. Maybe he was someone.

Chuck Alexander and Kurt were on the golf course at the Riviera Country Club. Chuck liked bringing guys like Kurt out there to play. That way he could be the big shot. Plus Kurt was the bartender with all the coke connections and knew all the women that came into the club. Chuck lit up a big Cuban cigar and sized up his tee shot. He pulled his driver out of his golf bag and teed up a ball.

"So, you've got to tell me? How is Jillian in the sack? I'll bet you she's a freak," Chuck said.

"Oh, she's a freak alright, but not in a good way. The bitch is frigid if you ask me. Cold as ice. I wouldn't fuck her again with your dick," Kurt said.

Chuck laughed and took a practice swing with his cigar still hanging out of his mouth. "I'll loan it to you. Have you seen the modeling pictures of her?" Chuck asked.

"That was twenty years ago. She's a dry cow now, and as my daddy from Texas said – you can't chase a dry cow up a hill," Kurt said. Chuck got a good chuckle out of that.

He hit his ball and it drifted off to the right and landed in the rough about 180 yards up. "Shit!" Chuck said.

Kurt teed up his ball. "You'd be better off just getting a high priced whore. That's what she is anyway. A coke whore," Kurt said, before taking a practice swing.

"I don't like the whole whore thing. You know, you can't kiss them and all that," Chuck said.

"You want to kiss that mouth after she sucked my cock?" Kurt asked, smiling.

"You're a sick bastard," Chuck said.

Kurt wailed on the ball and hit it 240 yards straight up the fairway.

"Excellent ball!" Chuck said. They put their clubs away and got into the golf cart.

"I'll spend a few hundred on the bitch to get into her pants, just to say that I did," Chuck said as they took off in the cart down the fairway.

"Now, that new hostess, Ashley, I'd eat a bucket of her shit just to smell her asshole," Kurt said. The men's laughter echoed throughout the golf course.

Jillian arrived dressed in her yoga gear. She ordered a glass of wine. She was chilly to Ashley and Ashley remained quiet as Chloe and Jillian talked it up. "So, how was your night with Kurt?" Chloe asked.

"Never again. I kicked him out of my place this morning. He's a loser," Jillian said.

Kurt, the bartender?" Ashley asked.

"Yes. That one," Jillian said.

"He is just gross. He has a big, crooked dick that curves to right and it hurts like hell," Jillian said.

"Ewwwww!" Chloe said. Ashley laughed nervously.

"His back is hairy too. He's just a disgusting ogre. A real douche," Jillian said.

Ashley's head was spinning; the wine was really hitting her. She knew she had to stop drinking because she had her acting class that night. She had to audition for the class, and now she was worried that she had already drank too much and wouldn't be sharp. Just as she was thinking that, a bottle of Veuve Clicquot arrived in an ice bucket.

"This is compliments of Mr. Levin," the waiter said as he opened the champagne and poured three glasses.

All three women looked over to the handsome businessman and waived. Jillian's face lit up and she turned on the charm until she realized that the bottle had been sent to Ashley and not her. Fucking little blonde hayseed bitch, Jillian thought. So this was how it was going to go from now on? The dumb twat didn't even know what to do, Jillian observed.

"I can't drink anymore, I have acting class this afternoon and I am already tipsy" Ashley said.

"Oh, don't worry about it. I have a pill that will fix you right up. Remind me before you go," Chloe said.

"Okay, I shouldn't though," Ashley said as she watched Chloe pour her a glass of champagne.

It suddenly occurred to Jillian that maybe she could exploit this young girl somehow. Make some money off of her. She needed money, and if she could exploit this girl, she would.

"That guy over there is Michael Levin, he's an agent at IPA," Jillian said. "I think he likes you."

Ashley looked at him and he smiled again.

"Jillian used to be a model," Chloe said.

"Really?" said Ashley.

"Yeah, a long time ago. You could probably do some modeling if you make some changes," said Jillian.

"Changes? What kind of changes?" Ashley wanted to know.

"Your hair for starters. It needs work. I mean, it's like ten years out of style," Jillian said.

"Oh, that's not true, Jillian! Maybe only five years," Chloe said, laughing.

"You want to play in the major league, you have to know the truth," Jillian said. "You have a great, natural look, but you need some finishing."

Ashley seemed hurt, but knew that Jillian was right. She finished her glass of champagne and Chloe quickly refilled it.

"Do you have pictures?" Jillian asked.

"No, I need to get them," Ashley said.

"I know a good photographer, but it's going to cost you a few hundred dollars. Maybe you can work out a "trade" deal with him," Jillian said.

"What kind of trade?" Ashley asked.

Jillian studied Ashley a moment," Who gave you the hickey?"

Ashley appeared embarrassed. Chloe answered for her and told the whole story about the stalker ex boyfriend.

"Get a restraining order," Jillian said.

The businessman finished his lunch and rose from his table. He approached the lady's table.

"Thanks for the champagne," Jillian said, smiling and flashing her eyebrows. Levin gave her a dismissive look and focused on Ashley.

"You're very beautiful. Are you an actress?" Levin asked.

Ashley turned bright red, her face already flushed from the alcohol.

"Uh, yes. I am trying," Ashley said. Levin produced a business card from his wallet.

"Give me a call. I may be able to help you out," he said. Ashley thanked him and he walked away.

"Look at you," Chloe said, "They're already attacking."

"Don't ever say you're trying. You're either an actress or you're not," Jillian said.

Chloe grasped Ashley's hand tightly. "Don't call him right away, give it a few days," Chloe said. Ashley's head was literally spinning. She felt like she might pass out.

Eight

Ashley woke up on top of her sleeping bag and her apartment was dark. She tried to piece together what had happened. She remembered being very drunk and going shopping at a few different stores in West Hollywood with Chloe. She remembered laughing uncontrollably at one store and everyone was looking at them. She kind of remembered peeing on the floor of a changing room when she couldn't find a bathroom.

They had seen a celebrity somewhere – maybe it was Tom Cruise, maybe Harrison Ford. Ashley couldn't remember. She vaguely remembered kissing Chloe on the lips in her car as she dropped her off. She was embarrassed. She looked at her clock. It was 6:15 and already dark outside. She had to be at the acting class at 7:30.

Ashley jumped up and was thoroughly disgusted with herself. This was not going to happen again. This acting class was too important. Getting into Jeremy Bone's class was very important, and now she might screw that up. She had to pull herself together. She saw the shopping bags sitting by the door. She couldn't even remember what Chloe had bought for her. She looked in the bags and pulled out a mini skirt and a white top. In another box was a pair of knee high leather boots. Ashley looked at the price tag - $418.65.

She saw a couple of pills lying on top of the breakfast nook. She stared at them a long moment. They were round and pink and they had the letters, *AD* on them. She remembered Chloe had given them to her and said to take one before her acting class. It would help her focus. Ashley was parched anyway and her head was throbbing from all the wine. She stared at the pill as she poured herself a glass of water. She popped it into her mouth, and then she stripped her clothes off on the way to the shower.

She took a quick shower and then hurried to put a little makeup on. She put on her new outfit and the boots. She didn't have time to linger and look at herself and she rushed out the door.

She got into her car and started driving. She had never been to the acting class before, but she knew it was in Hollywood on Franklin, just east of Vine somewhere. She thought she knew how to get there and she turned onto Sunset heading east. About that time the pill started to kick in. It was as if somebody just turned on jet engines inside Ashley's brain. Her hands were shaking and she was grinding her teeth. She nearly ran into the back of a car as it stopped on Sunset and Laurel.

Wow, what was this pill? Ashley did feel very alert all of a sudden and her wine hangover virtually disappeared. She revved her car's engine and shot around slower traffic in front of her. She was going to kill the monologue she had prepared for the class. She got over to Vine pretty quickly and then she turned north like she knew exactly where she was going.

She found the address on Franklin across from the Celebrity Center on Bronson. She found parking in the super market across the street and she hurried into the class.

Ashley found the class upstairs above a small theater. There were a group of actors gathered around a table in the front. They were signing into some sheet. A guy sitting at the table instructed anybody who was auditing for the class to sign in. Ashley was so wired and nervous she didn't look anybody in the eye, but noticed they were all pretty good looking people. She signed into the sheet and avoided eye contact with a flamboyantly gay guy who was in charge of the signup sheet. He scrutinized her as she signed in.

She walked into the classroom. There were probably thirty people sitting in chairs that were arranged into a half circle. The Instructor, Jeremy Bone was talking to some actor in the front of the room. Bone was short and thin, wearing a black turtleneck, and had a full head of wavy hair with one shock of gray in it. Ashley noticed him look at her as she sat down in the back row. Her heart raced and she was mad herself that she wasn't clear headed for this. She was obviously fucked up. The pill had ratcheted her into some other dimension where she had never been before. She didn't know if she could perform the monologue. She was terrified. The other actors around her were quietly talking and laughing. She forced a smile to a couple of them, but really couldn't see their faces she was so terrified.

Jeremy Bone was known as the acting guru around Hollywood for up and coming actors. He had written a book, "Jeremy Bone's Guide to

Making it in Hollywood," that had sold over 25,000 copies in its first year. He was a former casting director that had worked primarily on B-movies and discovered that he could make a lot more money teaching classes. Also, he had developed a minor God-complex since starting the class. Students hung on his every word and would do almost anything to please him. One of the biggest benefits of teaching the class was having access to a steady stream of the best looking young men in Hollywood.

Jeremy Bone had one of those counter/clickers beside his bed and he had recorded 223 clicks on it. That was the number of young men he had bedded – many of them "straight." Several of the people who had studied in his class were now working actors, working on television shows and getting minor movie roles. Jeremy had yet to turn out a major A-list star and he desperately needed to. He knew his stock would surely go down if he did not produce a major star soon. He wanted to be thought of in Hollywood as the new Lee Strasberg.

Tuesday night was audition night when actors who wanted to join the class had to audition to be accepted into the class. There were only so many spots and not everyone could get in. That night he was going to take just one new actor. Jeremy scanned the classroom for any new attractive male student. If a student was attractive and male he was almost sure to get in, but Jeremy had to be careful not to make it too obvious. He would have to admit some qualified female actors, and if they were super hot he would probably take them, because the super hot girls attracted the super hot straight boys and those were Jeremy's favorite challenges - because they probably wouldn't talk about his predatory behavior because they wouldn't want anybody to know about it.

"Okay, people, let's get started. We have several people auditioning tonight, so we can't waste any time," Bone said. The crowd quickly went silent. Bone scanned the room, scrutinizing all of the faces. "Let's take a moment and do our relaxation exercise. For those of you who are new here, this is how we do it. Close your eyes and imagine yourself slowly melting. Start from the top of your head and go slowly downward. Relax every muscle in your body starting from the top of your head, imagine it melting away...." Bone said, his voice taking on a hypnotic tone.

Ashley tried to do it, and she could feel her heart thumping inside of her chest and her head was racing and she felt an incredible tension in her jaw.

"Release the tension in your jaw, part your lips and let your mouth hang slightly open," Bone continued.

Ashley tried to do that and her mouth was incredibly dry, she didn't have any water and now that was all she could think about.

"Forget about all the traffic, all the bills, and parking tickets, and the DMV, and the boyfriends and the girlfriends and the nagging mothers, and the stoic fathers, and the bosses, and the asshole customers, let them melt into oblivion," Bone said.

Ashley remembered that Brady was in town and it unnerved her. When and where would he show up again? Maybe he had even followed her here. No, Ashley remembered he didn't have a car. But he could have rented one by now.

"Breath through your nose, exhale through your mouth. Let your heart beat slow down. Relax your arms, let them hang loose and release all of your tension through your finger tips. Just release it all," Bone was pacing slowly in front of the room.

Ashley tried to release the tension in her fingertips and realized that her pinky finger was twitching beyond her control. The intensity of the pill was not fading, and if anything it was increasing.

"Imagine all of your bodily functions slowly shutting down. Your heart slows down, your breathing. The tension rolls down your spine, though your genitals, down your legs and out the ends of your toes," Bone said.

Ashley thought of kissing Chloe in the car and was sexually aroused by it. She could feel her vagina throbbing and she remembered when Brady had climaxed inside her the night before. She thought of all the times she had swallowed his cum and sometimes they kissed afterward and she spit it back into his mouth.

"Okay, you are entirely relaxed now. All tension has melted away like candle wax and now you are just a puddle of warm creamy lifeless goo," Bone said. "Just sit there for a few moments and be nothing, do nothing, think nothing."

Ashley had done variations of exercises like this before. Bone's voice was very gay, but there was something hypnotic and seductive about it.

She thought of fucking the gay theater student back in college and wondered if she could seduce Jeremy Bone. He was an extremely handsome man, and she wondered what it would be like to fuck him and she thought of her incredibly dry mouth and her twitching pinky finger and her throbbing vagina.

"Ok, actors, let's come out of it," Bone said, "How does that feel? Is everyone ready now?"

Several people in the class vocalized that they were ready. Ashley was frozen with fear. She needed some water badly. She saw a water bottle sitting next to a student in front of her. She wanted to grab it and drink it in the worst way. She felt like she was in the desert and hadn't had water in days. Bone had called a male actor up to the front of the class, but their voices were just drones now. Ashley's heart was pounding and she needed water.

She suddenly bolted out of her seat and squeezed past several other actors as the student was performing his monologue. It threw the student off a little, but he kept going the best he could. Bone shot Ashley daggers with his eyes as she walked out. There was a water cooler in the front office and Ashley attacked it like someone who hadn't drank water for days. She quickly swallowed several small Dixie cups full of water and could hear ringing in her ears and her face felt numb. She did felt a little better after downing ten cups of water.

She listened at the door for the actor to finish his monologue. She heard clapping and then walked back into the room, trying to be invisible.

"Excuse me, young lady, what is your name, please?" Bone said loudly.

Ashley realized that he was talking at her and froze like a deer in the headlights.

"Uh, Ashley," she said. Bone looked on the sheet of paper.

"Ashley Duncan?" Bone said.

"Yes," she said, as every eye in the class was now upon her.

"Well, since you were thoughtful enough to interrupt another actor's fucking performance, then you must be ready to go right now," Bone said.

"Sorry," Ashley said.

"No, by all means. I'm sure you are a star in your own mind already, and you should be treated like one, right class?" Bone said and almost everyone laughed.

Ashley was frozen with embarrassment and humiliation. She didn't know if she should cry, scream, or run out of the class.

"You are the star of the show, so let's see what you are capable of. Get ready for your close up, honey," Bone said, then motioning her to come forward. "Come on, now!"

Ashley squeezed past several people and made her way to the front of the class and stood next to Bone. He draped his arm over her shoulder. "Nice sweater, honey, you look smashing," Bone said. Everyone laughed, but it was nervous laughter, as members of the class were embarrassed for her.

"What will we be performing for the class today, honey," Bone asked. Ashley looked into the sea of faces, and then glanced at Bone, who had a devilish gleam in his eye.

She introduced herself and her monologue from a "A little Shop of Horrors." It was a comedic monologue. She took a moment, and then went right into it. She lost herself in it and could hear her own voice but seemed to be outside of her own body looking down on herself.

Jeremy Bone watched her closely. She was obviously high on something he thought. Maybe crystal meth, and that was strange because she didn't look the type. There was something, *something* unique about her, Bone thought. He wasn't really paying attention to her acting, but was instead fascinated by her face. She had some kind of compelling quality that he couldn't quite put his finger on, kind of a girl next door with smoldering sexuality lurking underneath. Not in a slutty way, but she was definitely the girl everyone wanted to fuck. Bone thought to himself that *he* may even want to fuck her and he never wanted to fuck girls. In any case, she had some raw quality that people were going to like. Some quality that was going to translate into money in people's pockets.

The monologue took her two and half minutes to perform but seemed like it had taken hours, or milliseconds, Ashley couldn't decide. When she was finished, everyone was laughing and clapping, even Bone.

Bone leaned into her and hugged her. He whispered into her ear, "You're in, but I would rather see you do something dramatic next time."

Ashley floated back to her seat, not so sure what had just happened, but she surmised that she had pulled it off. She couldn't even believe it herself; she had never felt so entirely fucked up and out of it in her life. The pill was a gift that just kept on giving. She couldn't wait for it to be out of her system. She would never be so reckless again, she promised herself. Bone called another actor up, and Ashley tried to pull herself together and focus on the remainder of the class.

Jillian had scheduled a late appointment with Dr. Davis, her hypnotist/therapist. Dr. Davis had his office in Beverly Hills on the sixth floor of a Camden drive high rise that was full of medical offices, which housed the busiest plastic surgeons in America. Jillian's plastic surgeon was also in this building, and her gynecologist was just across the street.

Dr. Davis looked like the slick Beverly Hills doctor that he was, with perfectly coiffed and dyed hair with just the right amount of highlights, a gym fit sculptured physique, and perfectly tanned skin. He was 55, but looked years younger.

Dr. Davis had many wealthy, influential, and celebrity clients. He specialized in hypnotherapy that was designed to break people out of self destructive habits and behaviors. He was a licensed psychiatrist also, so in case the hypnotherapy didn't work he could prescribe the most effective drugs all day long.

Jillian saw him regularly, and Chloe called on him professionally as well. He didn't charge Jillian his normal rate and had been seeing her for years. Dr. Davis was an avid existentialist, meaning he made up his own morality as he saw fit. He sometimes took liberties with certain female clients that would probably be looked down on with great disapproval by the state medical board and other professional organizations, but he felt entirely justified because he was providing a "service" that his clients wanted and needed.

Jillian sat on the sofa in his spacious and plush office. She was his last client of the day and they both had made sure that was the case. Dr. Davis looked at her, smiling.

"So, Jillian. How was your week? Did any issues come up that you would like to talk about?" Dr. Davis said.

"My week was shit. I don't know how much more of this I can take. I only thought of suicide about four times a day, so I guess that was an improvement from the week before," Jillian said.

"Well, it's nice to know that you made improvement in that area. I am concerned, however. If the recurring thoughts become a "plan" then maybe we should consider putting you into an inpatient facility for thirty days or so, until you can perhaps get a clearer perspective," Dr. Davis said.

Jillian leaned back on the couch and sighed. "Oh please. I'm not going to Betty Ford again. My finances are a mess. Inpatient is out of the question, as divine as it sounds. I would love a vacation like that. The truth is, and you're the only person I have told that I'm 60 days behind on my mortgage. I have past due bills stacked up on my kitchen table. Things are getting a little critical," Jillian said with her eyes shut tightly. It killed her to divulge the extent of her financial situation.

Dr. Davis stared at her feet. "Jillian, I'm sure you understand that we all experience temporary difficulties with finances. There are always solutions, maybe some that we don't really want to face. Either we have to generate more income, or downsize our lifestyles."

"Yes, I don't want to face either of those options. I feel like a car with 300,000 miles on it. Highway miles. People might like the paint job enough to stop and take a look, but they keep moving on to the newer low mileage models," Jillian said, still squeezing her eyes shut.

Dr. Davis chuckled. "Well, Jillian, that is an interesting analogy. Perhaps you are just parking at the wrong lot, to take it a step further."

Jillian's eyes shot open, "So, you agree I have 300,000 miles on me! So, I am not imagining it. I'm just a worn out old hag that should be taken out to pasture and shot right now!" Jillian started to sit up, but Dr. Davis gently restrained her and pushed her back down on the sofa.

"Jillian, I appreciate your dramatics, but I think it is important to recognize certain realities and deal with them accordingly. None of us, none can be 25 forever. I experienced similar feelings just after I turned 40, but now I am in my 50's and I am closer to self actualization than I have ever been. It's important to know that these are normal phases and transition periods that are a part of life," Dr. Davis said as he put on latex gloves. He stood and walked over to his desk. He took a syringe that was already loaded and a rubber strap and walked back to his chair.

Jillian watched him with anticipation.

Dr. Davis took her left arm and wrapped the rubber strap around her bicep. "This will relax you," he said. "This will only hurt a second," he said.

He quickly found a vein and injected her. Jillian cringed, and then her eyes rolled back into her head as the drug quickly hit her.

"Remember, the solution will present itself when we are open to all of the possibilities," Dr. Davis said.

He watched her for a moment, as she shifted on the couch and rolled into a fetal position, smiling like a little baby with a blankie.

Dr. Davis pulled her shoes off and dropped them onto the floor.

"You are a very capable woman, Jillian. Very capable, shrewd, naturally and uniquely equipped to overcome the mundane, the petty, the provincial obstacles of life," Dr. Davis said as he was fondling her feet and it was apparent that he was enjoying his number one fetish. Jillian purred like a kitten has he sniffed and caressed her feet, while at the same time undid his belt and unzipped his pants.

"I feel soooo warm now, sooo good," Jillian purred.

Dr. Davis began sucking her toes and masturbating with his free hand. She moaned with pleasure and Dr. Davis was smothering himself in her feet.

By the time Ashley got home the pill was wearing off and she felt exhausted, but with an edge on. She drank the last Heineken in the refrigerator hoping it would bring her down. What was that pill? It was obviously some kind of stimulant. She looked at the other pill lying on her breakfast nook and picked it up to toss it in the trash, but then changed her mind and put it in the cupboard.

She hated the way that it made her feel, but she may need it again in an emergency. After all, she had pulled a rabbit out of the hat at the acting class. The instructor, who was so cruel to her in the beginning, was praising her on her way out. She was going to have to pay $600 a month to be in the class, but she figured it was a necessity.

She started to calculate all of her expenses in her mind. $1275 for rent, car insurance, $100, acting class, $600, utilities, $100, food, $300, gym membership, $50. She started to panic, how was she going to pay for all of these things? And she needed photos. Headshots. Jillian had said she could work out a trade deal with the photographer. Doing what? This was all a little overwhelming.

Then she remembered the man at Fred Segal, the agent who gave her his card. What did the man want? Could he really help her and would she have to sleep with him? He wasn't that bad, Ashley thought. If she did have to have sex with him to get his help, it wouldn't be so bad, and she might even enjoy it. He was handsome for an older man, and Jewish. She had never been with a Jewish man before and she had heard that they were good in bed.

She searched for his card in her purse and panicked when she couldn't find it. She finally poured out the entire contents of her purse and sifted through everything in a desperate search for the business card. She finally found it and breathed a sigh of relief. She stared at the card: MICHAEL LEVIN, SENIOR AGENT, IPA, with the address of his office and phone number. She remembered that Chloe told her not to call right away. She decided to take her advice and wait, so she put the card away in the cupboard with the pill.

Ashley took her beer and sat on top of her sleeping bag thinking. So, this was how it worked? You do your best to look "in" and stylish, you hang out at places where you will be seen by the right people. You take the right acting class, you eat and drink the right things, and you work out at the right gym. You take the right pills. You fuck the right people. It wasn't really about the "acting," or the "art," like her instructors back at the university had led all of the students to believe.

Had any of those instructors ever even been to Hollywood? They wouldn't cut it here. They wouldn't have the heart, nor the stomach for it. Art and acting had almost zero to do with the whole equation. Ashley was sure that there were hundreds, thousands, of capable actors that would never get a chance because they couldn't or wouldn't play the game that needed to be played. "Art," what a joke, Ashley thought.

Ashley decided right then and there that she would do whatever it took. She would play the game and play to win. It was do or die now. She would not return to Kansas like a whipped dog. She would not give all of those people who doubted her and snickered at her the satisfaction of her failure. She would not give her dad that satisfaction, and she definitely would not give Brady that satisfaction. Let him return like a whipped dog. He acted like one anyway.

He had looked pathetic standing out on the sidewalk the night before with his suitcase. He looked pathetic crying and groveling. He took advantage of her and basically raped her in her own apartment. He knew when he arrived that she did *not* want to have sex with him. He was probably trying to get her pregnant again, to keep possession of her, to destroy and diminish her dreams one sperm load at a time. Fucking bastard, he would deserve every bad thing coming his way. He was just a possessive, scared little boy who would never amount to anything, and certainly wouldn't if his dad didn't hand him a business.

Yes, he may have been the big quarterback in high school, but he couldn't even get college scholarship playing football. *Loser*. She never wanted to see or talk to him again. She never thought she would feel that way, but she did now. Before yesterday she had tender feelings for him, precious memories of their good times together, but they had all but evaporated overnight. He had forced himself on her one last time and that sealed the deal for him. In her mind he was dead and gone.

If she had to suck off some agent or some acting instructor to get in, she would do it. At that moment, Ashley's phone rang. It was 11:30, who could be calling, she wondered – it had better not be Brady. She saw that it was from the restaurant on her caller ID. She answered it. Kurt was on the other end of the line.

"Hi, Ashley, what are you doing?" Kurt said.

"Nothing. Getting ready for bed," Ashley said, wondering why he was calling and then she remembered what Jillian had said about him.

"Cool. I was just missing you here. It's been dead tonight. We had a little rush earlier, but now it's dead. What are you doing later?" Kurt said.

Ashley was now irritated, "I'm going to bed, I already told you that."

"Oh, ok. Thought you might want to hang out or something. I guess I'll see you tomorrow," Kurt said, his voice fading with rejection.

"Ok, bye," Ashley said hanging up before he could respond.

What an asshole, Ashley thought. Who did he think he was calling her at 11:30? She could have him fired, because he obviously got her number from the employee roster at work. Jean Pierre would fire his ass for calling her. She would monitor the situation and if he became a pest whatsoever she would turn him in. Ashley's days of being a

Pollyanna were over. She finished her beer and lay on her side, her mind racing.

Brady lay on the sofa in the back room of the pet shop. He could hear some of the puppies making noise in the front room. The smell of pet food permeated everything. He couldn't decide if he was on some great adventure or the biggest fool alive. He leaned toward the latter. Isaac and his wife had left around eight. Isaac had admonished him to be very careful if he went in or out and gave him a key. Part of the reason Isaac was letting him stay there was to prevent break-ins. A month earlier the store was broken into through a back door and several expensive puppies were taken.

Brady had taken a liking to one of the puppies. It was an apricot colored Cockapoo – the runt of the litter. The dog seemed to be looking to Brady to save it as all of the bigger dogs would just run over and nose the runt out of everything. Brady thought about how that was a microcosm of the world here in LA. Dog eat dog. He had never noticed the brutal competitiveness of life back in Kansas, where people tended to take care of each other. Here, it seemed like the weak fell to the wayside, while the strong spit dust in their faces as they blasted by in their expensive luxury cars. Everyone was competing for the job, the woman, the status, and it was as if they were all money hungry and desperate, and dangerous, even.

Trying to get their share of the disappearing pie. Most got a few crumbs, and some ended up dead in the gutters. Brady had not grown up rich, but his family was well off by Kansas standards. They never were short on food, or wondering how the next month's rent was going to be paid. Brady had seen people here living on the street wearing duct taped shoes with long matted beards and hair, and filthy ragged clothes eating out of garbage cans. There were a lot of them, and most of them seemed to be half crazy or full blown insane. He had talked to a few of the homeless people on the boulevard and handed out a few dollars, but realized pretty quickly that if he gave money to everyone who asked, he would be broke himself in no time. He wondered if any of them had backgrounds similar to his? Did they come here chasing a girl and end up homeless and crazy on the streets? He could see himself in that situation. Hell, he was half way there already.

If the people back home could see him now, laying in the backroom of a pet store in West Hollywood owned by Russian Jews, they would assume that he was already completely off his rocker. He could call the airline in the morning and see about getting a flight back home. But he promised Isaac he would give a notice. Well, it was better to bail out of this now, and the longer he stayed, the harder it would be to leave, he thought. He might even be able to make it home before his parents found out he was in LA, if they hadn't already. He shuddered with embarrassment at the thought of it.

Then he realized that nobody in the world knew where he was right now, in this pet store. And they would never know. This would be one of those humiliating memories that he would never tell anyone about, except maybe Ashley, if she ever came back to him. Then they would laugh about it, but otherwise nobody else would think it was funny.

He looked at his phone, it was 12:15. Ashley had not called. She must have received the flowers and she hadn't called. Fucking bitch. He could be dying and she wouldn't care. He *was* dying. Lying here in the dark in the back of a pet shop in West Hollywood, slowly dying of a broken heart. And she didn't care. He thought of calling her and telling her as much. He stared at his phone, teetering on the edge of calling her and telling her what he really thought. He resisted calling her minute by minute all day long. How could she so callously throw away a relationship that had lasted almost eight years? How could she so easily do that? If he could understand it, he could accept it, but he couldn't even begin to understand it. She would find out. She would find out what she lost and by then it would be too late. She would regret her decision for the rest of her life.

He heard something in the back of the store, like a trash can tipping over. He jumped up and went to the side window that was barred over. He tried to see where the noise was coming from. He listened and waited and could feel his own heart beating. Maybe he was going to die right here in the pet store by puppy robbers. How ironic would that be? Ashley would feel real good then. Everyone back in Colby would hate her and blame her, and her "career" would be sidetracked by the tragedy of it. He heard some more rustling coming from the alley behind the store. He thought of his obituary in the home town newspaper – "Local man dies in Hollywood Pet Store Burglary." The all star quarterback and homecoming king from the class of 99'. The promising son of local veterinarian, Henry Anderson. His mom would be devastated; she would never recover from it, always wondering where she went wrong, how her son could end up with such low self esteem that he couldn't let one girl get away.

Finally, Brady saw a homeless guy, crazy and foaming from the mouth stumble out of the alley and walk by the front of the pet store mumbling and cussing to himself. Brady's adrenalin level went down as the man disappeared down the street in search of his next garbage can or bottle. Brady almost wished he was an alcoholic or drug addict, because then he could escape from this horrible feeling that wouldn't go away. He heard the puppies yipping in the cages and he thought of the runt cockapoo. He made his way to the puppy cages and he saw the puppy staring at him with those sad eyes and wagging its little tail.

A smile came to his face and he picked the puppy up out of its cage. The other dogs clawed and clambered and barked for his attention, but he carried the runt away, who was by now smothering his face with kisses.

"How are you little boy?" Brady said.

He lay back on the sofa in the back room, snuggling with the puppy. It made him feel better for a moment.

Nine

Chloe's job was her identity. She was a representative for a huge pharmaceutical company. Her territory covered much of the LA Basin and parts of Orange County. Needless to say, Chloe had one of the best territories in the nation for drug sales, legal and illegal. The irony was that the federal government had spent billions fighting the war on drugs and now more people than ever before were hooked on legally prescribed narcotics: Pain killers, antidepressants, amphetamines, muscle relaxers, and anti-anxiety drugs. While other businesses were faltering and failing and subject to economic downturns, the drug business was booming.

Chloe had won all of her companies' top sales awards for several years in a row. She had one the best territories; only being beat out by the Bay area, New York City, and the Washington DC market occasionally. The brand new BMW Chloe was driving was leased by her company. She received a healthy expense account, and her salary, bonuses, and benefits package totaled more than $185,000 a year.

Chloe was a natural at the job. The doctors she called on loved her and she had a natural ability to schmooze, and to apply just enough grease and pressure to get those doctors to prescribe her brand of drugs nearly every time they pulled out their prescription pads. She was the face of her company in Southern California, and as long as she was the face, doctors would choose CoreGen Pharmaceuticals over other brands of drugs.

Chloe was driving down the 405 on her way to one of her best clients, a plastic surgeon in Newport Beach. The exclusive Orange County community that boasted more plastic surgery per capita than even Beverly Hills, or Palm Beach, Florida. She was listening to new age music as she weaved in and out of traffic, passing everyone in sight. She just wanted to zip down to Orange County, and make an appearance. Drop off some free samples of a new antidepressant, MoreCore, that the company was pushing, and then hurry back to LA before the afternoon rush hour.

She couldn't stop thinking about Ashley. She didn't remember ever being as obsessed with another woman. Her hair, her skin, her eyes, the sound of her voice. Her breasts, her legs, her hands, her wrists, her feet. Everything about her was just delicious. She was just so *fresh*. So adorable was her smile, and her cute little laugh. Her perfectly shaped butt. Chloe was getting so aroused thinking about Ashley as she felt the vibration of the road underneath her that she thought that she might have a spontaneous orgasm, and she almost rear ended a truck as traffic suddenly slowed in front of her. Chloe pulled herself together, feeling a rush of adrenalin mixing with the Adderall in her system. She took a deep breath and told herself to slow down. She was amped to the max and her obsession with Ashley was consuming her.

Chloe thought about her own sexuality. She was only really attracted to women, but hated to be labeled as gay. She had no interest in or allegiance to the gay community. She was sickened by the bull dykes, and in-your-face lesbians. She once had a brief relationship with a gay Latina, who was a part of the whole lesbian community in West Hollywood. They went to the annual Dinah Shore party in Palm Springs where thousands of lesbians gather every year. She felt like her girlfriend, Vanessa was putting her on display like a piece of meat at the Dinah Shore weekend and she hated it. They fought constantly all weekend and Vanessa was such a drama queen. Then there were all of those sickening, masculine dykes who looked like they were all some kind of mongoloid sisters, even wearing the same uniforms. The relationship between Vanessa and Chloe ended dramatically after they returned from Palm Springs. Vanessa stormed out of Chloe's condo and threw a potted plant through the window. Chloe took out a restraining order on her.

Chloe's parents, who lived in Virginia, did not know that she was "gay". Maybe they suspected it, because they never asked her if she had a boyfriend, or when she was going to get married. It was a don't ask, don't tell policy, she supposed. She did have boyfriends in high school and college. She even went out with one guy, Cameron for over a year and he was in love with her. She pretended to enjoy sex with him, but in reality she hated the cock. She was repulsed by those ugly, hairy, throbbing members that poked and spurted. Cameron eventually got the hint when they were drunk in Las Vegas and hooked up with some random girl for a threesome. Cameron saw how Chloe was a different person, almost possessed as she reacted sexually with the other women. The guy's fantasy of having a threesome with two women was shattered when he realized his girl liked other girls better than men in the sack. Chloe and Cameron had a bitter fight on the plane coming back from Las Vegas. That was the end of that.

Chloe began thinking of Ashley again. She assumed that Ashley was straight, but she had seduced straight women before. She had slept with many "straight" women, of course, including her friend Jillian. Most of the women enjoyed the experience sexually, but would back away quickly once anything resembling intimacy surfaced. Then they would retreat and act as if Chloe were some kind of evil bad influence, and would stop taking her phone calls. She hoped that it wouldn't be that way with Ashley. She hoped that maybe she could win the girl over by showering her with gifts and attention.

The girl seemed to be in desperate need of an LA mentor. Chloe had to insure that *she* would be that mentor. She had to keep the wolves at bay. Especially the male wolves. The Michael Levins, the Chuck Armstrongs, of the world. The sleazy predator men who were always searching for fresh meat to tarnish and exploit. Chloe realized that her main drawback as a mentor was that she was not in the entertainment business. Ashley was looking for someone to guide her career. Chloe was not in the entertainment business, but she was smart enough to recognize that Ashley had that something that everyone in Hollywood was looking for since the days of silent film. Ashley had that innocent all American girl next door that everyone, EVERYONE wants to fuck quality about her that translated into big dollars at the box office, in advertising, and on television.

As much as Chloe loved her career, and as much as it was a part of her identity, she realized that she had the skills that it took to succeed in any business. Maybe it was time for her to enter the world of entertainment. She was in the center of it already. Maybe it was time for her to stop pushing drugs and start pushing stars. Maybe it was time for her to take on Ashley as her first client. Maybe the stars were aligning to bring her and Ashley together so they could realize their fantastic destinies together. Chloe pulled into the carpool lane and sped around long string of cars building up to the 405/110 interchange.

Back in Kansas, word had reached Brady's parents that he was in Los Angeles after Ashley. He wasn't answering their phone calls and they were worried sick about him. Brady's father, Henry, was really upset. This was just so out of character for Brady. He had always been the perfect son; they had never had any trouble with him, except for that one time when he and bunch of guys from the football team got into trouble for trashing a motel room when they were away at a game. And of course, *the abortion.*

It seemed that the core of Brady's troubles had started and ended with Ashley Duncan. Henry always liked Ashley, thought she was adorable, but knew deep inside that Brady would never be able to hold her. Henry and Brady's mother, Margaret, were both relieved when Ashley and Brady broke up. They assumed that she would move to California, Brady would have a brief grieving period and then he would move on.

They knew Brady was despondent after the break up. Now, it seemed that Brady was having some kind of spiritual crisis and break down.

Henry liked Ashley's parents. They were good people and he had been their veterinarian for decades. Jim Duncan could be ornery and difficult, and there were times that he was slow paying, but Henry knew that Jim was ultimately a good guy. Ashley's mom, Ginney was the salt of the earth.

Henry Anderson decided to pay a visit to the Duncan household on the family farm just east of Colby to see if they knew anything. When Henry arrived in his veterinary truck, Jim Duncan was out by the barn working on one of his tractors. Jim watched curiously as the truck pulled up his driveway. The road was muddy from the melted snow of a few days ago. Several barking dogs ran up to greet Henry's truck, and he had vaccinated every single one of them.

Jim Duncan was a stout man with a ruddy completion and thick eyebrows. Henry Anderson was tall with an aging handsome and friendly face. He climbed out of his truck. "Howdy, Jim," Henry said.

"Howdy, Henry. What brings you out this way?" Jim said, still working on his tractor.

"Well, I'm a bit embarrassed to say the least," Henry said. Jim's jaw clenched in anger as he fought with a bolt on the tractor. Henry stepped closer to take a look. "It seems that Brady has gone and quit school and ran off to Hollywood after your daughter," Henry said.

Anger welled up in Jim's face as he broke the bolt free. He finally looked up at Henry. "Goddamn girl. She has the craziest Goddamn notions. She don't listen to anything I have to say. I give up," Jim said tossing a large wrench onto the ground.

"I heard this morning that Brady was out there from one of his friends. Both his mom and I have tried to call him, but he doesn't answer. I was just wondering if you knew anything about it, or if you had Ashley's number out there," Henry said as delicately as he could.

"I don't talk to her. Haven't since she left for California," Jim said. "Ginny!" Jim yelled for his wife.

After a moment, Ginny appeared from the house and came walking out. She smiled at Henry, but at the same time braced herself for some kind of bad news. "Hi Henry," she said. Henry smiled and nodded, though seemed embarrassed.

"Brady went off to California chasing after Ashley. You heard from her?" Jim asked. Ginny also seemed embarrassed and ashamed.

"Yes, I talked to her this morning. She said he was out there. She said she tried to convince him to come back, and that he left her apartment this morning. That's all I know," Ginny said.

"Goddamn kids these days don't know how good they got it," Jim snorted.

"Oh, would you behave," Ginny said to Jim. "I'm sorry about this. He must be broken hearted," Ginny said.

Henry stood there looking pained to even be having this conversation. Henry and Jim looked at each other, both embarrassed. Ginny stood by like a prop.

"Her and her Goddamn' big ideas. I don't know where she got them. Sure as hell wasn't from me," Jim said.

"Jim!" Ginny said.

"Kids make mistakes, I'm sure it will all come out in the wash," Henry said.

"Maybe for Brady, but I'm not so sure about Ashley. She's going to learn everything the hard, hard way," Jim said, and then started working on the tractor again as if he was done talking about it.

"He'll probably come back before long," Ginny said, trying to comfort Henry.

"She's working at a Goddamn bar," Jim said, "So much for being a MOVIE STAR,"

"Would you stop it?" Ginny said to her husband. "She said that she didn't know he was coming, and that she let him stay the night with her, but that he left in the morning."

"Thanks for the information, I really appreciate it," Henry said. "Please call me if you hear anything else. He's probably too ashamed of himself to talk to anyone right now. I thank you folks for your time."

He reached over the tractor to shake Jim's hand. Jim could barely look him in the eye he was so mad and ashamed. "See you, Henry," Jim said. Ginny gave him a quick hug and looked at him with sad eyes.

Henry drove off down their driveway being chased out by the barking dogs, and he hoped that he would never be as hurt and upset with Brady as Jim Duncan was with Ashley.

Ashley was in the Samuel French bookstore in Hollywood searching for a new monologue to do in acting class when her mother called to tell her that Henry had come out to the farm. Ashley was furious that she still had to deal with the Brady issue. Where was he? Now his dad and everyone else was looking for him and who was the *bad guy?* She was of course. She was the bad guy because she dared do something different, because she dared leave the safety and familiarity of her family nest and small town. Because she dared chase a dream that for most was unattainable. That she reject all of the values and ideals that she had been raised and indoctrinated with.

She loved her mother dearly, but she saw the way her mom walked on eggshells around her dad, yet doted over him night and day anyway.

Her dad, the moody and silent farmer was fine until you dared oppose any one of his desires or viewpoints about life. If you did he would write you off rather than come to some kind of understanding. Ashley felt terrible about the rift with her father. She woke up with it every morning and went to bed with it every night.

She had been the apple of his eye when she was a child. She was a tom boy and a daddy's girl. She helped him do the chores around the farm and he taught her to drive a tractor. She raised a steer for 4H and won a gold medal at the annual fair. She cried her eyes out when the steer was sold at auction and taken away to be slaughtered. She remembered how her dad had held her in his truck and told her it was going to be alright. The thought of that steer, "Bandit" being led away into a trailer still brought twinges of deep pain and guilt to Ashley every time she thought about it.

The main trouble with her dad started shortly after that, about the time she was 12, when she was reaching puberty. About the time boys started paying attention to her. Her dad couldn't handle it and started becoming way over protective and controlling. They started butting heads around that time and his way of dealing with it was to shut her out emotionally. The rift had started gradually way back then and now had grown so big that they were no longer talking to each other. She was still close with her mom, but Ashley considered her mom to be clueless and a pathetic codependent of her father.

Ashley looked around the book store and noticed a man probably fifteen years her senior looking at her. He smiled and she managed a little smile back, but did not want to encourage him in any way. What, did he actually think he had a chance with her? Men were always panting after her like dogs and wanting something from her and it was big time waster. She didn't have time to validate every man's ego. She was naturally friendly, but she had quickly learned to put up a wall around herself since coming to LA. She had to.

She wondered where that idiot Brady was and why he wasn't answering his dad's calls? She promised her mom that she would call him as much as she didn't want to. She knew the fool would probably answer her call on the first ring. That was if he didn't go off and do something stupid like kill himself. He had threatened to do that when she first broke up with him. She didn't take it seriously then, but if he was crazy enough to quit college and come out here following her, who knew what else he was capable of doing?

She had been browsing through various books with acting monologues trying to find just the right piece she could work on in acting class. Jeremy Bone had instructed her to do something dramatic and she really wanted to impress him. She finally found the play, "Hurly Burly" by David Rabe. She thumbed through the play looking for female characters. She finally found a character named Bonnie and a lengthy monologue to work on. Bonnie was a Hollywood "coke whore" who bounced from man to man. The monologue was just the kind of thing that would probably impress Bone. Ashley thought that it would really be a stretch for her, but she could pull it off.

She waited in line to buy the book. The man who had smiled to her earlier got behind her in line and she could tell he was dying for an opening. "Hurly Burly," he said, looking at the thin book in her hand. Are you doing a monologue from that?" the man asked.

"Yes," she said, irritated that she had to answer. She noticed the man's shoes that looked scuffed and tattered and he had one bad front tooth. He was obviously some actor wannabe. He was holding a play, "The

Tempest," by Shakespeare. He must be a real loser if he was still doing Shakespeare. That would get him a cup of coffee in this town.

"I did that play a few years ago at the MET Theater. Are you doing Bonnie?" the man asked.

"I was thinking about it," Ashley said.

"Interesting choice for you," the man said. Ashley didn't know what he meant by that. "Who are you studying with?" he asked.

Ashley didn't know how to answer that and looked like a dear in headlights. "What class are you in?" the man asked.

"Oh. I'm in Jeremy Bone's class," she said.

"Jeremy Bone. Impressive. I hear he is an abusive psycho," the man said.

"I just started," Ashley said, now wanting to be done with the conversation. It was her turn in line and she turned away from the stranger to pay for the book.

"Good luck," the man said as she was walking out of the store.

"Thanks," Ashley said, not looking back, leaving the man in the dust of her indifference.

At the pet store, Brady was busy helping to unload a truck load of pet food in the back parking lot. The Mexican truck driver stood in the back of the truck and tossed down fifty pound bags of dog food. Brady easily caught them and stacked them neatly. The driver threw the last bag, out of gas himself.

He climbed down from the truck sweating and panting. "Hay, cabron, you are muy fuerte!" said the driver.

"Back home we had to toss eighty pound hay bales all day long in the summer. That's work," Brady said.

"Where you from, cabron?" asked the driver.

"Kansas," Brady said, not sure if he should be proud or embarrassed.

"Oh, yeah, that's kind of by Chicago," the driver said.

"Kind of," Brady said as he counted the bags of pet food, checking them off on the invoice. Brady nodded to the driver that everything was there.

"Ok, Kansas, see you the next time," the driver said and he hurried to his truck cab, started it up and drove away. Brady started moving the bags of pet food into the back room of the pet shop.

Brady's phone started vibrating and he looked at it. His eyes lit up upon seeing Ashley's name on the screen, along with her picture. He let it ring twice, and then answered it.

"Hello," Brady said, too eagerly.

"Brady, where are you? People back home are calling me looking for you. What's going on?" she asked with a hint of irritation.

"Who? Who called you?" Brady asked, scanning up and down the street.

"My mom. Your dad DROVE out to the farm to talk to my parents," Ashley said with a bit more irritation.

Brady looked as though he had been punched in the gut. "Really. I'm sorry. They called me a couple of times this morning when my phone was dead. I was going to call them back later," Brady said.

"Where are you?" Ashley demanded.

Brady thought about it a moment and he didn't like her tone at all. "What difference does it make?" he finally said.

"Quit playing this stupid game, Brady. People are worried about you. Your dad had to drive all the way out to the farm because you are too chicken shit to pick up your phone,"

Brady cut her off. "Chicken shit? Chicken shit? Fuck you, Ashley. You're only mad because my dad went out to the farm and reminded your dad that you are out here and *you* can't handle it! You can't handle the fact that your dad is furious at you for leaving." There was a long moment of silence.

"So, you're still here. I fucking hate you. You couldn't just let it go, could you? I don't care what you do, just stay completely away from me, and call your folks before they go out looking for you at the farm again, ok?" Ashley said.

"Don't worry, I hate you too, you FUCKING CUNT!" Brady screamed and he smashed his phone on the parking lot next to the bags of pet food.

He picked up his phone, broken in two pieces, already regretting what he had said and done. When he turned and looked back he saw Isaac standing there looking at him.

"Is there a problem, Brady?" Isaac asked. Brady tried to pull himself together, but was obviously upset.

"C'mon, let's get these bags inside," Isaac said. He patted Brady on the back. Both men carried the bags of pet food into the store.

Ashley was livid. Brady was right: She hated more than anything that her dad had been reminded of something that was obviously painful and embarrassing for him. Brady had opened that whole can of worms again. Ashley hated him for it. She wished she could just find him and spit in his face. What was he still doing here? He was turning into a stalker, and it scared Ashley to think about it. Was he following her, watching her from across the street somewhere? Would he show up at the club? He had never acted irrational before, but he certainly was doing it now.

He had never called her a CUNT before, and in fact Ashley never recalled him saying that word at all. She had heard other men say it. It was the word they pulled out when they felt rejected and small. Brady's friend, Kevin had called her that when he tried to get a booty call out of her shortly after the "incident". She wanted to tell Brady about the incident now – that would make him hate her for sure.

Yeah, she fucked his best friend, and if that wouldn't ruin his obsession with her, she didn't know what would. But then he might go and do something really stupid and ruin every bit of progress she had already made. No, she would just try to stay clear of him and hope that he would go back home soon.

She picked up her phone and dialed the apartment manager, Larry. She explained to him that if he saw Brady hanging around the apartment to call her right away, and that if he caused any trouble to call the police. Larry urged her to get a restraining order and offered to go to the West Hollywood Sherriff's station to help her. She politely declined his offer and then rushed to the shower to get ready for her shift at Kraven.

Money was getting tight and she hoped for a busy night and a lot of tips. She might have to flirt more than usual to make more money. Chloe had called and said that she'd be coming in with her friend, Jillian. This Chloe was coming on awful strong, and Ashley felt a bit uncomfortable about it. What did she want? Everybody seemed to want something. She admired her naked body in the mirror for a moment before jumping into the shower.

Brady finished the rest of the afternoon in a daze. He felt incredibly guilty for calling Ashley a cunt. He had never said that word before. It sounded so ugly to him. He heard other guys talking in the locker rooms, out on hunting trips, and in bars throwing that word around like it was the most natural thing in the world. He had been taught by his father to respect women, and he loved women. He was not one of these guys who really couldn't stand women and only tolerated them because they had a vagina. It seemed that there were plenty of men like that and he hoped that he would never turn into one of them.

Ashley had a right to be mad at him, Brady admitted to himself. He still loved her, regardless of what she said to him. She was just stressed because of the thing with her father. He wanted to apologize to her, but was hesitant to contact her again because she told him not to. He felt terrible, and would have done anything to take it back.

He finally called his parents. He had to call collect from a pay phone because his phone was broken. It was an emotional call. Brady did everything in his power to keep from crying when he talked to his mom. They begged him to come home and get back into college. He told them that he needed time away from Kansas to find himself. He told them that he was done pursuing Ashley and that was not the reason that he wanted to stay. He told them about the pet shop and they didn't really understand. He convinced them that he just needed time in a new place to heal from the breakup.

His parents didn't think it was healthy that he was in the same vicinity as Ashley. He tried to convince them that LA was a huge city and the chances of running into her were slim to none. It was finally agreed upon between Brady and his parents that he would spend the winter in LA, then come back to college in Kansas for the Spring semester. They wanted to send him some money, but he declined. It was important to Brady that he finance his own sabbatical from Kansas.

Brady went to the gym and worked out hard. He pushed himself to the limit, trying to purge the anger, hurt and guilt from his body. The gym was in West Hollywood and was populated by gay males. He got hit on a few times, and he smiled politely, but offered them no encouragement. He took a long shower and saw men checking him out and saw two men jacking each other off in the steam room. Maybe men turned to this after being rejected by women he thought. Maybe this was what the world was coming to, where men and women were constantly at war with one another, and the two genders would have to drift to their own kind. Brady dreaded going back to the pet shop, but didn't know what else to do. He didn't have much money left, didn't really know anybody in town other than Ashley, and didn't really like going to bars by himself. He thought of going to the club where Ashley worked just to check it out. Maybe he could at least talk to her and apologize.

He got dressed and walked up to Sunset Boulevard. He had a hamburger at the famous Sunset Grill (written about in the song). He walked past the Roxy, the Whiskey, and finally went into the Rainbow Room. He sat at the bar and ordered a beer. The place was noisy and crowded and he felt entirely out of place. It was almost as if her were invisible. Everyone in the bar was tattooed, had long hair, piercings, weird clothing, or something that called attention to itself. He was just plain Brady from Kansas. The bartender barely even noticed him or said a word to him, and just slammed a beer in front of him. Brady drank the beer quickly and got out of there. He had never felt so alienated in his life.

He continued walking down the Sunset Strip and stopped in front of Larry Flynt's Hustler store. He looked in the window and saw displays of sex toys, lingerie, and other adult items in full view from the sidewalk. He saw hipsters browsing through the store and he thought about how decadent it all was. He had been inside sex shops in Denver, but they were sleazy, in the bad part of town, in windowless buildings. He wondered if Ashley had been to the shop and it sickened him.

He kept walking and stopped in front of the Viper Room, and remembered hearing something about that. Didn't some celebrity die there? He kept walking and then he saw Kraven across the street. It was as if some invisible force had driven him there.

His heart immediately started beating faster, knowing that Ashley was probably inside there. He saw a small crowd standing in line in front of a velvet rope and a burly doorman standing in front. The guy must have been 6'5" and 280 pounds. He also saw the sleazy paparazzi standing nearby smoking cigarettes. Valets were rushing expensive cars around the block to park them as glamorous looking people walked past the velvet rope into the club. Brady just stood there feeling about one inch tall.

How could he ever compete with this? Ashley was buying into all of this, hook, line, and sinker. She had changed already and she had only been in LA for a couple of minutes. Imagine what she would be like a year from now? Ten years? She was here for good; Brady tried to accept that fact. She was gone from him, gone from her parents and her home town that might as well be on another planet now. And there he was standing across the street, watching like a pathetic loser. He had never felt so small and meaningless in his life. What was he even doing there? But he could not leave.

It was as if he was frozen there on that patch of sidewalk, unable to leave or look away. It was if he was punishing himself. He felt out of control for the first time in his life. He could not seem to stop himself from doing what he was doing. What if Ashley came out of there with some director or movie star? Was that what he wanted to see to torture himself some more? What would he do, how would he react if he finally saw her with another man? Would he confront them and make a fool out of himself and be dragged away kicking and screaming by the police? Would that big bouncer put him into a headlock and choke him out?

Brady could only imagine bad outcomes from his being there. He literally could not move. Adrenalin was flowing through his veins giving him some kind of rush, some kind of buzz and he felt that he might pass out every time that door opened to the club and he imagined that Ashley was right there, just two hundred yards away from him. He could almost smell her. He could almost taste her and it was driving him crazy. Maybe he would never get the chance to kiss her or make love to her again. He couldn't imagine enjoying sex with any other woman, and he would always be thinking about her. His heart was nearly beating out of his chest. The light changed and he decided to cross the street to get a better look.

Ten

Ashley arrived to her acting class a half hour early. Only a couple of people were there and she didn't see Jeremy Bone yet. She was dressed in a low cut top, and a mini skirt. She wore more makeup than usual, especially around the eyes, and bright red lipstick. She looked like a whore and that was the idea. She had been rehearsing four days straight on the monologue from the play, Hurly Burly. She wanted to impress her class and especially Jeremy Bone. She was incredibly nervous. Even more nervous than the opening night of her first stage play. She felt that she had a lot riding on this monologue, like her whole Hollywood career, for instance.

It had also been several days since the incident at Kraven. Brady came into the club at the worst possible time. Ashley was busy seating a group of ten people from Paramount Studios and Brady burst into the club and started yelling, "I love you more than anything!" He shouted it over and over and was running toward her when the bouncer caught him and then dragged him kicking and screaming out of there. It had unnerved her. She knew that it was probably coming to that, but she didn't think that it would really happen. Afterwards, Chloe took her to the West Hollywood Sherriff's station to get a restraining order, and she had a court date the following week, where Brady would have a chance to refute it.

Ashley just hoped that Brady had finally hit a bottom in his vain pursuit of her. She told her mom about what happened, and as far as she knew he had not returned to Kansas. Her boss, Jean Pierre, told her he would have to fire her if it happened again. Chloe had invited her to a resort in Palm Springs to get away from town and forget about it, and Ashley took her up on it. They were leaving in the morning after the acting class.

Jeremy Bone arrived to class with an entourage of gay males who were also in the class. He made a grand entrance, and one of his flunkies took his jacket and scarf. Bone looked around the room and noticed Ashley, smiled briefly, but did not otherwise acknowledge her. Ashley suddenly felt very self conscious dressed the way that she was. She felt like she might hyperventilate and she had to slow down her breathing. At least she was completely sober this time. She thought about taking the pill that was still sitting in her cupboard, but she didn't.

She tried to look at the play in her hand and not focus on Bone and his minions, who were laughing about something very flamboyantly. Gays could be very catty and annoying, Ashley thought. They cried like hell any time somebody judged them, but they tended to be the most judgmental group of people she had ever seen.

Some of the other students started filing in and sitting down. A guy about Ashley's age came in and sat beside her. He smiled at her and took a double take. He was a hipster/skater type, gangly with a beanie on, long hair, and a scraggly half beard. Ashley smiled politely at him, but tried to focus on her material.

"Hi, I'm Owen," the guy said, extending his hand to her.

"Ashley," she said, taking his hand briefly.

"Are you new here?" he asked.

"Uh, this is my second time," she said.

"Oh yeah, I remember you now from last week. You did that comedy monologue," he said. "You look different. What are you doing this week?"

She showed him the play in her hand. He looked at it, but didn't seem to recognize it. Bone stepped up to the front of the class.

"Ok, kids, let's get started. We have a lot of ground to cover tonight," Bone said, scanning the room.

They went through their breathing exercises, and then Bone started calling on people to come up and do their monologues. Some of the people came up in pairs and did two person scenes. Ashley was so nervous she couldn't even see or hear the other students performing. Bone would make some of the students do the scenes more than once, and would give them direction. Sometimes, especially if it was an attractive male, and all of the males in the class tended to be attractive, Bone would adjust their posture physically. Some of his criticisms seemed pretty harsh.

Then came Owen's turn and he went to the front of the class. He explained that the piece he was doing was something that he had written himself. Ashley paid more attention because she felt somehow invested in him because he had introduced himself to her. He performed the monologue and it was a piece about him sitting in his room all day smoking pot and beating himself up about it because he hadn't accomplished anything. Bone praised the writing and commented that Owen was brave for doing a piece he had written, but criticized his performance as lifeless and boring. "I mean, do I really give a shit about this person? Not the way you're portraying him," Bone said.

Owen returned to his seat looking a bit beaten up. Ashley felt sorry for him and lightly grasped his hand, which seemed to pleasantly surprise him.

"Ok, Ashley Duncan. Our newest addition. Knock us out," Bone said. Ashley rose and made her way to the front of the class. She was so nervous that she felt like she might pass out. Bone looked her up and down and placed his hand on top of her shoulder. "How are we doing tonight, Ashley?" Bone asked, smiling warmly.

"Good," she said, barely squeaking it out.

"What will you be performing for us tonight?" Bone asked.

Ashley looked out upon the sea of faces that seemed to be scrutinizing her. "Uh, I'm doing a scene from Hurly Burly by David Rabe, and I'm playing the part of Bonnie," she said.

"Hurly Burly. Interesting choice. I can't wait," he said and then sat down, motioning her to begin. "Take a moment to get into character, then go for it," Bone said, sitting cross legged in his canvas director's chair.

She stood there and closed her eyes for a full minute, trying to get into character, and then she began. She did several lines from the monologue and felt that she was nailing it when Bone shot to his feet."Stop. Stop. Stop," Bone shouted. Ashley looked at him bewildered. He stepped onto the stage next to her.

"Honey, I don't think you have done your research. You have no understanding of this character. Zero. Zero. This is a character who has no self esteem, no self worth, who allows herself to be passed from man to man, because she equates that with love. She allows herself to be treated like an utter piece of shit, because that's what she knows is love. I don't think you can even begin to comprehend that," Bone said, almost in her face.

Ashley stood there, about to cry.

"When in your whole privileged, cushy life have you ever felt that way? I'll bet you shit sunshine and unicorns your whole cheerleader, class valedictorian life," he continued.

Ashley couldn't believe he was saying that and hot blood rushed to her face.

"You think you can come in here dressed like a whore, and you can convince me that you *are* a whore?" Bone shouted.

Ashley held back tears.

"You better go out and do some more homework before you come in here with a scene that is clearly way out of your league. This is the big times you're in now, honey. This isn't the sixth grade Christmas play back in Dubuque," He said. "Go sit down and think about whether you are really cut out for this. You have a pretty face, but guess what, honey – pretty faces are a dime a dozen in this town."

Ashley returned to her seat crying. She had never been more humiliated.

This time, Owen squeezed her hand. "He does that to everybody when they're new, fucking queen," Owen whispered.

"Do you have something to say to the class, Owen?" Bone yelled.

"No, sir," Owen answered with a hint of sarcasm. Bone smiled to himself, pleased that he had managed to break Ashley down so easily.

"Owen, since you seem to be Ashley's knight in shining amour, I want you two to do a scene together, sometime in the future," Bone said.

"Ok," Owen said.

"Is that ok with you, Ashley?" Bone asked.

"Yes," she said, still sniffling with tears.

Bone then called up the next student. Owen glanced at Ashley and she felt comforted by his presence.

The rest of the class went by and Ashley sat there hating Jeremy Bone for humiliating her like that, but she really hated him because she knew that he was right. She *had* lived a very sheltered, Pollyanna life. She had no idea what it was like to be hungry, or homeless, or even desperate. Doors had flown open for her all of her life because she was tall, physically attractive, naturally intelligent, and from a loving family.

She had no idea what it was like to be ugly, overweight, a minority, or handicapped in any way. She had no idea what it was like to be addicted, or even obsessed like Brady was for her. She suddenly felt very sorry for him, but she pushed that feeling down, thinking it better to remain mad at him.

She thought about the sources of pain throughout her life: Bandit the steer being taken away, the rift with her father, the abortion. Those were real and recurring, but seemed miniscule to the obstacles and problems a good majority of the world's population faced every day. Ashley knew that she would have to take Bone's words to heart if she wanted to make it in Hollywood. She would have to get some life experience to draw from, and that meant that she was going to have to drift closer to the edge than she had ever gone before.

Brady had been licking his wounds since the incident at Kraven. He worked days in the pet store in a daze. Isaac and his wife were nice enough, but they were always talking in their language. Other Russians would come into the store and they would be talking and laughing in Russian and Brady felt as if they were always talking and laughing about him because he was such a pathetic joke. Here he was with all of his potential, working at a pet store for minimum wage and sleeping on a cot in the back. They must be laughing at him, because it was pretty funny if it wasn't so pathetic. His neck still hurt from where the bouncer had choked him out and tossed him onto the Sunset Boulevard with all of those people watching.

It was a blur to him. He just remembered that feeling of not being able to stop himself. And now, why was he still in LA? What was holding him now? Ashley was clearly and unequivocally done with him. That came through loud and clear this time and he didn't blame her. He had gone out with a blaze of glory; he gave himself that much. He remembered her look of horror when he was running toward her in the club and he couldn't believe that she was actually afraid of him.

He, who had shared so much with her, was now just a creepy stalker that had to be restrained and tossed out like the trash. If ever he had a reason to return home and get on with his life, he had it now. Yet for some reason he couldn't do it. It was if some invisible and gigantic magnet was anchoring him firmly in California. He didn't know what it was, but he had to ride it out. Maybe California had something else in store for him?

He had gone out every night since the incident. He found a bar that he liked called Barney's Beanery and it was the only straight bar on the stretch of Santa Monica Boulevard known as "Boy's Town." There was a pool table and Brady was a pretty good shooter. He started to make a few friends and one of the bartenders was pretty cool. Brady had gotten blind drunk there three nights in a row and stumbled back to the pet store to pass out.

He was there again on the forth night. He had pulled some money off of his credit card and was drinking beers and shots of Jameson. He had flirted with a few girls since he first started coming to the bar. On that particular night, a short Filipina was watching him from across the bar. She was there with several of her girlfriends. Brady finally went over and talked to her. She was cute, he guessed, and as closing time approached she got cuter and cuter. She laughed at everything he said. She was no Ashley, but she had some nice tits, and she obviously thought that he was something special.

Brady needed that validation now more than ever. Before he knew it, Brady was out in her car with her and they were driving toward the beach. He had been in LA for over a week and had yet to see the ocean. The girl, Katrina, was driving him to the beach in Santa Monica, and he was shitfaced and yelling at cars and people on the street on the way down there. He just didn't care about anything.

They finally made it to Santa Monica and got out of the car. It was a cold night and he could smell the salt water and see the waves crashing onto the shore in the moonlight. Nobody else seemed to be on the beach at 2:AM. Brady took his shoes off and darted toward the water, throwing the rest of his clothes off on the way. Katrina chased him and shouted at him not to go into the water. He ran to the edge of the water, now naked and screaming like a maniac, "The great Pacific!" He stopped just at the edge of the water and marveled at the power of the waves. Katrina caught up to him out of breath.

They ended up on the sand with their clothes off. Katrina went down on him and she tried and tried like a trooper to get him hard, but his dick was like a cold salty wet noodle in her mouth. The harder she tried the smaller and softer it got. Brady then tried to get himself hard, in vain. Unable to rise to the occasion, he cussed himself and the wind and the waves and the planes flying out of LAX, and God. They drove back to West Hollywood in silence.

After class Owen invited Ashley for a beer at a bar close to the acting class on Franklin. The place was packed and many of the students from the class were there. It was very noisy and Ashley had a hard time hearing what anybody was saying, but several of the students told her that she wasn't that bad and that Bone did that to all of the new students to see if they would crack and quit. Owen bought her a Sierra Nevada Ale and acted like he was her appointed protector. She thought he was attractive in a geeky kind of way. He was so different from the boys back home or Brady for that matter. He seemed to be quite popular among the other class members and he carried himself with confidence. They ended up drinking shots of Cazadores and several Sierras and Ashley ended up dancing with Owen until closing time.

She was quite inebriated when the bouncers were pushing everyone out. She held onto Owen's arm and he escorted her to her car across the street in the market's parking lot. He offered to drive her home, or take her to his house for the night. Ashley was conscious enough to remember that Chloe was picking her up in the morning for the Palm Springs mini-vacation. Ashley was tempted to go home with him and have sex as she felt horny, but she wasn't going to do it that easily. He would have to work a little harder if he wanted it. He was talking to her, trying to be polite and respectable, and she just pushed herself onto him and pressed her breasts against him and kissed his lips hard. He seemed surprised, but he recovered and responded quickly. His hands were suddenly all over her and they were making out on the hood of her car in the parking lot of the Mayfair Market at 2am. She finally broke away from him, breathless.

"Thanks, I have to go now," Ashley said.

"Hey, don't leave me like this," Owen said.

He tried to pull her back into his arms, but she pulled away smiling seductively.

"We'll meet again," she said.

She got into her car, started it up and zipped onto Franklin bouncing her front bumper off of the pavement as she sped away.

Owen stood there watching her in awe. He walked away from the parking lot smiling.

Eleven

Ashley woke up in her apartment shivering. She was still in her clothes from the night before lying on top of her sleeping bag. She slowly became awake and then she shot up. She searched for her phone to see the time. She was relieved seeing that it was only 8:30. Chloe was coming to get her at 10. She tried to remember the night before and it slowly started coming to her. She remembered being humiliated by Jeremy Bone, then going to the bar on Franklin. Then she thought of making out with Owen in the parking lot of the Mayfair Market. She didn't really remember driving home and she panicked thinking about it. Had she driven home in a blackout? Where was her car? She jumped up and rushed out the door. She stumbled into the parking lot and was relieved to see her car in its assigned spot, sans dents or blood. It was a bit askew in its spot.

She breathed a sigh of relief and returned to her apartment. Wow, she felt a bit out of control. She could never let that happen again. She had never been so reckless. She went out drinking with friends in high school, and in college, but she was the one who was always in control. She thought about making out with Owen again. What else had happened? She wasn't too down on herself about that. There was something appealing about him. She was curious. Maybe she needed to cut loose a bit to move on from Brady.

Brady. Where was he now? Was he still lurking around West Hollywood, or had he finally gone home? It wasn't her problem, and that was the reason for this trip to Palm Springs. Chloe said that she would treat her to a weekend away from all of that. She felt a little funny accepting such an expensive trip and not being able to pay her own way, but Chloe had insisted. Ashley took her clothes off and jumped in the shower.

Chloe arrived to get her on time and they were off in Chloe's big BMW. Chloe shot in and out of traffic and passed everything in sight. Chloe told her that they were staying at an exclusive new five star resort called Hermosa Springs. Chloe had gotten a deal on it through her company. The room would have normally been $900 per night, but she had gotten it for $375. She talked a lot about money. How much her car cost to lease, $675 per month, her mortgage on her West Hollywood condo, $3500, property taxes per year, $7500, new Prada purse, $975. Chloe went on and on about money and how much she was making and tax attorneys, and investments.

Then, Chloe switched the topic to Jillian. How Jillian had not planned for her future and was now desperate and clinging to men like Chuck Alexander to save her. Chloe seemed to revel in the fact that Jillian was resorting to selling off many of her things on Ebay. Chloe talked about what a sad situation it was and how she had been much smarter and was never going to have to depend on any man. Ashley got the idea that Chloe didn't like men too much and she wondered if she was gay. Was that what this was all about, Ashley wondered. Why else would Chloe spring for such an expensive trip? Maybe she just wanted to spend a weekend with a girlfriend, Ashley told herself. Maybe she wanted Ashley to be her *girlfriend.*

Ashley watched her as she was talking and tried to figure it out. She was kind of cute, sexy in a way. Ashley guessed that if she was a lesbian she would probably be attracted to Chloe. Chloe kept smiling at her a little more than just friends would do, and she kept reaching over and touching Ashley's hand or arm as she was driving and talking. Ashley was starting to get the picture, but she decided she would just deal with it when the time came.

"Is the room a suite?" Ashley finally asked. Chloe looked at her strangely.

"Uh, yeah. There are two bedrooms. It also has a private Jacuzzi and patio," Chloe said smiling.

"Cool," Ashley said looking out the window.

"Are you ok? You seem a little distracted?" Chloe said.

"Yeah, I'm just a little hung over. I went out with some of the people from the acting class last night," Ashley said.

"Why didn't you say something?" Chloe said.

With that she shuffled through her purse with one hand while she was driving and came out with a pill and handed it to Ashley.

"What is it?" Ashley asked.

"It will make you feel better. Trust me," Chloe said smiling. Ashley hesitated a moment remembering what the last pill had done to her, but this pill was different looking. She swallowed the pill with a drink of Evian, not asking what it was.

A bit later they came over a hill and the desert and mountains were before them. There was a huge wind farm spread out across the hills with hundreds of wind turbines rotating. It was surreal and hypnotic and seductive. Ashley remembered seeing the scene in a music video. She felt an intense rush from it, and suddenly felt very happy and comfortable and warm; glad to be away from Brady, and her apartment with no furniture, and thoughts of drama back in Kansas, and Jeremy Bone, and driving drunk the night before, and the new guy, Owen. Ashley decided she would have a great time relaxing and getting away from all of her problems.

"It's so cool," Ashley said, commenting about the wind turbines and she touched Chloe's hand on the steering wheel. Chloe smiled to herself behind her $500 Dita sunglasses.

Brady was working in the pet store and his head ached from the night before. He thought of the incident at the beach with the poor girl who had tried so diligently to make him hard. Isaac was in a bad mood and seemed to be mad about something. The one bright spot of working at the pet store for Brady was the little puppy that seemed to love him. He had named the dog, Oatmeal, and he would walk by its pen every time he could. Most of the customers at the store seemed to be quite wealthy. A lot of gays came in with their little dogs and bought expensive canned dog food, little dog sweaters, chews, and other paraphernalia. Then, there were the hot actress types with their little dogs buying the same things.

They didn't seem to notice Brady much, and he wondered why. Back home, he was considered *the catch*. Was it because he was just another nobody working in a pet store? He had no tattoos or other accessories to make himself stand out. That was what people needed here in LA – to stand out. Otherwise, they just blended into the throngs of people crawling like ants all over the city. And so many people had tattoos and the counter culture uniforms that they no longer stood out and instead became conformists of another kind.

An attractive black woman came into the store. She certainly stood out. Her breasts were huge and she was dressed in a velvet Sean John track suit with a LA Dodger's cap, Ugg's and Christian Audigier sunglasses. She smiled and talked to Isaac, who seemed to know her. Then the woman and Isaac were looking at Brady from across the store.

"Hey Brady, come here a minute, please," Isaac said. That was nicest Isaac had been to him all morning. Brady walked over to the counter to where the woman was standing. Brady noticed her lift her shades to get a better look and literally check him out up and down. A woman had finally noticed him.

"Brady, take two of the fifty pound bags of Iam's out to her car, ok," Isaac said.

Brady grabbed one of the bags of dog food and followed her out. She had a firm, round ass that he focused on when he walked behind her. She led him to a brand new Black Range Rover parked on the street. Two pit bulls in the vehicle started barking as they approached.

"Shut up!" she yelled at them. She looked at Brady. "Don't worry about them, they're sweethearts," she said.

She opened the back of the Range Rover and he loaded the first bag into the back of it. She touched his bicep. "You're so strong, I could use you up at the house," she said.

Brady wondered what she meant by that. He wondered how old she was. He couldn't tell. She was over thirty he guessed, but could be as old as fifty. She was in good shape, and those breasts were at least 36 dd's and the nipples poked through the velvet track suit. They returned to the store for the other bag of dog food. "Isaac, can I borrow this young man for a bit, so he can unload these bags up at the house," the woman said.

"Of course, anything for you, Crystal," Isaac said. Brady felt a little bit like some kind of slave to be passed around, but he was glad to get out of the store.

As they walked back to the Range Rover, the woman shot him a smile. "I'm Crystal," she said.

"Brady," he said extending his hand. She handed him the keys.

"Can you drive?" she asked.

"Uh, sure," he said, a little surprised. She yelled at the barking dogs again, and Brady climbed into the driver's seat. He put it into drive and started driving. Crystal took off her sunglasses and checked him out. She had big brown eyes that looked somehow sad. Brady had no idea where he was driving to.

"So, what are you doing working at the pet store?" Crystal said.

"Uh, I just moved to LA. It was the first job I applied for," Brady said. Her eyes seemed to burn through him and it unnerved him. There was something mysterious about her. Brady detected a hint of a British accent.

"You just moved here, huh. You an actor?" she asked.

Brady laughed bitterly. "Hell, no!" he said.

"Where did you come from?" she asked.

"Kansas. I don't know where we're going?" Brady finally said.

She looked at him a long moment with a slight smile on her face. It was hard not staring at those huge breasts, and those nipples. "Turn left up here," she said.

Brady turned left on La Brea and drove the Range Rover toward the hills.

Chloe and Ashley arrived at the Hermosa Springs resort. It was an incredible new resort surrounded by high walls, palm trees and lush grounds that were adorned with giant fountains and statuary. Ashley had never seen anything like it.

They checked in and were doted upon by doormen, valets, and bellhops. Chloe acted like it was old hat for her, and handed out twenty dollar bills like they were candy to the various people. They arrived to their room which was on the ground level, but had a spectacular view of the grounds and the steep and barren looking mountains in the distance. The room was like something out of a movie. It had a bar and a huge television and was smartly decorated in a classic minimalist style. There were indeed two bedrooms like Chloe said, and also the Jacuzzi on the private patio just outside the room.

"Choose your room," Chloe said. Ashley hesitated, then moved into the smaller room and plopped down on the bed.

"Wow, this is so nice. It feels like heaven to be on a real bed," Ashley said loudly so Chloe could hear her in the other room.

"I'll have to admit, I'm impressed," Chloe said, walking into Ashley's room. She looked down upon her.

"That's right. You don't have a bed. We'll have to do something about that when we get back," Chloe said, as she laid on the bed next to Ashley, shoulder to shoulder. Ashley was now very aware of what was happening.

"I have scheduled spa treatments and massages for us later," Chloe said. There was a knock on the door and Chloe jumped up. "That must be the champagne." Ashley had to admit to herself that she was enjoying this first class treatment, even if Chloe was trying to seduce her.

Room service delivered the Dom Perignon on ice. Chloe tipped the man twenty dollars and he opened the champagne, poured two glasses and went away. Ashley walked into the main room to join Chloe for the champagne.

"I wanted to show you what the good life could be like. I want you to get used to it, because soon you will be somebody important," Chloe said. Ashley was embarrassed and surprised that Chloe had said that.

"I don't know about that. My acting instructor destroyed me last night," Ashley said.

"Don't listen to those talentless fucks. If they could act, they would do it, but they can't, so they teach. You have something that everybody is going to want, and all of the acting instructors in Hollywood can't stop that from happening," Chloe said, raising her glass to toast.

Ashley raised her glass, embarrassed, but wowed by the compliment. "Well, ok then," Ashley said. "To success!" Chloe said. They bumped their glasses together and laughed.

A large iron gate opened and Brady drove the Range Rover into a secluded Hollywood Hills property. The house was at the end of a long drive way and it overlooked the city. A black Silverado truck that was modified into a monster truck was parked in the circular driveway.

"Nice place!" Brady said.

"It was my husbands, he got killed last year," Crystal said.

"Oh, I'm sorry. What happened?" Brady asked.

"He was Billy Barnes, the stunt man. He got killed in a helicopter crash filming "Supercharged 3" last year. You probably heard about it," she said.

"Oh yeah," Brady said, not so sure.

They sat there in the driveway a moment. He could smell Crystal's perfume and her body language definitely shifted in his direction. Brady started getting aroused and he was glad that he still could after recent developments.

He carried the bags of dog food into the garage. Crystal kenneled the dogs and invited Brady into the house. Brady had never seen anything like it. The place wasn't that big but it had an incredible view of Hollywood and off to the side he could see all the way to the ocean.

The walls were covered with photos of Billy Barnes and various movie stars. An Emmy and an Oscar sat on the mantel above the fireplace. Brady stood in awe of all the photos. The man, Billy Barnes looked to be in his sixties in the pictures and was white. "So, you like working at the pet store?" Crystal asked.

"It's ok for now I guess," Brady said.

Brady turned and looked at her and she was leaning over a small mirror that had lines of cocaine spread out upon it. She snorted a line and leaned back, letting it hit her. "Hope you don't mind. You want a bump?" she asked.

"Oh, no," he said. He had never actually seen cocaine, and the sight of it scared him. She was now staring at him like he was a piece of meat.

"You want a beer or something?" she asked.

"I'll have a glass of water if you have one. Maybe we should be getting back," Brady said, now sweating a little.

She got up slowly and walked to the kitchen. She came back with a bottle of water and she pushed her breasts against Brady as she handed it to him. Her face was just inches from his and he could feel her hot breath.

"You ever fucked a black woman before?" she said.

Brady laughed nervously. "No," he said.

She turned away from him and returned to the sofa. She snorted another line, and then looked at him. "You want it, come and get it," she said almost nonchalantly.

Brady stood there looking at her and realized that his cock was rock hard. His heart was thumping inside of his chest and his mouth was suddenly very dry. He opened the water and took a long sip, and then he suddenly just moved right to her and they came together kissing.

She was rough with him and bit his lip and grabbed his ass hard. She obviously wanted him to play rough and he did – he pushed her back onto the sofa and split her track suit open with two hands and started sucking those humongous tits.

His hand went down the front of her pants and he jammed two fingers into her pussy.

"Do it!" she hissed.

She yanked his pants off and was sucking his cock, taking every inch of it in and gagging on. Within minutes he was fucking her hard and her pussy was sopping wet and she moaned so load they must have heard it down on Hollywood boulevard.

He fucked her hard missionary style for several minutes and she must have came two or three times, and then Brady pulled out and shot a streams of cum, porn star style from her stomach to her face.

"Oh, fuck yeah!" she said, and then she scooped the cum up and licked it off of her fingers.

The afternoon went by in a blur for Ashley. She got buzzed on the champagne and then they went for spa treatments. Chloe and Ashley each got massages, bikini waxes, manicures and pedicures. The spa was first class all the way and the women were pampered by the staff every step of the way. Ashley had never had a bikini wax before and even though it hurt, she was strangely aroused when the Vietnamese woman was feeling around down there. She felt like she was experiencing some new awakening as she was casting all of her small town notions of morality and modesty aside. Here in California, everyone seemed to just do what felt good at the moment, and Ashley had to wonder what was so wrong with that? Life was short.

Her own mom had suffered for years under the iron thumb of her dad. Her mom suffered in silence and never said anything when something was bothering her and just made the best of it. Her mom also never said an unkind word about anyone, but her dad was always bitching about people and judging how they lived their lives. Basically, that was anyone who lived differently than he did. She guessed that she would never heal her relationship with him. He would probably die of a heart attack or something on the farm and she would never have a chance to reconcile with him. A sharp pain went through her heart and she pushed it down. Weren't they supposed to be here to forget about all that?

Afterward, they went into town for dinner. Cloe took her to a small sushi place in downtown Palm Springs, where every dish was a creation that could have gone into a museum. Everything seemed so glamorous, and stylish, and chic and seductive. The waiters, the bartenders, the sushi chefs, all seemed to be putting on a performance just for them. Chloe taught Ashley how to order and eat sushi, since she had very little experience with it. And they drank big Japanese Asahi beers and hot saki. Chloe gave Ashley another pill and she took it without hesitation. They enjoyed their dinner and they laughed, and Ashley felt very comfortable with Chloe. Whatever she was doing was working.

They finished dinner and went for a walk in downtown Palm Springs. They stopped for a picture in front of the large Marilyn Monroe statue. They noticed a lesbian couple walking and holding hands and they both seemed a little uncomfortable by it, but Ashley felt a strong urge to take Chloe's hand, and Chloe felt the overwhelming urge to kiss Ashley in front of the statue, but she held back. They returned to their room and Chloe went out to the patio and turned on the Jacuzzi.

"I've got some good pot," Chloe said as Ashley took a couple of Heinekens from the mini bar.

Ashley had only smoked pot a couple of times and had not liked the way it made her feel, but she said, "Ok." Chloe took out a little glass pipe and loaded it. They both took a hit and Ashley coughed up a storm.

Chloe went to the bathroom for a few minutes and when she came out she was wearing a fluffy robe that was supplied by the hotel. She turned some electronic music on.

"I'm going for a soak," Chloe said, walking by Ashley and out to the patio. Ashley watched Chloe out on the patio and saw her take the robe off and she was naked as she lowered herself into the steam of the Jacuzzi. Ashley felt the pot hit her like a ton of bricks and it seemed as if every nerve ending in her body ended at her vagina.

She went and got into her robe and joined Chloe at the Jacuzzi. Chloe watched as Ashley shed the robe and joined her naked in the water. Their feet were touching in the water, the sound of the Jacuzzi motor and the music had a hypnotic effect. They sat there for several minutes and their thighs were now touching and Chloe was looking at her and before Ashley knew it she had her arms around Chloe and was kissing her.

They kissed each other hungrily and their hands were all over each other. Within minutes, they were dripping wet on Chloe's bed and Chloe went down on Ashley. She sucked and nibbled Ashley's freshly waxed pussy with a finesse Ashley had never experienced before and as Chloe inserted her fingers into Ashley's vagina waves of orgasm shot through her body.

They were soon in a 69 position and Ashley was eating pussy for the first time in her life. Ashley went into a blackout as she orgasmed again and again.

Ashley woke up naked the next morning alone in her own bed. She looked at the clock and it was almost noon. She looked around and couldn't see Chloe. The sun was already high and bright in the sky. Ashley remembered what had happened and it scared her.

She was crossing new boundaries every day, and the thing that scared her was that she enjoyed it. She was excited, she was aroused. She felt free and alive and artistically awake. She also felt out of control and didn't know where each day would take her. How was she going to face Chloe now? Would Chloe be all weird about it? Would it happen again, and would she end up being a lesbian?

Ashley couldn't see that happening. She experimented, she tried it, but she liked men. She loved men, and could never imagine going without them, but there was something very nice about what she remembered from the experience with Chloe. Her pussy was sore and tingling and she was aroused and felt the urge to masturbate or pee. She decided to pee. She went into the bathroom sat on the toilet and wondered where Chloe was. The toilet paper was embossed with the hotel's logo and that impressed Ashley.

Chloe was down in the hotel lobby at the breakfast bar. They had complimentary coffee, bagels, lox, cream cheese, and an elaborate fruit spread. Classical music played as the beautiful people staying at the hotel enjoyed the complimentary goodies. Chloe was enjoying her coffee and savoring the memory of the night before. Everything had gone down exactly as she had planned it, and Ashley was everything she had imagined and more. She had never experienced lesbian sex with a first timer who was as responsive and talented as Ashley. Wow, Chloe shivered and shuddered just thinking about it. Her vagina was in full activation mode. She couldn't stop smiling and the other people in the lobby noticed it and her smile was contagious. Chloe almost had to pinch herself to remind herself she wasn't dreaming. She sniffed her fingers and could still smell Ashley's sweet scent on them. Her head was still a little foggy from the drugs and booze the night before, but she felt better than she ever had in her life.

She took a valium from her purse and washed it down with coffee while she considered her next move, her strategy. She would have to back off now. She would have to pull the "take away". She would have to act like what had happened was spontaneous and she was embarrassed about it. As much as she wanted to just go back to the room and make love to Ashley all day long, she would have to restrain herself and think about the long term. If she came on too strong she would blow it – that had happened before. It happened with Jillian. Though, Jillian was nothing compared to Ashley. Ashley was the crown jewel of Chloe's entire sexual career. Could she hold onto her for longer than one night, that was the real question.

2000 miles to the west in a Maui five star hotel a similar situation was playing out. Jillian had gone on an impromptu vacation with Chuck Alexander. Just as Chloe had done with Ashley, Chuck pulled out all the stops in his quest to seduce Jillian. That was a tough order, because Jillian was as jaded as any human could possibly be and was not impressed by much. Maybe a billionaire would impress her, but she knew she was probably beyond landing one of those. She had flown in private jets before, had been to the swankiest places in London, Paris, Dubai, and Tokyo, so the Ritz Carlton in Maui was just old hat for her. The difference for her now was that she was broke and desperate for the first time in her life. She couldn't let Chuck Alexander know that, however. She had to keep up the façade that she had it going on. She had finally given herself up to him the night before after holding out for as long as she could. She also had to play the game as if she was into it, like she had to pretend that she enjoyed sucking his ugly Viagra enhanced cock beneath his hairy gut, even though she felt like she might throw up. The Xanax and champagne made it easier. She also pretended to have an orgasm and it took Chuck forever to get off and her pussy got sore as he pounded and pounded her, and she secretly wanted to just stab his eyes out. Finally she just had to jack him off.

The revolting pig fell asleep and snored his ass off all night, as Jillian lay there wide awake totally and completely disgusted with herself that her life had come to this point, but she had to remember the long term plan. Dr. Davis had helped her come up with it. Rope Chuck Alexander in, get him to marry her – stay married for a few years then get spousal support, and whatever else she could. Maybe the bastard would die somehow and she would get everything. She was tired of this whole game of playing the field and short term gains and just wanted to have some stability. Maybe she could learn to at least tolerate this loser, Chuck Alexander. She wondered how much he was actually worth. Less than ten million she guessed. He was real showy with his money and the big fish never did that. He probably was only worth about three million she finally decided. That would have to do. She could live with that.

At that current moment they were laying beside the hotel pool drinking Mai Tai's. Jillian looked at Chuck's fat hairy body that was shining in the sun and slick with oil. "How are you doing, babe?" she said, rubbing oil onto his back, surprised by her own generosity.

Chuck purred like a kitten as she rubbed the oil in. "I was thinking we could do one of those helicopter tours of the island, later," he said.

"Cool," Jillian said, trying to sound enthused.

While Chloe was gone, Ashley closed the door to her bedroom and called her mom and talked for awhile. She told her about the five star hotel and the spa treatments and said that a friend was treating her. Her mom mentioned that she had heard that Brady was staying in California for the foreseeable future. That angered Ashley but she didn't say anything. Her mom talked about crops, and the price of wheat and how they were worried about finances. Farmers were always worried, Ashley remembered. There were years growing up when a bumper crop had come in, but those were few and far between. It seemed as if her parents were always robbing Peter to pay Paul to keep that farm going. Ashley thought about how her mom was such a trooper and a strong women who toughed it out with her dad no matter what.

Ashley felt guilty laying there in the lap of luxury and thought about how her parents would literally die if they knew about her shenanigans from the night before. Her parents got up at the break of dawn every morning to start their chores and here she was lying in bed at 1:00 pm and she had eaten another woman's pussy the night before. She hung up with her mom feeling a little guilty and confused and angry that Brady was still hanging around LA. She heard Chloe come into the room and she finally gathered enough courage to go out and face her.

Ashley came out of her room smiling, wearing the hotel robe and looking half asleep. Chloe was fully dressed and sitting on the sofa watching the business channel on the large screen television. "Good morning," Ashley said.

"I brought you a coffee," Chloe said, pointing to a cup on the bar.

"Thanks," Ashley said, going to retrieve it. There was an awkward moment of silence.

"Last night got a little crazy. I am so embarrassed," Chloe said, playing as coy as she possibly could.

Ashley smiled and tried to think of something to say. "I don't remember much. It's no big deal, I guess. I don't want it to ruin our friendship," she finally said.

Chloe smiled. "Exactly. I think we were just a little buzzed and over stimulated."

They both giggled. "It seems a little cold to lay out by the pool. I thought we could go shopping. They have this new mall out here that I wanted to check out," Chloe said.

"Sure," Ashley said. "I'll get ready."

They went shopping all afternoon and Chloe bought several new outfits for herself. Ashley looked at several things and tried them on, but didn't really have the money to buy them. Chloe resisted buying her anything, but did finally buy her a pair of tennis shoes. They laughed and had a good time with each other. The sex that they had the night before did not seem to be some weird issue between them. Chloe was still very much aroused just being in Ashley's presence, but was careful not to reveal that. Ashley was confused; she felt an attraction toward Chloe that she had never felt toward another woman. She decided that she would just go with the flow and try not to over analyze it. If it happened again, it happened again. Ashley was not going to let herself be restrained by traditional mores ever again. She was an artist, and artists lived free.

Twelve

Things got surreal quickly for Brady. He sat by the pool at Crystal's house drinking a Corona high in the Hollywood Hills looking down on the city below. Was this really happening? Was he really doing this? Never in his wildest dreams did he imagine something like this would happen. He thought of how fast things had happened in the past 24 hours. After he had gone home with Crystal to help her with the dog food, they returned to the pet store where he abruptly resigned. Isaac was furious and started yelling at him, telling him what a piece of shit he was and how he was just like all of the others. Brady just stood there and took it, feeling like a scumbag for quitting without notice like he said he wouldn't do when Isaac hired him.

Brady retrieved his things from the back room while Isaac watched him like a hawk. Brady saw the puppy Oatmeal scratching at his cage wanting him to go and get him and Brady offered to take the puppy as payment for the money Isaac owed him. "You are not getting that fucking dog," Isaac said. Isaac pulled out three hundred dollar bills from his wallet and shoved them at Brady. "Get out of my store," he said.

Brady put the money in his pocket and he could hear the puppy whining as he walked out. Crystal was waiting for him in the passenger seat of the Range Rover. Brady put his things in the back of the Range Rover and then drove back to Crystal's house, where he moved in.

Brady did cocaine for the first time that day. He did cocaine and had marathon sex with Crystal all day and night. She was possessed and couldn't seem to get enough. He did things with her he had never thought of doing. She liked it rough and wanted him to choke and slap her. He played along with it as much as he could but got the feeling he didn't go far enough for her. She wanted him to pee in her mouth and he refused to do that. She pushed his legs back and licked his asshole, not just lightly tonguing it, but pushing her entire tongue up in there. She would take his entire balls and cock into her mouth until she gagged. She called him "sir" and "Mr. Anderson," and she requested that he call her "nigger whore," which he refused to do.

She wanted him to fuck her in the ass and when he did she just went crazy and her eyes rolled back in her head, like she could not get enough. She made him go down on her and wanted him to bite her pussy and clit and she wanted him to stick his whole hand up in there. They snorted line after line watched the nastiest pornos that Brady had ever seen. Crystal had the remote and would just keep reversing and forwarding certain scenes over and over again. Finally, Brady couldn't get it up any more and Crystal started fucking herself – she had the bottom of a Corona bottle stuck up her vagina and the long neck of another bottle pushed up her ass. That was something Brady had never imagined witnessing, and could not unsee.

She was sleeping now. Finally, after 18 hours of fucking, sucking, and snorting. Brady was wide awake and wired like he had never been before. There was still some coke smattered on the mirror in the house and he thought about going in and doing it. So, this was the big deal -

cocaine? He had to admit, he liked it a lot. It made him feel like superman when he took the first snort. The rush that hit him and the instant euphoria, and the feeling of omnipotence that followed was something that he had only come close to experiencing when as a quarterback he threw the pass that won his high school team the state football championship. And here he was with this Nubian queen, this Amazon woman, this sexual dynamo, fucking the bejesus out of her in the Hollywood Hills. If only his high school teammates could see him now. If only Ashley, that fucking bitch, could see him now. He thought of the puppy, Oatmeal back at the pet store and it pained him deeply. He walked into the house and snorted another line.

The rest of the Palm Springs trip was mostly uneventful for Ashley. As much as they tiptoed around it, the sexual episode between her and Chloe made things awkward. They went out to dinner again, then went back to the hotel, watched a movie and went to bed in their own rooms. Ashley backed off on the pills and alcohol. She just wanted to get back to LA and keep working on her monologue for acting class. She was also scheduled to take pictures with a photographer that Jillian recommended. She felt that she had at least gotten some "life experience" out of the Palm Springs trip.

Chloe's constant talk of money started to irritate Ashley. The real kicker was in the car on the way back. Chloe started talking to Ashley about her career, about how she would need a manager. Chloe talked about herself and what a good sales person she was and that although she did not have direct experience in the entertainment business, that she would be a natural at it, "I mean, what is the difference between selling drugs and entertainment?" Chloe said. Chloe said that she would quit her job to become Ashley's full time manager. Ashley didn't know how to react; she suddenly began to wonder about Chloe's sanity. Why would a woman quit a $200,000 a year job to become *her* manager? She hadn't even had her pictures taken yet. Ashley knew that realistically it might be years before she started making money as an actress. She was not that delusional to think that she would just be an overnight success. She had read all of the biographies.

Ashley politely turned Chloe down, and she got the feeling that when she got out of the car that Chloe was hurt and mad even though she hugged her and gave her a Hollywood kiss on the cheek as they parted. What had started as an adventure ended as a downer. Maybe it was because they were coming back to reality as they arrived back in West Hollywood.

Chloe *was* hurt and mad as she was driving away. She was mainly mad at herself – she had exposed her hand too soon. She played the night before perfectly, but couldn't keep her mouth shut on the trip home. Now, she had probably scared Ashley off with the manager talk. Chloe was furious at herself for blowing it, and she blamed it on the pills she was taking. The pills made her too talkative and out of control. She was going to have to stop taking so many. She knew that was going to be hard. She started to wonder if she was addicted to them. A friend of hers had to go to the Betty Ford Center to get off of pills and hadn't been the same since.

The thought of this terrified Chloe. She had always been so in control of everything, and here some naïve Kansas farm girl had caused her to come undone. Well, she had that one night of bliss with her, so in that respect she had been successful, but how could she ever recover from that? Knowing that she would never get the chance again? Chloe parked in her parking spot in front of her condo. A sinking feeling enveloped her. A dark depression arrived like certified mail. Chloe hung her head on her steering wheel and thought about suicide. A moment later she reached into her purse and took another pill.

Thirteen

Jillian recommended the photographer, Cliff Cooper to Ashley. He had been a famous fashion photographer in the 80's, but screwed up his career with drugs. Jillian didn't tell Ashley that part. Cooper had once been a model himself when he was in his twenties.

He was now in his fifties and years of hard living had diminished his once studly looks. Ashley met him at his studio loft in downtown LA. Cooper was desperate to make some kind of comeback and Jillian had played Ashley up real big as the vehicle for that.

When Cooper saw first saw Ashley he believed that Jillian was right. Ashley had that special quality that everyone was looking for. They shot all day long and Cooper took over 800 photos. Finally they took a break and Cooper opened a bottle of champagne and lit a joint. He turned on some Muddy Waters for atmosphere.

"The shoot is going fantastic. You are incredible, Ashley. The camera loves you," Cooper said.

Ashley giggled, already feeling the weed and champagne. "Thank you. It's been so much fun," she said.

"I'd like to take a few more just for fun. Do something more artistic," Cooper said.

Ashley giggled," Artistic. What does that mean?"

"Nudes," Cooper answered matter-of-factly.

Ashley contemplated it a moment as the super strength ganja took effect. She smiled and started peeling her clothes off.

"Let's do it," she said.

Cooper shot another 400 photos as Ashley twisted and contorted her body in every way he suggested. At one point he pulled his dick out and jacked off for about two minutes as he was still taking photos. He shot a stream of cum about four feet and it splattered on Ashley's neck and shoulders. Cooper tossed her a hand towel and kept shooting. She was completely uninhibited for the first time in her life and was getting off on it. She masturbated as he kept shooting pictures.

They finally finished around midnight. It was agreed that he would take the pictures for free, but would be able to use them for his portfolio. When the photo shoot was over, Ashley pecked him on the cheek and he got a charge from it. She had to be one of the most desirable girls he had ever seen or photographed in his life. He would hang onto the nude pictures and cash in on them later. They were like money in the bank, and he couldn't believe how easy it was to get her to do them.

Meanwhile, things were going good for Brady. After the initial drug fueled orgy with Crystal things had settled down in the Hollywood Hills. Crystal helped Brady get a job working with a famous animal trainer, Les Ford, who supplied exotic animals like lions, chimps, and bears to the movie studios. Brady hit it off with Les right away. He jumped right into working at the ranch out by Santa Clarita, feeding the animals, cleaning their cages, etc., and helping Les transport them to movie sets. Brady also got to hang out on the movie sets and meet the various crew members and watch films being made.

He was gone most of the time, so his exposure to Crystal was kept to a minimum. When he did spend time with her she was very needy and her sex drive never waned. She required sex at least three times a day and Brady was always happy to get back to work, because she was damn near fucking him to death. She allowed him to drive her deceased husband's big Silverado to work. Brady was making over a grand a week and that was good money for him. He talked to his parents a couple of times and told him what he was doing. They were secretly broken hearted as they realized he probably wouldn't be coming back to finish school or work in his father's veterinary practice.

Brady still thought of Ashley quite a bit, but was in acceptance mode, realizing that she would probably never come back to him. He did not ask his parents if they had heard anything about her and he tried not to think about her. She was not on any of the movie sets he was working on, but there were plenty of hot girls that were. Some of them had even flirted with him and made eyes at him. Brady was starting to get his confidence back.

Ashley's pictures came out great and she started submitting them to various agents and managers. Most of the nudes were not included in the proofs that Cooper gave her. She was too embarrassed to ask him about it. She pushed the whole incident into the back of her mind, hoping it wouldn't come back to haunt her.

She continued working at Kraven and taking acting classes. She finally nailed the monologue from Hurly Burly and Jeremy Bone was now treating her like a full-fledged member of the class. She had only seen Chloe a couple of times at the club with Jillian and it was awkward. She had no resentment or bad feelings toward Chloe, but it seemed that Chloe did towards her as much as she tried to hide it. Jillian was dating Chuck Alexander and it seemed like things were getting hot and heavy between them.

Ashley finally bought some furniture for her apartment and was settling into her life in West Hollywood. Christmas was approaching and her mom tried to convince her to come back home. Ashley told her she was too busy and would have to come back in the summer instead. She still had not talked to her father. She heard from her mom that Brady was working "in the movies" and she was deeply curious about what that was about, but she wouldn't dare call him.

It angered her that he had followed her out to California and was now latching onto her dream. He never cared about movies and was for the most part bored with them. Had he been genuinely interested in movies, or drama, or art, they might still be together. He wasn't and Ashley realized that despite being together for several years, they really didn't have much in common other than sex. In that department, Ashley had men hitting on her all the time, at the club, on the street, in the acting class, but she declined all of their offers. She focused on her classes and goals at hand. She was supposed to start working on a scene with Owen, and they were going to get together to do that.

Ashley finally called that big time agent, Michael Levin, who gave her his card, but he never returned the call. Ashley was starting to get the picture that people in California were flaky and they didn't always do what they said they were going to do. In Kansas, there weren't enough people to go around that you could screw a different one over every day and still have plenty to choose from. Here, people were a dime a dozen and you could use them up and discard them, and ten more would be in line to eagerly get sodomized.

Chloe and Jillian got together for lunch at Fred Segal one day like they had for years. They spent the morning shopping all of their usual spots, and were now having their noon time wine. Jillian had pulled out of her financial slump and was now spending Chuck Alexander's money. He gave her a credit card to go shopping with and she had paid her rent with it.

Chloe was not her bubbly self and had slipped into a dark depression since the trip to Palm Springs. She was no longer happy in her job and her sales had slipped considerably as she was just going through the motions. She often would go home after work and go straight to bed. The mixture of pills she used for every up and down in her life no longer seemed to be working. She tried to stop using them all together, but became paralyzed with fear within hours, irritable, and unable to function at all. Jillian talked about herself for awhile and realized that her friend was not herself.

"What is wrong with you, anyway?" Jillian finally asked.

"I don't know. I'm depressed and nothing is working to snap me out of it. I'm thinking about checking into Betty Ford," Chloe said.

"Don't do *that*. Go see Dr. Davis – he'll get you back into shape," Jillian said. "He did wonders with me."

"I don't know. It is more serious than that. I've never thought about suicide before, and I've been thinking about that a lot lately," Chloe said, letting it out.

Jillian looked at her a long moment. "I was like that a month ago, and it passed. You just have to ride it out. Seriously, if it wasn't for Dr. Davis, I wouldn't be sitting here right now."

"Really. You didn't say anything," Chloe said.

Jillian shrugged and lit a cigarette. "Look, this thing I got with Chuck isn't like, my ideal situation, but Dr. Davis got me to see things clearly. He got me to accept reality and deal with it. He helped me come up with a plan and implement it," Jillian said. "You don't want to go away for a month and spend fifty grand at Betty Ford, do you?"

"I guess not," Chloe said.

"Hey, where's that wannabe actress chick, what's her name?" Jillian asked.

"Who knows. She thinks she's hot shit, but she's clueless," Chloe said.

Jillian studied her a moment and a sly smile came to her face. "That's what this is all about, isn't it?"

"No! Are you nuts?" Chloe said. Jillian started laughing.

"Yeah, now I get it. You've been acting funny ever since you got back from Palm Springs. Please, she is a hot piece and everything, but you're going to let that chick do you in?" Jillian said laughing.

Chloe stared at her salad and didn't say anything.

"You just need to get back into the saddle. Call Dr. Davis today," Jillian said.

When Brady arrived home from work he noticed a GMC Denali in the driveway that he had never seen before. He parked the big Silverado where he usually parked it and went into the house. A large menacing looking black guy was inside the house talking to Crystal. Brady could see them through the window. They appeared to be arguing about something. Brady had heard Crystal talking on the phone and she was very "ghetto" but when she spoke to him she always used proper English and even had the hint of an English accent. Brady could hear her using the ghetto voice when she was talking to this man in the living room. The large black man looked over and saw Brady. In a moment, the man and Crystal came walking out.

"Oh, hi Brady. This is Derek," she said, switching back to the English accent.

Derek nodded to Brady, didn't smile and kept his hands in his pockets.

"Hi," Brady said.

"He was just leaving," said Crystal.

"Later," Derek said, as he got into his Denali. He backed out of the driveway and disappeared out the gate. Brady didn't ask Crystal who he was or what it was about and she didn't offer it.

Crystal threw her arms around Brady and kissed him.

"Hi, baby! I missed you," she said slurring her words.

She was drunk as she usually was. She drank at least two to three bottles of Kendal Jackson chardonnay per day, and she smoked blunts. She would take all of the tobacco out of a cigar and pack it with marijuana. There were piles of tobacco sitting in ashtrays all over the house.

Brady thought about it – Crystal was usually half comatose, except when she had coke. He hoped that she didn't have any because he didn't want to go through another two day binge with her. At the same time he wished that she did have it and he almost salivated thinking about it.

They went inside the house and Crystal got Brady a beer and sat on his lap on the sofa.

"How was your day, baby? I missed you," she said, stroking the side of his face.

"It was cool. We took one of the big cats to Paramount studios for a shoot today," Brady said.

"That's so cool, baby. I'm proud of you," she said. She leaned her head against his shoulder. She was wasted.

"Who was the dude?" Brady finally asked.

"The dude? The dude? Oh, you mean Derek? He's just an old friend, he stops by sometimes," Crystal said.

She started rubbing Brady's crotch and squeezing his balls. She did it a little rough and it hurt him.

"Ouch!" Brady yelled.

"Fuck you!" she said and slapped him. Brady slapped her back and she fell back onto the coffee table.

"Motherfucker!" she yelled and hit him again.

She continued hitting him and he had to restrain her. They ended up rolling around on the floor and knocked over a lamp and potted plant. Finally Brady had to get on top of her and held her down kicking and screaming. She spit in his face.

"Fucking bitch!" Brady said and slapped her again. Then he saw that she was getting a thrill from it. His cock got hard. He yanked his belt off with one hand and twisted it around her neck.

Soon, he was fucking her mouth with his cock while he had the belt wrapped tight around her neck. Brady couldn't believe himself, was shocked by his own brutality and the thrill he was getting out of it. She was gagging on his cock and he came down her throat. He pulled out and released the belt and saw that she was completely satisfied having been abused by him.

Brady went into the bathroom to wash his cock off and catch his breath. He was disgusted with himself for taking such an eager part in her sickness.

Crystal laid there a moment, looking at the dirt and broken vase beside her. She had come a long way from the streets of Compton where she grew up. The guy Derek was her half brother, a lifelong member of the Ghost Town Crips, a notorious Compton street gang. She had a tumultuous relationship with him – but he supplied her with drugs and she supplied him with money. She had told him to stay completely away when her husband Jimmy was alive.

Derek started coming around again after the funeral. Crystal really didn't want any remnant of her life in Compton to be around, and he was the only thing that remained. She hadn't been to the city of Compton in over fifteen years and she had no plans of ever returning there. She pulled herself out of there when she was fifteen and had worked as a stripper and prostitute off and on for most of her life until she married Jimmy. She had met him at the strip club she was dancing in on the Sunset Strip. They married a month later and when he died she got the house and part of an insurance policy, while Jimmy's kids got his life savings. Crystal would never have to strip or turn tricks again. When it came to men, Crystal only liked white men. She felt that she could control and manipulate them better, and they seemed to be more enthralled with her while black men saw her as just another girl from the neighborhood. There was no sense of mystery there.

Crystal had recurring nightmares about her mother's boyfriend who would come into her room drunk when she was only ten years old and have sex with her. At the time, she even grew to like it, but was confused and scarred for life by it. She had been placed on psychiatric holds several times and had been through a couple of court ordered rehabs. She even did a six month stint at Cybil Brand detention center for a cocaine possession beef in the early nineties. There had been half assed suicide attempts and pill overdoses over the years.

She finally had a sense of stability when Jimmy was alive, and despite what all of his friends probably thought, she really loved him and missed him desperately. She had not recovered from his sudden death and she was just using this kid, Brady to get over it. She only hoped she could hold onto Brady a bit longer and was terrified he would leave her right then. She jumped up and joined him in the bathroom. He was standing in there brooding and staring at himself in the mirror. She put her arm around him and leaned into him. They stared at each other in the mirror instead of facing each other directly.

"I don't really get into that rough shit. It gives me a bad feeling," Brady said.

"I'm sorry, baby. I'm just a little out of control. I'm still hurting over Jimmy's death," she said.

He looked at her another moment in the mirror, wondered how abuse equated to comfort, then turned and hugged her.

"Let's go get some steaks or something. I'm buying. We can go to Chasen's," she said.

"Ok," Brady said, "I'll buy this time," still hugging her.

Fourteen

Ashley had the day off and was supposed to start working on a scene with Owen for next week's acting class. She called Owen and they agreed to meet at his place in the Korea Town section of LA. He was living in an old house with two roommates just off of Western Boulevard and Beverly. She arrived and was surprised that everyone was at home on a week day, in the middle of the day. That was one thing Ashley noticed – nobody seemed to work in LA. Or they barely worked, or were working all the time. It was so strange compared to what she had grown up with. Her dad usually worked from sunrise to sundown and her mom was just as busy with the household chores.

The three roommates including Owen had a band together and they were rehearsing when she arrived. Owen was the lead guitar player and singer, his roommate Karl was the bass player. The other roommate, Griz played drums. Ashley watched them for a few moments and was impressed. They were a death metal band and they really put out a lot of sound.

Owen wrote all of the songs. He explained to Ashley that they played gigs in back yards and a few small clubs around town and that they had a small hardcore following. The roommates said their hellos to Ashley, but were largely bored or too cool to really acknowledge her. Owen took her up to his room on the top floor of the old house. The walls were covered with posters for his band, Che Guevara, and Bukowski.

Ashley sat on his bed and he sat in a beanbag chair across from her. He handed her a scene he had written for the class.

"You wrote this?" she said.

"Yeah, thought it might be fun. I'm really more of a writer than an actor, I just take the class for kicks," he said.

Ashley read the scene while he watched her read it. The beat of the drums from the guys practicing down stairs reverberated up through the floors and Ashley unconsciously tapped her toes to the rhythm. The scene that Owen had written was about a serial killer, who had picked up a hitchhiker and was planning on raping and killing her, but she was crazy and it throws him off. It was a dark comedy. Ashley finished reading it and smiled.

"Wow, that is dark," she said.

"What do you think? You want to do it?" he asked eagerly.

"Sure, it's a definite challenge. Jeremy is going to love this" she said.

They worked on the scene for a couple of hours as they laughed and flirted and touched each other a bit. Ashley found herself getting aroused just being in the bedroom with Owen with the door closed. That was something that her parents had never allowed in high school, even though she was going steady with Brady. She guessed that he had made her pregnant in the back seat of his car. The painful thought of her abortion returned to her and she used it in the scene they were rehearsing. Owen was impressed.

"Wow, that was great! That was just what I was imaging the girl to do, when I wrote it," he said.

"Thanks," she said, not letting him in on her secret. Owen stared at her looking directly into her eyes. Ashley was wearing a low cut blouse and shorts and her bare legs were looking fantastic and were driving Owen crazy, though he tried hard not to show it.

"You want to do it again?" Owen asked.

"No, I think that was enough for today," she said.

"Okay," he said standing, "Maybe we can meet again next week before the class."

"Sure," Ashley said. "What are you doing today?"

"Uh, well, nothing I guess. Why, you want to do something?" Owen said.

"I thought you might want to go out for a beer or something?" Ashley said.

"Shit. I'm kind of broke right now. I'm waiting for my unemployment check to come in, but I have some beers downstairs," Owen said.

"Okay," Ashley said smiling.

"I'll be right back," Owen said, hurrying out.

Ashley looked around the room. She knew what was going to happen, but she couldn't stop herself. She had been lonely for the last few weeks. She was trying to be strong and focus on her career, but she had felt empty and lonely. She realized that was the life she had chosen for herself – one above relationships and traditional family. Artists were meant to suffer and that was where they drew their inspiration from. It was a lonely life and she wondered if she would be able to hack it in the long run. Christmas was five days away and she had told her mom she couldn't come home this time. She even missed Brady and restrained herself from calling *him* every day.

She liked Owen and felt comfortable with him. She guessed he was probably good in bed and she had already made up her mind that she was about to find out. Besides that she was beginning to wonder if she wasn't a lesbian, because her last sexual encounter had been with Chloe and she couldn't even get that out of her mind. She wondered why Chloe had not called her, and she thought about calling her several times, but stopped herself. She was tired of being such a *good girl* and decided she would cut loose with Owen.

Owen returned with a Senor Frogs bucket full of Modelos on ice, with some cut limes, a bottle of Don Julio tequila, a salt shaker, and two shot glasses.

Ashley laughed upon seeing the presentation, "Wow!"

Owen poured two shots and handed one to Ashley.

"Merry Christmas," he said. Ashley looked at the shot with hesitation.

"I don't know how I'm going to get home, but Merry Christmas!" she said and she tapped her glass against his and drank the shot, shuddering as it went down. Owen opened some beers and then took down his acoustic guitar and started playing. Ashley sipped her beer and settled in, fascinated by his guitar playing.

Chloe didn't take Jillian's advice and call Dr. Davis. She went home, flushed all of her prescription pills down the toilet and called a friend of hers who she knew was a member of Alcoholics Anonymous. Chloe knew that she was addicted to the various pills and was tired of being dependent on them. They weren't making her feel any better, and she had strong thoughts of suicide throughout her day.

Her friend, Steven, a gay male was surprised to hear from her, but invited her to a meeting on Robertson in West Hollywood. Chloe was afraid that someone she knew would see her at the meeting and wore a cap and large dark sunglasses. She explained to Steven on the trip over to the meeting that she wasn't an alcoholic, but needed help getting off the pills.

"Honey, please. I've drank with you, are you forgetting that?" Steven said laughing.

"I was doing about twenty Percocets a day and drinking my ass off," Steven said, "I have over a year sobriety now and have never felt better."

As they parked the car, Chloe had second thoughts.

"Maybe I should just go see a therapist, I mean, these meetings are for people who have real problems," Chloe said.

"People like you and me," Steven said, waiting for her to get out of the car. Chloe finally did and they filed into the meeting looking for a seat.

The meeting was packed with people from all walks of life. There were many West Hollywood types and tattooed hipsters, as well as a few older grandfather and grandmother types. Chloe was nervous and suspicious. Everyone seemed so happy, and they were laughing. She noticed one fresh faced girl, probably in her early thirties at the front of the room. The girl smiled at Chloe. Steven got a cup of coffee for Chloe and sat next to her, holding her shaking hand.

When the meeting got started, the leader asked if there were any newcomers and Steven nudged Chloe. "Stand up and say your name," he whispered.

Chloe reluctantly stood, "My name is Chloe, and I'm an drug addict," the words squeaked out of her mouth.

There was thunderous applause and everyone at once said, "Hi Chloe!"

Chloe's knees were knocking together, she felt like she might pass out, and she sat back down.

Ashley was seriously lubricated from the tequila and beer. She listened to Owen play his guitar and sing, and they talked about Jeremy Bone and the acting class gossip. Finally, Owen sat next to her on the bed and he kissed her. She didn't stop him, but didn't really reciprocate either. He backed off and stared into her eyes.

"You are so incredibly beautiful. I got a physical charge when I first saw you, you know that?" he said.

She stared at him, the tequila and beer surging through her brain. "Thank you," she said and she kissed him. They started making out and then heard a commotion coming from below. Owen's best friend, Gabe had arrived to house and was talking to the roommates downstairs. They heard him coming up the steps. "Owen, what's up, dude?" he yelled through the door.

"Oh, shit, I forgot he was coming," Owen said.

Owen got up and opened the door. Gabe was tall and good looking and wore the hipster uniform that they all wore – skinny jeans and t-shirt, and a little beanie cap. He was carrying a guitar case. Gabe walked into the room and was surprised to see Ashley sitting there. He took a long look at her and smiled.

"Wow, sorry to interrupt," Gabe said, "I can leave."

"This is Ashley from my acting class," Owen said.

"Oh yeah," Gabe said, shaking her hand.

"Stay," Ashley said.

The events that followed were very cloudy in Ashley's mind.

The two guys played some songs on their guitars. Gabe sang a song that he had written, and then they played some cover songs from Nirvana and Ashley sang along to them. They all continued drinking and then Gabe took out some ecstasy tablets. Ashley had never tried that but she took it and then things got real freaky.

She somewhat remembered having sex with both of them. She sucked Gabe as Owen was fucking her from behind. She became animalistic and couldn't get enough, and seemed to be outside of herself watching as the two men took turns and switched off on her. Some weird music was playing really loud.

Music was ringing in her ears and she woke up suddenly. Owen was asleep naked beside her. Beer bottles littered the room. The music was still playing on an Ipod. She reached over and shut it off. It was still dark outside, but all of the lights were on in Owen's room. Gabe was gone. Ashley got up foggy, naked and shivering and she looked outside at the darkness. She could see some Christmas lights blinking on a palm tree across the street. She tried to remember what had happened and she wondered if it had really happened, and then she decided that it had. Careful not to wake Owen, she quietly got her clothes on and slipped out of the room.

She walked to her car cautiously. It was 3:30 am. She got into the car and started it. She drove down Santa Monica Boulevard and turned up Western. The streets looked empty, except for a homeless man dragging a grocery cart full of empty bottles across the street. He looked at her with vacant eyes as he crossed in front of her car. Ashley turned the heat to high in her car. Her windows were fogged up and dripping. She was freezing. She had crossed another boundary and gained another life experience. She felt out of control again, but tried not beat herself up for what she had done. That was what people in Hollywood did, right? *She was not in Kansas anymore.* She stopped at another light by the Hollywood Freeway and wondered where Brady was at that moment.

She turned onto Hollywood Boulevard and noticed two transvestites fighting on the corner. They looked so ragged and desperate and it reminded her of a scene out of a B-movie. Ashley realized she was still feeling the effects of the ecstasy. The lights were trailing and colors were vivid and she suddenly felt anger at herself for taking the pill and anger at the boys for giving it to her. They had taken advantage of her and "raped" her. She never would have done what she did if she hadn't taken that pill. She would avoid Owen in the future. What a dirtbag, Ashley decided. She started to panic and realized she was in no condition to drive, but was afraid to stop. She saw a red light coming up but she blew right through it.

A moment later she saw the flashing red and blue lights behind her. She was being pulled over by the LAPD. She pulled the car over and her hands were trembling on the wheel. An officer approached the car and tapped on her window. She rolled the window down and was blinded by his flashlight.

"License, registration and insurance," the officer said. She could not see his face.

"Yes sir," she said as she hunted in the center console for the documents.

"Where are you going?" the officer asked.

"Home, West Hollywood," she said. She could now see the officer's face. He was tall, Latin, and good looking, probably about thirty years old.

"Have you been drinking alcohol?" the officer asked.

"Uh, I've had a couple of beers at my friend's house," Ashley said, on the verge of tears.

The officer studied her face for a moment. "Step out of the car, please," he said.

Ashley got out of the car and now tears were running down her cheeks.

"Please, please, don't arrest me. I've just moved to town and I was over at a guy's house and I just had to get out of there," she said.

The officer looked at her a long moment.

"You realize that you ran that red light back there? You are in no condition to drive," the officer said. Ashley began sobbing.

"I'm so sorry, please don't arrest me. I made a big mistake," she said between sobs. The officer looked around.

"Ok, get into your car and park it on that side street," the officer said. "I'll take you home."

Ashley parked her car on a side street off of Hollywood Boulevard and the officer followed her in the patrol car. After parking her car, she got into the car with the officer.

She tried to direct him back to her apartment. He asked her how long she had been in LA, and if she was an actress. Ashley still felt very fucked up from the pill and was trying to act sober. The officer smiled at her and obviously thought she was cute.

Ashley realized she was once again being cut a big break because she was an attractive girl. Most everybody else would be on their way to jail right now, but instead she was being given a ride home in the front seat of the patrol car. Calls kept coming in over the police radio. Ashley noticed the officer's wedding ring. He was a good looking guy, kind of like a young Pancherella from the TV show CHIPS. The officer stopped in front of her apartment building.

"Ok, is this it?" he asked.

"Yes, thank you so much, she said, and then she surprised herself when she leaned into him and kissed him. He was surprised too, but quickly started making out with her. Then a call came over his radio. The officer had to push Ashley back.

"I've gotta go," he said. He took a card from his front pocket and handed it to her. "Call me," he said.

Ashley stared at the card a moment, then got out of the car. She watched the LAPD squad car speeding off down the street.

Ashley woke up in her bed to her cell phone vibrating. She looked at it and saw it was Owen calling. It kept ringing and she finally answered it.

"Hello," she said, barely able to keep her eyes open.

"Ashley, where did you go?" Owen asked.

"Home," she said, laying there.

"I was worried about you…" he said

"Fuck you. You're an asshole," she said. There was a moment of silence.

"What's wrong?" he finally said.

"You know what's wrong. You and your friend took advantage of me," she said. There was a moment of silence.

"And, I almost got arrested last night. The cop brought me home, but I don't remember where my car is," she said, shooting out of bed.

"What? I'll come and get you. We'll find it," he said.

"Fuck you. Lose my number," she said, hanging up.

She wandered into the kitchen and poured herself a tall glass of water and drank it down. She noticed the cop's card sitting on the counter and she looked at it – EFRAIN VELASQUEZ, LAPD, it said. She started to throw it in the trash, and then realized that it might come in handy if she got into trouble again. She would not call him to ask where her car was though. She thought that she remembered where it was. Off of Hollywood Boulevard somewhere. She thought of who she could call to help her find it, and she thought of Chloe. She hesitated a moment, then found Chloe's number in her contact list and dialed it.

Chloe picked up after two rings.

"Hello," Chloe said.

"Hey Chloe, how are you?" Ashley said trying to sound cheerful. As she was doing this she went to her cupboard and fished out the one pill she had saved. She stared at it a moment and then took it.

"I'm ok. What's up? I'm at an AA meeting," Chloe said.

"An AA meeting? Alcoholics Anonymous?" Ashley said.

"Yes," Chloe admitted.

"That's a little extreme, isn't it?," Ashley said.

"Maybe, but something has to change," Chloe said. Ashley explained about what happened with her car and asked Chloe to come and help her find it. Chloe agreed to come and get her after the meeting. Ashley though it was strange that Chloe was going to AA meetings. She felt the pill starting to surge through her system. She stripped out of her bra and panties and walked into the shower. She wondered if she should get tested for STD's after the events of last night.

Brady sat in a tattoo parlor on Sunset Boulevard about to get his first tattoo. The tattoo artist known as Buzz Lightyear had specially designed a tornado with Ashley's initials hidden in the eye of it. They would be hard to see unless you were looking very hard. Brady was having it put on his forearm. He braced himself as the needle made first contact. It hurt and Brady thought about how the pain represented the pain that Ashley had caused him.

He felt hardhearted. He felt nothingness. He had anesthetized himself beyond the point of caring. He was making money and enjoying his job and just getting lost in it. He would go home to Crystal and have sex with her and get drunk and smoke blunts, and it was bearable.

He would move out and get his own place soon. He worried that Crystal might kill herself if he did that. That would be her problem. He hadn't signed up to take care of her for life. She was so needy. And who was that guy, Derek who kept coming to the house? Something funny was up.

Brady worried that she would get cocaine again, and then his job would be in jeopardy. Brady's boss knew Crystal and told him that she used to be a prostitute and a stripper. Brady had been with her for a few weeks and knew almost nothing about her. She didn't reveal much, or even talk much about anything than other than what was happening at the moment.

Brady watched as Buzz Lightyear tattooed the outline of the tornado onto his forearm. Kansas seemed worlds away now. Christmas was three days away and Brady was not going home. Brady had talked to his parents a couple of times. Every time he did he felt guilty and terrible afterwards, so the calls were getting fewer and farther between.

Chloe came and got Ashley and they drove up to Hollywood Boulevard to find her car. Chloe told Ashley that she had started going to AA meetings because she thought her pill use was getting out of control. She said that she had seven days sobriety and that she had to spend three days in a detox unit. Ashley didn't tell her about taking the pill that morning, or about the ecstasy, or the threesome with Owen and his friend, or about making out with the cop. Ashley admitted that she had gotten drunk with Owen and that she tried to drive home.

"You can come to a meeting with me and check it out," Chloe said as they circled block after block looking for Ashley's car. Ashley was growing increasingly anxious as the search continued. Finally she spotted the Kansas plates of her car on Van Ness Avenue just beside the 101 freeway. "There it is!" Ashley said. Chloe pulled up next to the car. It was parked next to a ratty apartment building that overlooked the freeway. Ashley hugged Chloe and they agreed to have lunch another day. All of the feelings came rushing back to Chloe as Ashley got out of the car.

Ashley got into her car thinking that she had dodged a major bullet. She didn't get arrested and she found her car. No harm done. She would stay away from that loser, Owen. He was a wannabe and she needed to avoid wannabe's. The town was full of them. Her acting class was full of them. Maybe she should start looking for a new class. She thought of the agent who had never called her back and that maybe she should call him again. Be more flirtatious. Whatever it takes. She pulled into a gas station off of Hollywood Boulevard and started to fill up when a large, lifted black Chevy Silverado truck pulled into the station and stopped in front of the opposite fuel island.

She barely recognized Brady when he climbed out of the truck. He did not see her. He was wearing a Dodger's cap on backwards, and a tight muscle shirt. The fresh tattoo on his forearm was covered with plastic. Ashley couldn't believe her eyes. Brady gassed up his truck and was totally unaware that she was watching him. Ashley quickly finished filling up her car and got into it. She wondered where he got that truck and the tattoo. He looked completely different from when he first arrived to Los Angeles. She wanted to go talk to him and she just sat there watching him. Someone behind her honked and she realized that she should move. She pulled out looking back at him. He didn't see her and she just drove off down Hollywood Boulevard.

Fifteen

Brady noticed Ashley as she was driving away from the gas station. He saw the Kansas plates and then recognized her car, but only caught a glimpse of her. His heart started thumping in his chest. Adrenalin rushed through his veins. She still had that effect on him. He looked down upon his tattoo as he pumped gas. He wondered if she had seen it, and if she had even recognized him. Had she seen the truck and what did she think of that? The truck was definitely over the top and Brady felt it was stupid to be driving a big raised up 4wheel drive in Hollywood. He remembered seeing trucks like this and feeling angry even because they were such a waste of energy and resources.

Here he was driving one, and he had to admit he felt a little special driving it. People certainly noticed it and looked, wondering if it was a movie star or someone important driving that truck. The curiosity must be killing Ashley if she saw him. Brady wondered what she was doing for Christmas. He had to remind himself that she had a restraining order on him. The bitch. She did not want to see him or have anything to do with him. *After all he had done for her*. Brady finished gassing up the truck, climbed back into it and headed back to the hills and Crystal.

Ashley arrived to the acting class early to meet with Jeremy Bone. She had called and made an appointment with him. She arrived looking gorgeous and he took her into his office. She appeared nervous and he scrutinized her. She smiled at Bone, realizing that was what always worked.

"So, you look good. How is Hollywood treating you?" Jeremy Bone asked.

"Ok. It's a big adjustment," she said.

"I need to have Sydney help you make a website. We need to get you going out on auditions. You need to get a reel started, and you need to get into SAG," he said.

"Yes, I want to get started as soon as possible," she said. He looked at her a long moment and knew that something else was bothering her.

"So, what's really going on, honey?" he asked.

She hesitated a moment, then finally let it out, "I don't want to do the scene with Owen."

He studied her a moment. "What happened?"

"He and I are not compatible," she said.

"Well, honey, you're going to find out that in the business, actors aren't always compatible, that's just something you have to deal with," Bone said.

"He took advantage of me when we were rehearsing," she said. "He drugged me."

"He slipped you a roofie?" Bone asked.

"Not exactly. I didn't know what I was taking and things got a little weird," Ashley said.

Bone stared at her. Her face was flushed and hot. "Ok. He's gone. I'll put you with somebody else," Bone said.

"I don't want him kicked out of the class, I just don't want to work with him," she said.

"No. He is out. I don't want him in the class anymore. I want to have a safe space for actors to work together and he abused that. He is gone, do you understand?" Bone said.

"Ok. Yes," Ashley said, not so sure about it.

"So, that is it?"

"Yes," Ashley said standing. Bone hugged her and kissed her on the cheek.

"Oh, honey, did you get your pictures back?" he asked.

Ashley thought of the wild photo shoot and grimaced inside. What had she been thinking? The photographer had called her a couple of times late at night sounding wasted and she hadn't returned his calls.

"Yes, I have them," Ashley said. She laughed and walked out, not feeling too good for getting Owen kicked out of the class, but she was glad she would not have to see him again.

When Brady returned home Crystal was watching the DVD of the movie her husband was making when he was killed. She watched the movie over and over again. She was drinking her Kendall Jackson chardonnay and smoking her blunts. Brady grabbed a Corona from the refrigerator and joined her on the sofa. Brady felt sorry for her. She looked so sad sitting there.

"Hi babe," he said.

She noticed his tattoo. "Oh, shit. Look at you," she said, grabbing his arm to get a better look.

"What is it?" she asked.

"It's a tornado, can't you tell?" he said.

She looked at it a long moment, then let his arm go. "Oh, yeah," she said. If she noticed the initials, she didn't say anything. They watched the movie for a few moments, not saying anything. Brady sipped his beer and looked around the place.

"You know what we need? A Christmas tree," he said.

"For real?" Crystal said.

"Yeah, Christmas is two days away and we have nothing at all to get us in the Christmas spirit," Brady said.

"Fuck Christmas," Crystal said.

Brady rubbed her shoulders. "Don't say that, baby. We're going to have a good Christmas this year. Let's try to, ok?"

She looked at him a long moment. "Ok," she said. He smiled at her and kissed her.

"You know, you can be yourself around me. You don't have to put up some kind of front," he said. She stared at him, wondering where that was coming from.

"C'mon, let's go get a tree," he said.

The class was assembled at Jeremy Bone's acting space. It was five minutes after the time the class usually started when Owen came ambling in. Ashley was sitting in her usual seat. There was an empty seat next to it. Owen saw Ashley, nodded at her and started toward the empty chair.

"Owen, don't even bother to sit down," Jeremy Bone called out.

Owen turned and looked at him. "What?"

"Just turn around and go back out. You're late," Bone said.

Owen shrugged and started toward the seat. Ashley avoided looking at him.

"I said, you can leave! I'm not kidding." Bone said.

Owen turned and looked at him, anger rising to his face. "What the fuck? What is this really about?"

"Just leave, please. You are done here. This is the way it is in the real world, folks. You're late, you're done. You're fired!" Bone said, now appealing to the entire class.

"You can fuck yourself, queen. I've been in this class for two years," Owen said.

Sidney, a large gay black man, who was one of Bone's assistants, jumped to his feet and got in Owen's face. Everyone in the class was mortified.

"Leave now!" Sidney said, towering over Owen.

Owen glanced up at Ashley. She avoided looking directly at him.

"Fuck it!" Owen said loudly, and then walked out, slamming the door behind him. After a moment some of the class members started clapping and talking in a burst of nervous energy.

"Ok, class! Let's focus now. Owen is a loser and not the caliber of actor we want in this class," Bone said. Ashley was sure some of the actors in the class gave her a dirty look.

A few moments later Ashley got a text message from Owen, "Fuckin bitch. Karma is a motherfucker." Ashley was unnerved by the text, but tried to focus on the class.

On the day that followed, Christmas Eve, Chloe boarded a plane and flew back to Virginia to be with her parents. As much as she hated it, Jillian went with Chuck Alexander to Las Vegas to spend time with his kids from his first marriage. Brady and Crystal were settled in with their Christmas tree and the dogs high in the Hollywood Hills. Ashley had to work at Kraven on Christmas Eve and she tried to make the best of it, though she felt very lonely and homesick for the first time being in LA.

She heard news from home there had been a cold snap, the temperature dropped to twenty below zero in her hometown, and there was a foot of snow on the ground. The temperature had been in the high seventies in LA. It didn't feel like Christmas, even though Sunset Boulevard was glittering with Christmas lights.

Ashley was setting up the hostess station before Kraven opened, when Kurt walked over from behind the bar. He reeked of alcohol and Ashley wondered if he was high on cocaine, the way he was fidgeting and acting.

"Hey, what's up, Ashley?" Kurt said, sliding right in behind her a little too close for comfort.

"Not much," Ashley said, just hoping he would go away quickly.

"So, you're stuck here too. Seems like everyone has left town," Kurt said.

"Yes. Maybe I'll get home next year," Ashley said, not looking at him and cleaning the menus with Windex.

"Hey, well if you're not doing anything after we close, you should come over and hang out. We can watch movies and drink some champagne,"

Ashley cut him off, "I am never going to hang out with you, Kurt. We work together and that's it, ok?" she said.

Kurt was surprised by her directness. "Well, excuse me!" he said, looking directly at her. "I am sorry for even standing in your shade, your majesty."

Kurt slammed a menu down and walked back to the bar. "Merry fucking Christmas to you!"

Ashley didn't engage with him and just let him seethe behind the bar. The whole rest of the night he avoided her, but she could see him glaring at her from across the room. The night just dragged on. It was slow and hardly anybody came in, but just before closing, a group of ten hipsters showed up for dinner. So the whole crew ended staying for another two hours. Ashley hated the group of hipsters for doing that to them. She just wanted to go home and go to sleep. Jean Pierre gave all of the employees a gift certificate for a free turkey at Ralph's super market. While the Mexican bus boys seemed grateful for the free turkey, Ashley felt insulted by it. She was feeling sorry for herself and pissed at the world.

The whole day she had been slipping into darkness and loneliness. She spoke briefly to her mom and wished everybody back home a Merry Christmas. After a virtual eternity, Jean Pierre let Ashley go home. She walked down Sunset Boulevard feeling lonelier than she ever had in her life. She looked at the Christmas lights hanging on the Palm trees and thought about how very far away from home she really was. A car drove by her and someone yelled out the window, "Whore!" Ashley saw the car disappearing into traffic on Sunset and thought she saw Owen driving it with his roommate in the passenger seat. This added to the already sick feeling she had and she hoped that Owen was not going to turn into a bigger problem for her.

She returned to her apartment and sat in the dark watching the blinking Christmas lights on the 12 inch tall tree she had purchased, wanting to have some kind of Christmas spirit. She drank a Heineken and wondered what Brady was doing. He obviously hadn't gone home for Christmas. Chloe was gone. Ashley suddenly realized that she had no friends in LA – only acquaintances. Chloe had shown up for her to go find the car, but Chloe wanted something from her, so she didn't count.

It seemed that everybody in LA wanted something from Ashley. The other actors in her class all seemed to be in competition with one another, and the other girls seemed to be very catty. All the men that Ashley knew seemed to want to have sex with her, and the gay men were very flighty. She talked to some of her old friends back home from time to time, but the distance between them was growing. Ashley realized that she was completely on her own for the first time in her life. She would just have to get stronger and tougher. She couldn't let something like being alone at Christmas break her.

Ashley could have hung out with the loser, Kurt. Pretended to have a good time, even though she secretly despised him, all to avoid being alone. A lot of people did that. They would rather be with somebody they despise than to be alone. She thought about Owen and felt a little guilty for getting him kicked out of the class. Then she thought of him driving down Sunset with his loser friend and her guilt quickly dissipated. She took an Ambien that Chloe had given her and washed it down with beer, hoping that visions of sugarplums would soon be in her head.

High above Hollywood Boulevard in the hills a different type of Christmas celebration was taking place. Brady was naked on all fours and Crystal was behind him naked on all fours eating whipped cream out of his ass, while jacking him off. She would squirt whipped cream into his ass crack with a canister, then lap it up like it was an ice cream sundae. "Oooh, that's so nasty," she kept saying. Hard core porn was playing on the wide screen television, loud rap music was playing. A plate of cocaine sat by the fireplace with care. She pulled his cock straight back sprayed whipped cream all over it, then sucked it up making loud slurping noises. The look on Brady's face registered somewhere between embarrassment and bliss. Crystal's two pit bulls laid nearby looking bored.

Ashley slept until after noon. The sun was bright outside and it was a balmy 80 degrees in Los Angeles. Ashley opened her eyes and laid there a moment staring at a cobweb in the corner. She could hear some birds chirping outside her window, and that in fact was what had woken her. She saw that her phone was blinking beside her bed. She looked at it and saw there was a missed call from her mom.

Ashley remembered it was Christmas day and it depressed her. She just wanted the holidays to be over with, and her website to be done. To be back in acting class, going on auditions and moving forward with life. The holidays were just an irritating obstacle to her goals. She groaned and rolled out of bed and then stumbled over to the refrigerator. She opened it and saw that there were two Heinekens left and not much else. She opened one.

She would get back to the gym and start taking care of herself tomorrow, but today, she felt like getting drunk and staying that way until the day was over with. She recalled a vivid dream she was having the night before. She tried to recall who was in the dream. She kept seeing the cop. The one who brought her home. The one who she made out with in the police cruiser.

She had his card in the cupboard.

Ashley sipped her beer and thought about him. He was a good looking guy. It might be interesting to have a fling with a cop. It would certainly be "life experience" she could use in her acting. What if she had to play in a thriller, or a cop movie? She would know that much more about it. She would not be pretending, because she would know what it was like to fuck a cop. He would tell her all the juicy details about his job. And he was a Latino – she had never been with a Latino.

The Mexicans at the club were always hitting on her, but they were unsophisticated and gross.

The cop, he was different. He was well groomed, suave, handsome, and a perfect gentleman. Who knows, she might even want to have something long term with him. He could be her knight in shining amour. Her dad would be suspicious of him because he was Mexican, but would like the fact that he was a cop. Ashley went to the cupboard and dug out the cop's card and stared at his name: EFRAIN VELASQUEZ, LAPD.

She thought about calling him, but then decided not to. Not on Christmas Day, that would seem too desperate. She really, really wanted to call him and see him again. She wondered if he was as handsome as she remembered. She had to restrain herself not to call him.

She was hungry and realized she hadn't eaten anything since yesterday afternoon. She tried to put something together to wear. She turned on the TV and watched the news; they talked about a cold snap moving on and possible rain. They were making such a big deal about it and it was twenty below zero back home with a foot of snow on the ground. They did a feature story about celebrities feeding the homeless on skid row in downtown LA. Ashley thought about driving down there and volunteering. Maybe that would be a good networking opportunity.

She got dressed and walked outside. There was a chill in the air and it felt colder than she had yet experienced in California. It looked like it might rain. She thought about returning for a jacket, but she didn't. She walked down Palm Avenue to where she had parked her car and stopped in her tracks upon catching the first glance of it. The words, WHORE, and SLUT were written in shaving cream all over the windshield, hood, and side of the car.

Ashley's heart started racing – who could have done such a thing? Brady? No, he wouldn't do that. He had never done anything like that. Then she remembered the car from last night. She thought it was Owen and his friend. She didn't walk closer to the car and a couple of guys who were walking up the street looked at it and commented, though she didn't hear what they said. They glanced at her and quickly looked away, probably realizing it was her car and they were embarrassed for her.

What a scumbag Owen turned out to be. He was mad because he got kicked out of the acting class, and now he was taking his revenge. She could call the police, but what good would it do, Ashley thought. This was LA and they had much bigger fish to fry. Owen had gotten his revenge and probably wouldn't do anything else, but if anything else did happen she would have to get a restraining order or something.

Only in town three months and already two restraining orders, Ashley almost laughed thinking about it. She stared at her car and wasn't as affected by the vandalism as the vandals probably hoped that she would be. At least they didn't slash the tires or break the windows. She returned to her apartment, got a jacket and some paper towels, then returned to the car and wiped the offensive words off. "Sticks and stones will break my bones, but words will never hurt me," Ashley thought to herself over and over again.

She drove down Santa Monica Boulevard and found a coffee shop that was open and went inside. Nobody else was in there and the kid behind the counter looked like he resented having to work. Ashley wished him a Merry Christmas and he looked at her like she was from outer space. Ashley sipped her coffee and nibbled on a bran muffin, wondering how she was going to make it through the day. She saw a homeless man shuffling down the sidewalk and tried to be grateful that she wasn't him.

Afterward, she went to Gelson's Market on Beverly Drive and wandered around aimlessly. She saw a few people in small groups, doing some last minute shopping for their Christmas get togethers and that only made her feel more alone. She finally picked up a magnum bottle of Bare Foot Chardonnay, a People magazine, a bag of potato chips, and a roasted chicken from the deli section. She decided that she was just going to drink herself into oblivion to get through Christmas.

Fuck Owen and his friend. She couldn't believe that she *had done that* and had enjoyed it. She remembered how turned on she was fucking both guys at once, but she couldn't remember that much about it. Only bits and pieces. The same thing about her tryst with Chloe. It was as if she was in a blackout throughout both experiences. She remembered the orgasms, she remembered sucking two dicks at once... Was that because she was so fucked up, or was she so excited that her mind shut down. Or, was it guilt? Was she guilty for what she was doing?

Ashley suddenly thought of killing herself. She could drive down to the beach and jump off of the Santa Monica Pier. Maybe she would go see a shrink after the "holidays". She wouldn't kill herself. Maybe it was chemical imbalance. Maybe it was Mercury in retrograde. Maybe it was bad karma, as Owen said to her. Something was fucked up in the "universe" as they say in LA. She felt fucked up – depressed, angry, anxious, afraid, lonely, and even desperate.

Ashley had never felt desperate in her entire life. She guessed that was because life had been handed to her on a silver platter. She had a wonderful childhood on the farm, despite whatever differences she had with her father. She had many wonderful Christmas celebrations with her extended family – aunts, uncles, cousins, and grandparents. Her poor great grandmother sitting in that nursing home with dementia, waiting to die. Her old dog, Scooter, was probably curled up in a pile of straw out in the barn.

She thought of a wonderful Christmas when she had gone on a skiing trip to Colorado with Brady and his family. She thought of Brady's dad and what kind and generous and upstanding man he was. He was so much different from her own father, who was grouchy and controlling and overbearing. It made her sad to think that Brady had left his nice family to come out here and be doing who knows what.

She looked at an obese girl standing in front of her and felt sorry for her. What did Ashley really have to feel sorry about? How ungrateful could she possibly be? Doors had always swung open for her because she was blessed with good looks and intelligence, but they weren't exactly swinging for her here and her only Christmas "present" was the vandalism on her car. She decided that she would revel in this dark feeling and remember it for her acting. Life would not always be a bowl of cherries. She listened to "Little Drummer Boy," by Bob Seger that was playing in the store and started crying as she was waiting in line to pay for her wine and other items. The clerk, an older lady behind the counter was looking at her, trying to not to cry herself.

Back at the house in Laurel Canyon that belonged to the famous Hollywood stuntman it was past noon and Brady and Crystal were sleeping off their coke fueled orgy that lasted most of the night. The house was a mess and littered with sex toys, whipped cream cans, wine bottles, beer bottles, and dog shit, because nobody let the dogs out the entire night.

Brady and Crystal were asleep together in the master bedroom. Crystal could sleep all day after a coke binge, but Brady usually woke up much earlier. He crawled out of bed and stumbled into the living room where he immediately smelled the dog shit, and saw the mess from the night before. Brady cussed to himself and then let the dogs out. Brady was an animal lover, but he found it difficult to like the pitbulls and was a bit afraid of them. One of them had growled at him and bared teeth, even after he had been there a couple of weeks.

Brady cleaned up the dog shit and flushed it down the toilet. He was disgusted with himself. He looked around the place and wondered if he could make it one more day there. He felt as if he was being held hostage, but he was a willing participant. Here it was Christmas day and he was stuck in a cycle of depravity. His boss had invited he and Crystal over for a Christmas dinner, but Brady knew he couldn't get Crystal up to go. He knew he should call home and wish his parents a Merry Christmas, but felt too guilty to do that. He dreaded calling them. What would he say? He would tell them how well he was doing working at the animal sanctuary. But it would all be charade and what was left unsaid would be the main conversation.

The one that went on inside everyone's head. The one that nobody was willing to talk about it. Brady's head was throbbing from the booze and coke. He felt jagged like a piece of broken glass. Maybe he should just leave right now before Crystal woke up. Go back home. He looked out upon the city and it looked gray and bleak. He could see the Christmas tree on top of the Capital Records Building, but it didn't raise his spirits. He looked at the plate of cocaine on the coffee table and saw a smattering of white powder left on it. He knew that would give him some relief for the time being and he sat down and meticulously formed a fat line on the plate with a credit card. He picked up a glass tube and snorted the line into one nostril. It burned as it went through his nasal cavity and entered the back of his throat and the surge hit him almost instantly. He felt warm and energized and his outlook improved dramatically and instantly.

It was twenty below back in Kansas – why go back now? At least wait until the end of winter. He could work and make as much money as he could and then go back to finish college. That is what he decided he would do. Work here until May or June, then return and help his dad during the summer and return to college in the fall. He could move into his own apartment until then to get away from Crystal.

He picked up a half full warm beer and drank from it. The cocaine was dripping onto the back of his throat. His face was numb and the warm beer wet his barren mouth. Crystal wasn't so bad, he thought. He had experienced more sexually with her than he ever dreamed he would. If only some of his buddies back home could hear what they did. Crystal was a hurricane of sexuality, while Ashley was a summer breeze. Yes, he still thought of Ashley daily, if not moment by moment. He looked at the whipped cream cans lying on the floor and cringed thinking about it.

Brady had to pull himself together and call his folks and sound sober enough, not to get them worrying. He searched for his phone and found it stuck down in the sofa. He looked at it and saw that there were six missed calls from back home. From his parents. Six calls? Why so many, he wondered. They wouldn't call that many times just to wish him a Merry Christmas. They weren't like that. He stared at his phone suddenly paralyzed with fear.

Ashley arrived back home after her mini breakdown in the store feeling a little better. She had cried and got it all out. She decided she would make the best of the remainder of the day. She would watch a Sopranos marathon on TV, drink wine and then tomorrow Christmas would be over and people would get on with their lives. She had called her mom and once again wished her a Merry Christmas and told her everything was fine and lied. She said she was spending Christmas with friends, so she was surprised when her phone rang an hour later and it was her mom again. Maybe it was her dad finally calling to wish her a Merry Christmas, Ashley thought as she answered it. It was her mom. "Hi honey. Sorry to call you with bad news, but we just heard that Henry Anderson was killed in an accident this morning," Ashley's mom said.

"What? No, you're kidding?" Ashley said, stunned.

"No, we heard he was on his way out to check on some horses at the Spier's place. I guess it was a head on collision with a semi. The roads are as slick as snot," Ashley's mom said. "Have you talked to Brady? He's still out there."

"No. No. We haven't talked. I was just thinking of Mr. Anderson this morning," Ashley said as she welled up with tears.

"He was a nice man, for sure. A great veterinarian. Your dad is really upset about it," Ginny said.

"I've gotta' go, mom. Thanks for calling," Ashley said.

"I thought you should know," Ginny said.

"Yes, thank you, talk to you soon. Merry Christmas," Ashley said as she hung up the phone.

She sat there not knowing if she should cry, call Brady, or get packed to go home. What an eerie coincidence, she thought. She hadn't thought of Brady's dad much at all. Then, this morning she was thinking about him and now he was dead and gone. Right away she called Brady and it went straight to voicemail. Ashley sat there and had a drink of wine, not knowing what to do.

Brady scrambled around the house trying to throw some things together to go home. He was sobbing loudly. The news of his father's death instantly burned the cocaine right out of him and he felt a pain greater than he had ever felt in his life. Nothing else mattered now, he just had to get home as soon as possible. He had seen the call come through from Ashley when he was on the phone to his uncle. He wasn't going to call her back. The bitch had a restraining order against him, and now she was calling because his father died? He had called the airlines immediately after getting off the phone with his uncle. He spoke briefly to his mother, but she was still in shock and could barely talk.

The accident had happened because of slick roads. Apparently his dad was rounding a corner and lost control of his pickup, causing him to slide into oncoming traffic. He hit a tractor trailer rig head on and was killed instantly. Brady continued to sob, he felt responsible in some way. He had broken his father's heart by coming out here and now his dad died with a broken heart. He found his bag and started shoving dirty clothes into it. Crystal heard him sobbing and stirred awake. She laid there watching him load his suitcase and it suddenly occurred to her that he was crying and packing to leave. She shot up.

"What is wrong, baby? What is happening?" she said.

Brady continued sobbing and stuffing things into his suitcase. Crystal jumped out of bed and hurried to comfort him. She started rubbing his neck.

"What is wrong, baby?" she asked again.

"My dad was killed in an accident this morning," Brady finally said between sobs.

"Oh, my God! I'm so, so sorry, baby," Crystal said, trying to be as empathetic as someone still under the influence of cocaine and large amounts of alcohol could possibly be.

"I'm going home. Can you take me to the airport?" Brady asked.

Crystal hesitated answering.

"Forget it. I'll call a cab," Brady said, zipping up his bag. He had finally stopped crying.

"Are you coming back?" Crystal asked.

Brady looked at her coldly. "I don't know."

Brady walked out of the bedroom and dialed his phone, trying to get a taxi. Crystal followed him into the living room and went directly to the plate of cocaine. She snorted a line as Brady was talking to the cab company. He looked at her with disgust.

"What is the address here?" Brady asked. She snorted the cocaine down and thought a moment as he was waiting.

"1340 Granito Drive," she said.

Ashley drifted deeper into the dark hole she was already in. She had been crying for a half hour ever since she heard about Brady's dad. She gulped down a tall glass of wine and was already feeling the effects of it. She looked out the window into the court yard and it looked cold and gray outside. The leaves were falling off of the tree out there. What should she do? Call and get a plane ticket? Henry Anderson was not her father, but the father of her ex boyfriend. Why was she so affected by it? What had she given up to come here? She lost the relationship with her own father. She lost the relationship with Brady and his family. She wouldn't see her mother, but only about once a year. She was thousands of miles away from all the people who really loved her. She was totally alone on Christmas with no friends, no boyfriend, and no prospects on the career front.

Would she become another casualty of the Hollywood dream? Would she join the legions of wannabe's who never made it? Would she enjoy some short period of success, get a taste of it, and then fade into oblivion like so many did? Like Jillian, who was now bitter and desperate, and alone. Women only had a short window of time to "make it", unlike men.

Ashley realized that she was gambling with her life, her time, and her very soul. Maybe she should get out cheap and ditch the whole thing right now. Pack up her shit and get the fuck out while the getting was still good. Ten years from now it would be impossible to go home. She could go home now, attend Henry Anderson's funeral, and reconcile with Brady. Get married and settle down in Colby and be Brady's wife and have children and live a normal, happy, and conventional life. She sipped her wine thinking about it. Who was she kidding? She would kill herself if she had to do that.

She poured herself some more wine, filling the glass all the way to the brim. She was just having a bad couple of days, and she was already throwing in the towel? It was tragic about Henry Anderson getting killed and all, but what did that really have to do with her? Quitting was not an option. She had to recommit to her dream, her goal. She was born to be an actress. She was born for bigger things than Colby, Kansas, and a husband, and kids. She was born to be here in Los Angeles, among the stars, the directors, the producers, the artists. She would become successful and have homes all over the world and she could fly her parents in to spend weeks with her if she wanted. Her dad would be proud of her then. He was only mad because he thought she was wasting her time chasing a dream. She would show him. She would show everybody. She would show Jeremy Bone, she would show Brady and all of the people back in Kansas. She would show that fucking dweeb that vandalized her car. She would show Chloe, and Jillian, and the people at Kraven. Kurt would tell people, "I used to work with that chick." Her professors back in college would brag that they used to teach her. She would be the most famous person to ever come out of Kansas. She would give interviews on the talk shows and they would joke about it – the girl from Kansas.

Ashley was not about to let somebody dying on Christmas day derail her destiny. She would send a card and some flowers to Mrs.

Anderson. People die. Shit happens. People have to be alone sometimes. Nobody said it would be easy. Anyway, she could have any man she wanted, and why should she be stuck with just one? She refilled her wine glass, then got up and walked across the room to get cop's card. She stared at it: "Efrain Velasquez, LAPD."

Sixteen

Brady sat at the bar in Terminal Five at LAX. He booked a flight to Denver and his cousin was going to make the four hour drive to pick him up. He was still a little wired by the cocaine so he ordered a large Budweiser draft and a shot of Cuervo Gold. He cried in the cab all the way down to the airport and now he felt he was cried out. His dad was gone, he would never get to see him again. He would have to accept that. Well, now he wouldn't have that pressure to go back to Colby and take over his father's vet practice. His mom wouldn't pressure him to do that. She would sell the practice to someone who wanted it. Brady couldn't see himself going back to Colby now.

It was only less than a month ago that he arrived in Los Angeles, but it seemed like five years ago. Everything had changed. Everything that he thought he knew was wrong. Everything that he thought he wanted he no longer wanted. Everything he thought he believed he no longer believed.

Brady had a good foothold in LA working with the animals in the movie business. It was exciting and different every day, and the money potential was fantastic. The guy he was working for liked him and trusted him. Brady ordered another beer and a shot. The bartender asked him if he was ok, and Brady assured him that he was. Brady thought about Crystal and decided he would break it off with her when he returned. There was no love between them. She was using him and he was using her. She was more concerned about herself when he left than her fake concern for his loss. She was more concerned about taking another snort of cocaine. She probably had already called some other guy to come over and fuck her.

Wow, sex would never be the same though, would it? Once you go black, you never go back, they say. Brady didn't know about that – Crystal was pretty intense, but it was all mechanical. There was no real passion behind it. Not like he had with Ashley. Not like he had with Ashley. Not like he had with Ashley. Brady heard his name being called over the PA system, "Last call for passenger, Brady Anderson." Brady snapped out of his day dream and grabbed the bar bill to pay it.

Ashley was pretty drunk now. She felt like she was in a gray out. Like she was operating, but outside of herself. She called the cop's number and he answered and she could hear a baby crying in the background and a woman talking. The cop had gone outside of wherever he was to talk to Ashley. She guessed that he was probably married, and she asked him, but he denied it. He was surprised and happy to hear from her. He told her that he would be working the night shift and would stop by. She had used the incident with her car as the reason for her call. It was the perfect excuse for him to come over also.

Ashley now felt a sense of danger and excitement and it brought her out of her doldrums. She moved around her apartment straightening it up and cleaning. She knew that within hours she would probably be having sex with the handsome Latino cop. She was really horny and couldn't wait. Her vagina was activated, even though her senses were dulled by the wine. Her inhibitions were down and she decided she would go all out with the cop. She would skip all the small talk and pretense and just go straight for his cock the moment he came into the apartment. If he was married with a child, that wasn't her problem. What she didn't know wouldn't hurt her.

She looked through her closet, trying to find the right outfit to wear. She had to make herself so irresistible that he would have no defense. She slipped out of her panties and put on the mini skirt that Chloe had bought her. She looked at her bikini waxed pussy and she slipped her finger into it, then took it out and smelled it. She put a small top on that exposed her midriff, and then she put on some thigh high stockings and high heels. She went into the bathroom to prepare her makeup.

Brady's flight to Denver finally took off and he was sitting in a window seat. The plane was nearly empty on Christmas Day and nobody was sitting next to him. The plane took off over the ocean, then turned back over Malibu and went straight over the San Fernando Valley. Brady looked out over the massive city, and all the houses and buildings, and highways for as far as the eye could see and it fascinated him. He was returning to a town you could drive across in two minutes. The land was so flat you could see for miles on a clear day. The only air pollution was from dust stirred up by the relentless wind, or tractors plowing the fields. There hadn't been a murder in Colby for at least ten years. There was hardly any crime to speak of except for drug and alcohol related crimes. There had been a bit of a meth problem in recent years.

Brady remembered thinking that people who used meth were such losers, and now he was using cocaine on weekly basis. One of his friends from high school had gotten hooked on meth and had been in and out of trouble. The cocaine that was currently in his system was wearing off and he felt like shit. His dick hurt. Crystal had nearly sucked it off last night. He also had anal sex with her unprotected. He was worried that he might have gotten HIV. Who knew who else she had been with? Who was that scary looking black guy that came around? The thought made him shudder. Well, if he was HIV positive, he would just go out with a blaze of glory. He would party and fuck until he dropped dead. What mattered now? He decided he would get tested when he got back to LA.

He thought of his father and the pain hit him like a sharp knife in his guts. He looked for the flight attendant. He needed a drink badly. An attractive flight attendant was walking up the aisle and he caught her eye. "Are you ok?" she asked.

"Yeah. When is the drink cart coming?" Brady asked.

She looked at him a moment. "We're preparing it now," she said.

She moved on and Brady stared out the window. They were now over the clouds. Brady's uncle told him that the projected high temperature for Colby was 4 above zero.

Efrain Velasquez pulled up in front of Ashley's Palm Avenue apartment and parked the LAPD squad car. He had been on the force for three years after a four year stint in the Marines, and a tour in Iraq where he saw some combat. He had been married for two years to a girl he knew from high school in Montebello. They had a new baby boy together. He had never cheated on his wife except for kissing Ashley a few days ago.

He looked at himself in the mirror of his squad car. Constant noise kept coming from his police radio. Here he was, outside of his patrol area, on Christmas Day meeting with a young white girl who was very desirable. He had gone to mass with his wife, Sylvia, and his new baby just that morning. He had said the Lord's prayer, "Deliver us from temptation," but here he was. He assumed she would never call him again when he gave her his card, and was stunned when she did call.

He had been with white girls before. They were crazy. A different kind of crazy than the emotional fiery Latinas that he was used to. The white girls he had been with were cold, crazy. Amoral. Hedonistic. This girl fit the mold for sure. Efrain pulled his wedding ring off and put it into his front pocket.

Some people walking by looked at him in the patrol car. People always acted differently when they saw the squad car. This was one time he wished he wasn't in it. He straightened his hair and took a deep breath. He called in on his radio to let them know he was going to be out of his car for few minutes. He got out of his car and walked into Ashley's apartment complex. He knocked on her door and after a moment she answered it. She was visibly drunk and dressed like a party girl on her way to a night club. She threw her arms around Efrain.

"Oh, I'm so happy you showed up!" She said, slurring her words. She smelled of perfume and Efrain worried that his wife would smell it on his clothes. "Somebody vandalized my car this morning," Ashley said, grabbing her wine glass. She sat on the edge of her bed and Efrain could see that she was not wearing any panties underneath the mini skirt.

He didn't say anything else and just went to her and started kissing her and his hand roamed beneath her skirt and he was fingering her. Her mouth was hot with wine and his tongue was right in there with hers. They fell together onto the bed and he was on top of her in full uniform. His radio was squawking as calls came in. She pulled at his uniform as he was sucking her breasts, and soon the gun belt and everything was dropped to the floor. Efrain pulled the mini skirt off and he was licking down her stomach to the bikini waxed sweet spot, and soon he had her whole pussy in his mouth and his tongue was probing the inside of her vagina.

His cock was rock hard and she was grabbing for it. They rolled into a 69 position and she stared at his uncut cock. She had never seen one before. She looked at it curiously for a moment, and then started sucking it. After several minutes of serious oral, Efrain mounted her and she gasped as he pushed his cock into her sopping wet pussy. He fucked her hard for several minutes and she pulled at his ass cheeks. "Go ahead, come inside me," Ashley moaned as she was climaxing.

He yanked his cock out at the last moment and sprayed cum all over her stomach and breasts. He kissed her and they were both breathing hard, and Ashley was moaning and laughing.

Efrain looked at her. "What is so funny?"

"Nothing, nothing, that was hot" Ashley said. Efrain rolled over and stared at the ceiling catching his breath. He could hear the constant traffic of his police radio coming from the floor. Ashley got up and took a drink of her wine and walked naked to the kitchen to wipe the cum off of herself with a paper towel.

Brady drank three whiskies on the plane. He was in a daze as he disembarked. He could feel the frigid air as he stepped onto the jetway. He walked the long hallway of jetway and emerged into the strangely empty gate area where a few people were waiting around all dressed in their winter gear. Brady had his North Face ski jacket on that he had left with. He made his way down to the baggage claim area where his cousin, Jerry, was waiting for him. Jerry was wearing a heavy parka and a farmer's cap and muddy snow boots. Jerry was a few years older than Brady, and was now a farmer in Colby. His face broke into a smile upon seeing Brady.

"What the fuck, cuz, they tell me you've gone Hollywood," Jerry said.

Brady attempted a smile. They shook hands and made brief eye contact. "I don't have any bags checked," Brady said.

They walked out of the terminal to the parking structure where Jerry's truck was parked. The air was frigid and it was hard to breath as the jet fuel and exhaust from busses and cars hung in the arctic air. "Fuck," Brady said as they walked into the parking structure. "Forget what it was like already?" Jerry said laughing.

They drove away from the airport in Jerry's truck that smelled like dirt and cow manure. The sun had gone down and the Christmas lights of Denver were twinkling in the distance and they got on I-70 heading east across eastern Colorado into Kansas. Jerry once again told Brady all of the details of his father's death. He said that his mother was holding up ok, and was trying to be as strong as possible. He told him that his body was at the County coroner's and would be transferred to the funeral home in the morning. The funeral was scheduled to be held in a couple of days. Brady didn't say much of anything until they stopped at a truck stop for gas. "Let's get some beer, ok?" Brady said.

"Sure," Jerry said.

Crystal called her half brother Derek over to sit with her. She had an intense fear of being alone. She couldn't stand to be alone for any extended period of time, especially when she was doing cocaine. Since Derek was her supplier of cocaine, calling him only made sense. She could be herself around him. He spent most of his time talking on the phone to his homeboys in the gang or his various girlfriends. Crystal passed the time clicking through reality TV shows, snorting lines, and guzzling Kendall Jackson. She continued talking to Derek, but he wasn't listening because he was talking on the phone. Crystal wondered if Brady was coming back, or if she was going to have to start looking for a new hostage.

Ashley felt a little better after Efrain left. She felt a lot better. She was basically floating on air as she straightened up her apartment. She had sobered up a little after that intense sex. Christmas was almost over and she had gotten through it. She told Efrain about her car being vandalized and about Owen and his friend. Efrain said that he would deal with it. She wondered if Efrain was married. She didn't ask him, but something told her that he was. Maybe that would be better, anyway, Ashley thought. She didn't need a "relationship" right now while she was pursuing her career. If he was married, he didn't say anything about it and what she didn't know wouldn't hurt her. The sex was fantastic, and she wouldn't mind getting some more of that. Her vagina was still tingling.

Efrain had rushed out to a police call and said that he would call her later. She could tell that he was pretty happy too. Christmas Day wasn't so bad after all. Then she recalled the death of Henry Anderson, and the sharp knife of guilt stabbed her again. Oh, yeah, *that*. She poured herself another glass of wine. The big bottle was nearly empty. She wondered where Brady was. He had never called her back. She would have flowers and a card sent out in the morning. She was supposed to meet the gay guy from the acting class in the morning and build her website. Big things were going to happen for her in the New Year.

Jerry and Brady drank Budweiser's as they drove down 1-70 into Western Kansas. Country music twanged on the truck's AM radio. They were only fifty miles from home and it was about 10pm. There were a lot of big trucks on the road.

Brady was a little drunk now and he bragged about working in the movie business to Jerry and told him about the big cats and the bears that he worked with. He admitted to Jerry that he was living with a black woman. "You're fucking a nigger?" Jerry said. Brady laughed it off, "Don't say it like that," he said.

Jerry told him about the farm business, crop prices, and the local gossip of Colby. Brady was bored by all that, but he tried not to show it. "So what happened with you and Ashley out there?" Jerry finally asked.

"Fuckin' bitch. I hate her," Brady said, smashing a beer can and opening another. Jerry slowed down as the exit to Highway 24 that went to Colby approached.

"Hey, Mom's probably already asleep. Let's stop into Tornado's for a beer," Brady said.

"Ok," Jerry said, turning onto Highway 24. The lights of Colby, Kansas were visible in the frigid distance.

They pulled up and stopped in the parking lot of Tornado's bar. A couple of muddy pickups were parked outside. Brady looked at the bar, "Nothing changes, huh?" "Nope," Jerry said and they climbed out of the truck and walked inside.

Brady shook the cold off as he walked inside the dark establishment. Two men, farmer types were sitting at the bar. Some Christmas lights were blinking. Sherry, a girl Brady knew from high school was behind the bar. She was a few pounds overweight, but had a pretty face and huge breasts. Jerry and Brady took some seats at the bar. It took the other men a moment to recognize Brady.

"Howdy, Brady," one of the men said. "Sorry about your dad."

Brady nodded, and the pain hit him again. "Get him whatever he wants on me," the man said.

"Buy the house a round," said the other man. Sherry looked at Brady with sad eyes and she put down five shot glasses on the bar. "I'm so sorry, Brady," Sherry said as she poured five shots of Jack Daniels. She distributed them to the four men at the bar, including Jerry and Brady.

Jerry raised his glass, "To Henry," he said. They all drank down their shots and slammed them on the bar, including Sherry. They followed the shots with Budweisers. Sherry looked at Brady. "Nice to see you back," she said.

"You're out in Hollywood, now?" she asked.

"Yeah," Brady said.

Jerry put some music on the jukebox. "Pour some more of those fuckin' shots," Brady said.

Sherry smiled and refilled the shot glasses. Brady looked at her a long moment and admired her cleavage. She caught him looking at her and smiled. "You hear from Ashley?" she asked.

"Nope," Brady said, tipping up his shot glass.

Efrain Velasquez was parked in his police cruiser down the street from Owen's Koreatown house. He was watching Owen's car that was parked on Gramercy Place. He was conflicted about what he was doing, but also getting a rush from it. He had cheated on his wife for the first time and he felt a little guilty, but at the same time felt like he had really scored. This girl Ashley was the finest white girl he had ever laid eyes on, and her pussy was just as sweet and tight as he imagined it would be. He could still smell her perfume on him, and her pussy on his hands. He would have to do something about that before he got home. His wife Sylvia was attractive too, but in a different way. In a mom, kind of way.

He had found himself less sexually attracted to his wife after she gave birth. Not only did she gain fifty pounds during her pregnancy, now she was devoting all of her time to the baby and breast feeding. It now seemed that her sexual organs were being used for a different purpose, and as much as he hated to admit it to himself, he just wasn't very turned on by his wife any more. She was a great mother, and probably always would be, but the sexual being she once was, was now replaced by the mother. He knew his wife would be devastated if she knew what he was thinking about her. He was even glad that she couldn't have sex for several weeks after the baby was born, because frankly, he just wasn't attracted to her with the extra weight on and the constant cooing over the baby.

Efrain had gotten his rocks off good all over Ashley and now that was all he could think about. Where was this going to lead? It couldn't be good, he shuddered to think. Now, here he was doing something shady with his job. Just as he was thinking that he saw a guy walking to the car he was watching. He knew that it was Owen's car because he ran the plates, and he ran Owen's record. Owen had been arrested for possession of Marijuana twice, and currently had an outstanding traffic warrant for a failure to appear on driving without insurance charge. Owen was a long haired hipster and just the type of guy that Efrain hated the most.

Efrain's adrenalin was pulsing as Owen got into the car, started it and pulled away from the curb. Efrain followed him onto Western Boulevard. Efrain noticed the light bulb on Owen's license plate frame was out, and that was probable cause to pull him over. Efrain hit the lights and siren. He saw Owen looking at him in the rear view mirror. Efrain yelled in the loud speaker, "Pull over!" Owen pulled his beat up Toyota into a parking lot on the corner of Western and Sixth Street.

Efrain didn't call the stop in and got out of the car. He walked up to the driver side window and looked at Owen. "License, insurance, and registration," Efrain said.

Owen squinted as Efrain shined a flashlight into his eyes. Owen scrambled to come up with the paperwork. He didn't say anything and looked scared. "Do you know why I pulled you over?" Efrain asked.

"No," Owen said, handing Efrain the paperwork.

"The bulb over your license plate is out," Efrain said. "Do you have any warrants?" Efrain asked.

"Uh, I think so," Owen answered.

"Have you been drinking tonight?" Efrain asked.

"I've had a couple," Owen said. Efrain ordered him to step out of the car, and Owen stepped out looking defeated. Everyone who was driving and walking by watched with curiosity.

Efrain shoved Owen roughly against the car and started patting him down. Owen seemed surprised by his aggressiveness. Efrain put the cuffs on him so tight it felt as if his hands would go numb. "Do you have anything on you I should know about?" Efrain said right into Owen's ear.

"No, what is this all about?" Owen finally said, as Efrain shoved him against the car. "Stay right there," Efrain said as he started looking through Owen's car. Efrain found something in the side pocket of the door. It was a pill.

"What's this?" Efrain said. "I don't know," Owen said.

"Looks like X to me," said Efrain. Owen didn't say anything, and hung his head, completely defeated.

Efrain got right in his face. "You know a girl named Ashley?"

"Uh, I know a few Ashleys," Owen finally said.

"You know who I'm talking about, punk!" Efrain said glaring into his eyes.

"Where are you from, dirtbag?" Efrain shouted.

"What do you mean?" Owen asked, now thoroughly frightened. Efrain shoved him hard against the car.

"Where the fuck are you from, shitdick?"

"Uh, here. I'm from LA. I grew up here," Owen said.

"I think it's time for you to get out of town for awhile. You got somewhere you can go?" Efrain said.

"Uh, I don't know…maybe…," Owen said.

"I think tomorrow is a good time to leave, otherwise I'm going to be your worst fucking nightmare, got it?" Efrain said in a hushed tone.

Owen nodded. Efrain yanked Owen's arms up and took the cuffs off, then gave Owen a little shove toward his car. "Get the fuck out of my sight, faggot."

Owen stumbled into his car and drove out of the parking lot. Efrain got back into his squad car feeling a power rush he had not felt since being in combat and killing his first man in Iraq.

The bar crowd at Tornado's thinned out to just Jerry, Brady, and the bartender. Brady and Sherry were making eyes at each other. Sherry took Brady's arm and looked at the new tornado tattoo, which was still healing. Sherry touched Ashley's initials on the tattoo, but didn't say anything.

Jerry was tired, drunk and bored. "Brady, I gotta' go. I've been up since 5am, Cuz," Jerry said. "Go ahead. I can get home," Brady said.

"What about your bag?" Jerry said. "I'll get it," Brady said.

The two men got up to go get Brady's suitcase out of the truck. Jerry was obviously a little disgusted with Brady. Brady followed him out, got his bag, thanked Jerry and returned into the bar as he drove away. It was now almost two am and ten below zero. Christmas was over.

Brady went back into the bar and drank more beers as Sherry cleaned and closed up the bar. Brady went home with Sherry and they ended up in her bedroom feeding wood into a pot bellied stove. They made out and collapsed onto the bed. Brady got rough with Sherry and forced his cock into her mouth until she gagged. She was a little shocked, but she went with it.

He fucked her hard and then pulled out and then came in Sherry's open mouth. Immediately after coming, Brady rolled off of Sherry and passed out. She wiped the mess off her chin and laid there wondering if she had just been used. She was used to it.

Seventeen

Brady woke up early in the morning entangled in Sherry's naked body. It took him a moment to remember where he was. He cringed upon seeing Sherry. The house was freezing. The pot belly stove had burned out overnight. Brady pulled himself out of bed and got dressed quickly. Sherry stirred a little, but pulled the covers over her head. Brady hoped he could get out without having to talk to her.

The realization of why exactly he was in Colby hit him hard – his dad was dead. His dad was killed in an accident just yesterday, and here he was waking up to a local bar marm that would tell everyone in town about what had happened. Brady felt like the biggest piece of shit in the world. What was happening with him? He just couldn't stop himself from doing stupid things that he regretted afterward. He blamed it on Ashley. He was lost and it was entirely her fault. Now, this thing with his dad. Brady blamed Ashley for that too.

If Ashley had not gone to California, then he never would have followed her there, and his dad might still be alive. Brady seethed with hatred toward Ashley. Brady noticed Sherry's big yellow dog watching him from the corner as he slipped his shoes on. It occurred to him that his dad had probably been the dog's vet and he felt like crying. He patted the dog's head and tip toed out, hoping he could get home before his mom woke up. He stopped at the edge of the room and put a couple of pieces of wood into the pot bellied stove before he left.

He had to face reality soon enough and that hit him as soon as he stepped out into an Arctic air mass that was hovering over the entire Midwest. It was twenty below zero as Brady started walking down the deserted street to his mom's house. He had no gloves or hat on.

New Year's Eve was just one week away and Ashley was scheduled to work that night. She just wanted the Holidays to be over. She had made it through Christmas and went the next morning to meet with Kendall from the acting class, so he could build her website and make her a resume. Kendall was a large gay black man who stood at least 6'5" and was built like a tank. Ashley was glad that he was gay, because she could work closely with him and not worry about him hitting on her. He was a master with computers and HTML code. He quickly put together a workable website – ASHLEYDUNCAN.COM. He used several photos from her photo shoot and a few others she had from college productions. Cooper, the photographer had sent her most of the pictures but had excluded the nudes. Ashley just wanted to forget about the "artistic" shots, but it was in the back of her mind that they would come back to haunt her.

Kendal added some snazzy graphics. He made it look very professional and Ashley was impressed. She sat watching over his shoulder the whole time. They talked and gossiped about people in the acting class and Jeremy Bone. They laughed it up like two close girlfriends.

Kendall was very flamboyant and Ashley got a big kick out of him. Kendall had gotten a few parts on some soap operas and had his SAG card.

Kendall put together a resume for Ashley based mostly on her college acting experience, and he advised her to go out on some student films so she could get some footage to make a reel. By the time Kendal was through, Ashley had her own completed website and she felt elated. She felt like she was finally getting somewhere. She hugged Kendall tightly and kissed him on the cheek and promised that she would "take care of him".

"I heard about what happened to Owen," Kendall said as Ashley prepared to leave.

"What?" Ashley asked.

"The cops kicked him out of town," Kendall said.

"What? You're kidding?" Ashley said.

"No. He called Jennifer from the class this morning and told her. Said he was leaving for Seattle. I guess he was pretty bummed," Kendall said.

Ashley was stunned. She couldn't believe it. What had Efrain done? She hadn't heard from him since yesterday, but she couldn't get him out of her mind. She thanked Kendall again and walked to her car with her head spinning from the news.

By the time Brady reached his mom's house he was almost frost bitten. He rushed into the door, rubbing his ears and hands, and was instantly enveloped by the warmth of the house. The foyer was filled with flowers, and cards. Brady could see plates of cookies, cakes, and other covered dishes sitting around. He was almost frozen to death and had yet to process he was returning home for the first time since his father's untimely death. He stood there, lightly stomping on the floor to get the blood flowing through his frozen feet as he continued to blow on his nearly frost bitten hands. Brady's mom, Margaret, walked out of the kitchen and was shocked to see him standing there and she let out a little scream, and then was relieved when she saw that it was her son.

"Oh, my God! Brady! I thought you were coming last night. I waited up for you," Margaret said. She moved to him and hugged him. He immediately started crying in her arms.

"You're freezing! What did you do?" she said, standing back and taking a look at him. Brady couldn't look her in the eye and continued sobbing.

"I'm so sorry, Mom," he said.

"Come in a sit down, let me get a fire going and I'll get you some coffee," she said, pulling him into the living room. She sat him beside the fireplace and then she began making a fire. She was holding up very well considering what had happened. She put on the stoic front that Midwesterners do in the face of tragedy.

"Everyone has been so kind. Everybody. You see all the flowers I received. We're going to have the service on Saturday. Hopefully it will warm up a little by then," she said as she started the fire.

Brady just hung his head and continued sobbing. "I'm sorry, mom. So sorry…"

She looked at him and sat beside him stroking the side of his face. "Your father loved you and was proud of you no matter what," she said.

"If I hadn't gone to California, this never would have happened," Brady said, between sobs.

His mother looked at him, and tried to comfort him. "You can't say that, Brady. It was a freak accident. Things like this can happen to any of us, at any time," she said.

Brady leaned against her, his teeth chattering. "Have you been drinking?" she asked.

Brady sat upright, "Last night," he said.

"Go take a hot shower and I'll make some breakfast. You'll feel better," Margaret said.

"Thanks," Brady said, "I love you, mom."

"I love you too, honey," she said.

Ashley went to a florist shop to send flowers and a card to the Anderson family. She picked out a nice arrangement and a card. She stood at the counter, thinking about what to write. She got emotional and started crying a bit thinking about Henry Anderson and the ski trip they all went on together. She thought of Brady too, and remembered his laugh back when he was happy. Back when he thought that they would always be together. Ashley felt a tinge of guilt about Henry Anderson's death, like she in some way was partially responsible. She pushed that thought out of her mind.

She finally wrote on the card: *Dear Margaret, I am so very sorry for your loss. I have nothing but fond memories of Mr. Anderson and your family. I will always cherish the memory of the ski trip we all went on together. I sincerely regret not being able to attend the funeral. Send my regards to Brady as well. Love, Ashley.* Ashley handed the card to the clerk and paid him. She was off to meet Jillian and Chloe for lunch at Fred Segal. They were back in town and Ashley was looking forward to it. She had been lonely when they were gone.

She arrived at Fred Segal and got a table outside; Chloe and Jillian were not there yet. The waiter showed up, flirted with Ashley a bit, tried to entice her to order wine or champagne, but Ashley ordered mineral water, trying to lay off the alcohol for awhile. She had been getting out of control lately with the drinking and she didn't like what it was doing to her. She wondered if Chloe was still sober. Then she saw Chloe getting out of her BMW and letting the valet take the car. Chloe dropped her cigarette on the ground and waved at Ashley. She was wearing some big sunglasses. She walked over to the table and

Ashley stood to hug her. Chloe hugged her tightly and kissed her lightly on the lips. Ashley felt a little uncomfortable and the whole incident in Palm Springs came rushing back to her.

"You look great, honey. Did you have a good Christmas?" Chloe asked.

Ashley contemplated telling her about Efrain, but decided not to.

"I'm just glad that it is over with. I worked on my website, that was about it," Ashley said. "Did you have a good trip?"

"Oh, it was so cold in Virginia! It was just unbearable. I got through it, and sober for a change. It was tough being around my family, sober, you know? And, they all drink like fish!" Chloe said.

The waiter arrived with the mineral water and greeted Chloe by name. She ordered a mineral water also and talked Ashley into sharing some oysters on the half shell with her.

"It's tough being around family. There's all these weird dynamics going on. My mom is trying to hold everything together, and my dad is a rageaholic. My brother can't stop talking about how much money he's making. They're just all insane. I realized that for the first time," Chloe said.

Ashley thought it was funny that Chloe mentioned that about her brother, because that was exactly what Ashley thought about *her*. At that moment, Jillian arrived and turned her car over to the valet. She looked very svelte, dressed to the nines, Raybans, designer purse, skirt, etc. She smiled slightly and walked over. Ashley and Chloe both hugged her. Jillian sat down and noticed the mineral waters sitting on the table. She looked at Ashley.

"Oh, please, don't tell me you're doing the "sober" thing too?" Jillian said.

Ashley glanced at Chloe embarrassed for her. "No, I just have things to do this afternoon and need to be sharp. Jillian flipped her hair. "Well, I'm having a cocktail," she said.

The waiter came and Jillian ordered a Kir Royale. "So how was your Christmas with Chuck and family?" Chloe asked with a hint of sarcasm. Jillian lit a cigarette.

"I made it through without killing the little fuckers," Jillian said. She went on to tell about how they had stayed at Caesar's Palace in Las Vegas with Chuck and his two children, ages 9 and 11. She had to pretend like she liked them, they were so spoiled and she loathed every minute of it. There had been tension between her and Chuck when he accused her of being moody and distant. "Luckily, the little monsters went back to Colorado to their mom. Chuck only sees them five times a year. I guess I can live with that," Jillian said. The waiter brought her Kir Royale and Ashley's mouth watered upon seeing it. Chloe tried not to react one way or another.

"So, things are moving right along with you and Chuck, then?" Chloe asked.

"So far so good. We're doing New Year's Eve at Kraven," Jillian said.

"Oh, I should make reservations too! I was supposed to go to this AA thing, but I may cancel out on that," Chloe said. "You working?" Chloe asked Ashley.

"Yes, unfortunately," Ashley said. "Every holiday."

"I heard the pictures came out good," Jillian said to Ashley as she sipped her Kir Royale like it was nectar from the gods. "Sure you don't want one of these?" Jillian asked Ashley.

Ashley looked at Chloe, "Do you mind?"

"Go right ahead, don't worry about me," Chloe said, trying to act like it didn't bother her. Jillian waived at the waiter and ordered a drink for Ashley.

"How long are you going to do the AA thing? I mean, you don't really have a problem do you? Dr. Davis could fix you up in a few sessions," Jillian said.

"I *do* have a problem, Jillian. I think I need to stay sober for awhile and see what happens," Chloe said.

"Next thing you know, you'll be volunteering at a homeless shelter or some lame shit like that," Jillian said.

"Who is this Dr. Davis again?" Ashley asked. The waiter brought her the Kir Royale, and Ashley took it eagerly.

"I gave you his card, didn't I?" Jillian asked.

"I think so," Ashley said.

Jillian went on to tell Ashley how much Dr. Davis had helped her with anxiety issues and how wonderful and brilliant he was. As they were talking, the agent, Michael Levin walked in and sat down at his usual table with his Daily Variety to read. Chloe grabbed Ashley's arm. "There he is!"

Ashley glanced at him and he smiled and nodded to her. Ashley smiled and gave a little wave.

"I called him and he didn't return my call," Ashley said in a hushed tone.

Jillian glanced at the agent with boredom. "It's all a game and a power trip. Right now he holds all the power – you have to find away to take that from him," Jillian said.

"He's definitely still interested," Chloe said. Ashley could feel the champagne working on her brain and she suddenly felt warm and fuzzy. She smiled at Levin again. This was her shot and she knew it. All the websites and pictures in the world could not do what that man could for her with one phone call and Ashley was shrewd enough to realize that.

Levin was talking to the waiter and he pointed to the ladies table. The waiter looked over and nodded. "Isn't he married to that chick on channel 5?" Jillian said.

"Oh yeah. That's right. The Asian weather girl, what's her name? Jennifer Kim," Chloe said.

"The dragon lady," Jillian said laughing. The waiter appeared at the table with a bottle of Dom Perignon in an ice bucket, and three glasses and told them it was compliments of Mr. Levin. Chloe looked like a deer caught in the headlights. The waiter started filling the glasses. All three women looked over at Levin and smiled and waved to thank him. He smiled and continued reading his Variety like it was no big deal.

Brady showered and sat to eat breakfast with his mom. She served him some biscuits and gravy, with scrambled eggs and sour dough toast with homemade choke cherry preserves. He scarfed it down like he hadn't eaten in ages. His mom watched him with sad, but loving eyes.

"Do you want some more? There's more. You look thin," Margaret said.

Brady pushed his completely cleaned plate aside. His eyes met his mothers for a moment, but he quickly looked away.

"No thanks, mom. I'm stuffed. That was the best meal I've had in a while," he said.

She looked at him and put her hand on top of his. "Are you coming back?" she asked.

He avoided eye contact with her.

"I don't know, mom. I was thinking I would stay the rest of the winter out there. The guy I'm working for, kind of needs me for the rest of the season," Brady said.

"I guess I'll decide what to do with your father's business later. Roy Hendricks called and wanted to buy it," Margaret said.

Brady immediately broke into tears. He just collapsed onto the table with his head in his arms openly sobbing. Margaret rubbed his head and shoulders and let him cry it out.

"I'm so sorry, mom," Brady sobbed.

"It's ok, honey. Your dad loved you no matter what. I love you no matter what," she said. "Are you going to come with me to see the funeral director this afternoon?" she asked.

Brady sat up, rubbed his eyes and tried to pull himself together. "Yes. Yes," he said.

After breakfast Brady got into the warmest winter gear he could find and he took his mom's car into town. He drove to the local wrecking yard and he got out of the car, shaking with cold and fear. The man who ran the wrecking yard recognized him and pointed him across the yard to where is father's truck was. Brady approached the wrecked vehicle cautiously. The whole front of it was a complete mess of mangled steel and plastic. The front windshield and parts of the cab were smashed in. Brady stood a distance from the truck and could see blood on the broken windshield and seat.

He stood there crying in the snow a bit and his tears froze immediately on his face. The reality was upon him that his father was gone forever and it kept slapping him right in the face. The feeling that *he* was responsible would not leave either. No matter how many times people explained away the "freak" nature of the accident and blamed it on the slick roads and weather, Brady knew that if his dad had been in the right frame of mind and not worried about *him*, then it would not have happened.

He returned to his mother's car and cranked up the heat, trying to get a hold of himself. He checked his cell phone to see if he was getting any reception and decided he would call Crystal. He didn't know why. He didn't miss her, but he felt he should talk to someone and she probably understood him better than anybody at this point. He called her and after a few rings she picked up. She sounded drunk, she sounded out of it and he could barely understand what she was saying. She kept asking him when he was coming back and didn't seem too interested or understanding of what he was going through.

He hung up realizing that she wasn't really capable of doing any better. She was very sick and her sickness seemed to be contagious. He realized that he would have to move out and get his own place if he returned to LA. He looked out at the steam rolling off the wrecking yard and the barren snow covered fields in the flat distance. He wondered if he could actually live in Kansas again. He looked at his watch: it was 11:22 am and Brady realized he was in bad need of a drink. He drove off toward Tornado's.

Chloe tried to resist the glass of champagne that was poured for her, but ultimately said, "fuck it," and gave into temptation. Now, the three women, buzzed on Dom Perignon and indulging in raw oysters were laughing it up and having a great time. Ashley glanced at her cell phone and saw that she had a missed called from Efrain. At the same time she kept glancing over to see if Michael Levin was looking her way. He was talking on his cell phone, but he was looking her way. Chloe and Jillian noticed this too.

"Go get him," Jillian said.

Chloe grabbed Ashley's arm and looked into her eyes.

"Jillian's right, honey. This is your chance, this is your audition" Chloe said. "Go over there."

Ashley looked at him a long moment, waited for him to put away his phone. He finally did and Ashley stood. She was scared out of her mind, but she didn't want Jillian and Chloe to see that. She walked casually over to Michael Levin's table. He smiled as she approached. She held out her hand and he took it. Jillian and Chloe watched from their table.

"Thank you for the champagne," Ashley said, mustering every ounce of charm she could.

"It's nothing," Michael said. "Would you like to have a seat?" he said and motioned for her to sit. She glanced back at Jillian and Chloe, and then sat down across from Levin.

"So, you're an actress, right?" Michael said.

"Yes, I'm trying," Ashley said. Levin's eyes bored into her.

"Don't ever say that. You either are an actress or you're not," he said.

Ashley felt stupid and nodded.

"Do you know who I am?" Michael asked. Ashley nodded. At that moment, his cell phone rang.

He looked at it. "I have to take this," he said and he answered it. He went into a long conversation about a movie deal, and a script, and a ten million dollar offer for Jack Wrangler to star in the movie. Michael was dismissing the deal and basically telling whoever was on the other end that the project wasn't right for Wrangler and that the offer was mediocre. Ashley couldn't believe what she was hearing.

Jack Wrangler was washed up in her eyes, but he was still getting ten million dollar offers? Ten million dollars. What could she do with ten million dollars? She could buy her parents a ranch in Montana. She could have her own home in the Hollywood Hills. She would settle for one million. Michael finally finished the call and smiled at Ashley. "They'll think about it and call back," he said. Ashley giggled. Michael waived to the waiter and he came over. "Bring us a bottle of Dom and two glasses," Michael said. The waiter went off to get it. Michael stared at Ashley.

"So, can you act?" he asked. Ashley nodded.

"Who are you studying with?" he asked.

"Jeremy Bone. I'm in his class," she said, thinking that would elicit a positive response.

"Jeremy Bone. Jeremy Bone. I think I have heard of him. We'll have to get you into Dina Solomon's class," Michael said and his phone rang again. He answered it.

Ashley's head was spinning now. Dina Solomon was the most famous acting coach in Hollywood. She had instructed all of the top actors in LA. She thought about poor Jeremy Bone and what hopes he had for her, but she had to take care of her own best interests. The waiter returned with the champagne and opened it to pour two glasses. Chloe and Jillian were watching every move from their table. Ashley glanced at them and smiled. Michael was talking to whoever he was on the phone with before.

"Twelve million is a good number. Twelve million is something that Jack could probably live with, but he is probably going to want a rewrite," Michael said into the phone as he winked at Ashley. "Ok. Send the script over and I'll get it to him over the weekend. I can't promise anything, because its New Year's for Christ's sake. Ok, honey, Ciao." Michael put the phone away and smiled broadly. He raised his glass to toast, and Ashley joined him.

"To success," he said.

"To success," Ashley said and they clinked their glasses together, then they both took a drink. Michael leaned into her smiling and took her hand.

"I'll be honest with you, Ashley. You have the look that we're looking for. You definitely have the look, but a lot of girls have that. A lot of girls have *talent*," he said motioning around the patio where almost every woman looked fantastic. "The question is, do you have everything else it takes? Do you have the temperament, the guile, the *cajones*, to do what it takes?"

Ashley looked into his eyes. "I do," she said. Michael started laughing and he again clinked his glass against hers. He opened his phone and speed dialed his office.

"Natalie, please cancel all of my appointments this afternoon, I have a personal matter to take care of," Michael said, then looked to Ashley with a big shit eating grin on his face. "Do you have to be anywhere this afternoon?" he asked.

"No," she said, smiling and taking another gulp of champagne. She knew that this was her defining moment, and she had to ride the wave wherever it took her.

Jillian and Chloe looked at each other and knocked their glasses together.

"Looks like our girl is learning," Jillian said. "What are you doing this afternoon?"

Chloe laughing sipping her champagne "Guess I'm not going to the AA meeting," she said.

"Good, I have Chuck's credit card. We can go for spa treatments," Jillian said. The two women high fived each other. "Do you have any Adderalls?" Chloe asked.

"No, but I have a little blow," Jillian said. Chloe finished her glass of champagne and refilled it.

"I guess that will do," she said.

Across the patio, Ashley and Michael leaned into each other, staring into each other's eyes.

Brady sat at the bar at Tornado's bar in Colby, Kansas. He was the only person in there, except for an extremely overweight female bartender who was watching Maury Povitch on the television behind the bar. Brady sat there nursing a Budweiser and a shot of Jack Daniels. He felt better once the warm feeling of the booze engulfed him. He glanced at the television with disgust at some white trash couple who were battling on the show with Maury Povitch as the referee.

Brady realized that everything in show business was about exploitation. Even the animals they used in movies and TV were being exploited. He walked to the jukebox and picked out some songs. He chose, "Wanted," by Bon Jovi and it was a song that reminded him of Ashley. He chose some Nirvana, some Metallic, some Rat, and Lynard Skynard. The music started playing and it drowned out the toxic noise of the television.

Brady had called his best friend Kevin, who was in town for the funeral, back from college. Kevin was on his way down. Brady needed someone to talk to who would understand him, someone who could give him some perspective. Brady was at a total loss on what to do with his life. Should he go back to college and finish vet school and then take over his father's practice? Should he return to Hollywood, to the ghost of his relationship with Ashley, to his ultra sick relationship with Crystal? Should he stick around awhile and help his mom close out his father's affairs? Should he do something completely different? He had no idea what to do.

Brady thought of Isaac, and when he quit. Isaac said that he was a flake just like all the rest. Brady never thought of himself as a flake, had not been raised to be a flake, but couldn't help feeling like a flake now. A couple of farmers walked into the bar. They squinted in the darkness until their eyes adjusted and they recognized Brady.

"Brady, how the hell you doing?" one of farmers said.

"I'm ok. Thanks," Brady said.

"Mary, get him whatever he wants on me, and get us our usual" the farmer said to the bartender. The bartender pulled out three Budweisers and set them in front of Brady and the other farmers. Brady attempted a smile and raised his beer.

"Sorry about your dad. He was a good man," the farmer said.

"They don't make em' like that anymore," the other farmer said. Brady could have gone without hearing that. He almost started crying, and then Kevin walked into the bar. He saw Brady and his face lit up. The two guys met each other halfway and hugged.

"Good to see you, bro," Kevin said. Metallica was playing on the jukebox. The two friends looked at each other a long moment, then bellied up to the bar.

Chuck Alexander and Kurt were out on the golf course sitting in a golf cart waiting for a group in front of them to finish the hole. They were smoking cigars and Chuck was dressed in the latest, most colorful flamboyant golf wear. Chuck had just finished telling Kurt what a bitch Jillian was to his kids on their trip to Las Vegas.

"I'm going to give her just enough rope to hang herself. I gave her my American Express card to use in case she needs something – let's see what she needs," Chuck said laughing.

"You better check that fucker right now, because she always needs something," Kurt said.

Chuck took out his cell phone and called. He pressed a series of numbers into the keypad and then listened to the account activity. He smiled at Kurt, and then pressed a number that connected him to customer service.

"Yes, hello, I want to place a hold on my account. I have some unauthorized charges on there and I want the account frozen," Chuck said winking at Kurt. He cupped the receiver.

"The bitch just spend $275 at Fred Segal this afternoon," Chuck said to Kurt as he was on hold.

Chloe and Jillian were at the Bon Ivy day spa getting full spa treatments including massages, manicures, pedicures, facials, and waxes - $495 a person and Jillian gave the spa Chuck's credit card to hold for payment. They enjoyed themselves all afternoon, as the spa attendants pampered and primped them. When it came time to leave however, Jillian got the wakeup call. The credit card was declined and the spa had orders to hold the card. Chloe, reluctantly ended up paying the nearly $1000 bill.

"This is fucking great! I blew my sobriety thanks to you, and now I have to pay for this nonsense?" Chloe snapped.

"Don't blame me for your stupid sobriety," Jillian said as they walked out.

"As far as I'm concerned you owe me $1000, Jillian," Chloe said as they stood on the sidewalk of little Santa Monica in front of the swanky day spa.

"You can get in line," Jillian said bitterly. "I'm going to cut that fucker's balls off when I see him."

Jillian repeatedly tried to dial Chuck Alexander but he didn't answer.

Ashley stood in the lobby of the Peninsula Hotel in Beverly Hills with Michael Levin. Everyone who worked there seemed to know him and called him, "Mr. Levin." The man at the front desk handed him a room key and Michael slipped the man a $20.

"Come here often?" Ashley asked, feeling insecure.

"I've been here a couple of times," Michael said smiling. He put his arm around her and escorted her down the hallway to their room.

They went into the room and Ashley looked around. It was tastefully decorated in the manner she was quickly growing accustomed too. She looked at the large bed and thought to herself that she was doing what was necessary. She was doing what had to be done. Michael took his jacket off and hung it up in the closet. He took his tie off and started unbuttoning his shirt.

Ashley sat on the bed and watched him. He was probably close to sixty years old. Even older than her own father. She had never been with a man that old before, but this wasn't just any man. This was a man who had just secured a twelve million dollar offer for washed up Jack Wrangler. She noticed that Michael moved with a spring in his step. He smiled at her.

"How are you doing? Nice room, huh? They're bringing a bottle of Dom over," He said with a hint of a Brooklyn accent.

He sat down beside her and started stroking her hair and looking at her. His eyes were hungry and he kissed her. She let him, at first not reciprocating, but then she leaned into him and kissed him back. His hand moved up her thigh. A knock on the door interrupted them.

Michael jumped up and went to open the door. A room service attendant was there with an ice bucket and the champagne. It was a young Latino guy in his twenties. He walked into the room with the champagne in an ice bucket and glanced at Ashley on the bed and appeared to be embarrassed for her. He seemed to be nervous as he opened the champagne bottle as Michael was watching him. He glanced over to Ashley and smiled at her. She smiled back.

Brady and his friend Kevin were still sitting in Tornado's at the bar. Brady had been telling Kevin about his whole situation in LA. What had happened with Ashley. They were on their forth beer and had just as many shots.

"I think I'm finally done with her. I saw her at the gas station about a week ago, and I didn't feel anything. Nothing," Brady said, as if trying to convince himself. At that moment, Sherry, the bartender from the night before, came into the bar and saw Brady sitting there. The two of them shared a look which did not go unnoticed by Kevin. Sherry went about her business and was bringing a shipment of beer into the bar.

Kevin looked at Brady a long moment. The farmers were playing Garth Brooks, "Thunder Rolls," on the jukebox.

"I never told you, but Ashley wasn't exactly the good girl you thought she was," Kevin said. Brady looked at him and cracked a slight smile like he was ready to hear anything.

"Go ahead, you can tell me now, I don't give two shits about her," Brady said, laughing coldly.

Brady ordered more beers and shots, and the fat girl behind the bar huffed and puffed as she scurried to get them. Kevin took a gulp of beer.

"Well, that one summer when you were away, you know, when you went to Arizona, Ashley and I ran into each other at a party out at the ponds," Kevin said.

Brady was watching him as adrenalin started rushing into his body. Brady braced himself for what he was about to hear.

"Anyway, we were drinking and one thing led to another.....I can see why you are kind of obsessed about her. She is one hot piece of..."

Kevin didn't get the words out before Brady punched him right off of his bar stool. Kevin fell backward onto the floor, and Brady immediately kicked him right in the face. One of the farmers rushed over and grabbed Brady from behind. Brady got one more kick into Kevin's face before the farmer dragged him kicking and screaming out the front door.

Once outside in the blinding light, Brady and the farmer scuffled and fell to the ground and were lying in the snow in the gravel parking lot. The big farmer was on top of Brady and his face was beet red as he struggled to restrain him.

"What is the matter with you, Brady? What the hell are they teaching you out in LA? You don't take the boots to a man when he is down," the farmer said. Brady kept struggling, trying to escape. "Let fucking go of me!"

Sherry and the other bartender came out to see what was happening. Kevin walked out holding his bleeding face.

"I'm going to kill that motherfucker!" Brady said upon seeing Kevin. Steam was rolling out of Brady's nostrils.

"Kevin, go on. Get out of here!" The big farmer on top of Brady shouted. Kevin stumbled toward his SUV, got in and drove away, spinning gravel on the way out.

"Let fucking go of me!" Brady screamed again, now crying.

"I'm calling the police," the fat bartender said.

Sherry stopped her, "His dad just died."

The farmer rolled off of Brady and let him up. Brady's whole back side was covered with snow and dirt. Brady jumped into his mom's Cutlas Ciera and spun gravel out of the parking lot, fishtailing onto the main highway. The farmer and the others watched, and shook their heads and returned into the bar.

Ashley was lying partially undressed on the bed. She was drunk from all of the champagne and her head was spinning. Michael was in the bathroom. She heard the toilet flushing and a moment later he came out wearing a robe from the hotel. He had a small bottle in his hand and he held it up to his nostril and snorted hard. His eyes seemed to roll back in his head. He looked at Ashley.

"Take your clothes off," he said as he snorted on the little bottle again. Ashley slipped off her panties and kicked them onto the floor. Michael slipped his rope off and he was naked underneath. His cock was half hard and he had man boobs and white hair on his chest. Regardless of that, he was strutting around like a 20 year old stud. He came to Ashley and presented his half flaccid cock to her mouth. He snorted from the little bottle again.

"What is that?" Ashley asked with his cock on her chin.

"Poppers. Try it, it will give you a rush," Michael said. He handed her the little bottle and she held it up to her nostril. "Breath it in hard," Michael said. She sniffed from the bottle.

A hot rush went straight to Ashley's head and it seemed to spread straight to her vagina. She grabbed Michael's cock and took the whole thing into her mouth.

"Oh, fuck yes!" Michael mumbled as he reached down and slipped a finger into Ashley.

Brady sped down the icy streets of Colby and he spotted Kevin's SUV in the distance. He careened through a gas station parking lot and took chase. Kevin was driving out of town past a big grain silo when Brady caught up to him laying on the car horn. Kevin sped up and Brady pursued him. Brady kept honking and screaming and tried to cut around the SUV, but Kevin swerved to keep him from passing.

"Pull over you chickenshit, motherfucker!" Brady kept yelling at the top of his lungs. Finally, Kevin made a quick right turn down a dirt road and Brady tried to follow him, but spun out and went off the road, plowing over a country mail box and into a snow drift. Steam from the broken radiator spewed out from under the hood.

Brady's car was hopelessly stuck in the snow drift as Kevin disappeared in the SUV down the dirt road. A moment later a Thomas County Sheriff's car pulled up with lights flashing. Brady hung his head on the wheel of his mom's wreaked car, defeated.

Ashley laid in the bed woozy from the champagne and a little whacked out from the amyl nitrate. Michael was showering in the bathroom. Ashley felt like she had just crossed some kind of invisible line that bordered on prostitution. She felt a little guilty, but at the same time invigorated. She was going to make progress one way or another. The man showering in the other room had the power to make things happen for her with one phone call.

Many actresses may not be willing to cross the line she just crossed, but those people would be working as hostesses and waitresses until their expiration dates had passed. Ashley knew she only had a short window of opportunity to secure her place in Hollywood history. Seize the moment. She had seized the moment, and she had done it quite nicely. Now, she had to keep that moment going. She heard the shower shut off. A moment later, Michael walked out toweling himself off. He smiled at Ashley.

"I'd better get back to the office," he said.

"That was fun," Ashley said, giggling.

A broad smile broke across his face. "Hey, you're welcome to hang out here until check out time tomorrow morning. Order room service, whatever. Just don't throw any wild parties, ok?"

He sat on the edge of the bed and caressed her hair, looking at her.

"I promise, I won't," Ashley said in her best little girl voice. She leaned forward and kissed him. He stared at her a moment. "Wow, you really are something else. Give me a call tomorrow at the office, ok?"

"Sure," Ashley said. Michael pulled his socks on and then slipped into his pants, not able to stop smiling. Ashley pulled the covers over herself and squeezed her eyes shut, smiling.

Michael left her in the room and she stayed the night there. She ordered the Ossobucco with a heart of palm salad and a glass of Far Niente Chardonnay from room service, and watched a pay per view movie. After the movie, she was bored and horny and in the $500 hotel room. She called Efrain and he came over after his shift at 2:00 am. They fucked twice and he got kind of jealous, asking a lot of questions about who paid for the room, etc., and Ashley just told him to "deal with it." He fell asleep in the room and didn't get home to his wife and newborn child until 6:00 am. He kissed his wife and told her he had a crazy hectic night at work and that he was booking a suspect until five am. His wife wanted to believe him but she could detect a hint of perfume on his shirt.

In Colby, Kansas, Brady benefitted from the fact his dad had been one of the most beloved men in town. The deputy who arrived on the scene of Brady's "accident" drove him home, told him to sleep it off and let him off with a warning. A tow truck pulled his mom's car out of the ditch. Brady's mom had to get a neighbor to drive her to the funeral home and finish the funeral arrangements without her son by her side.

Eighteen

It was the day before New Year's Eve that the funeral was held. The service was held at the Colby United Methodist Church to a standing room crowd. Nearly the whole town was in attendance. The cold front had gone away. The temperature was nearly 40 degrees and it was sunny. The casket was closed, and Brady and his mother sat in the front pew. Brady wore sunglasses and cried softly throughout the whole ceremony. His mom sat next to him and attempted to comfort him the best she could. She was handling the whole affair much better than he was.

Sitting in the crowd was Jim and Ginny Duncan, dressed in their Sunday best. Also in attendance were Kevin's parents, but he wasn't with them. The pastor gave a sermon and spoke about how generous Henry Anderson was; often performing veterinary services for free to countless citizens of the town who couldn't afford to pay him. Story after story conveyed that thought. There was the time he put a pace maker into a dog that belonged to a ninety year old woman and didn't charge her a dime. Then there was the time that he helped a horse give birth to a colt that was stuck in the birth canal and he saved the mother and the colt. Other people got up to speak, including the town's mayor, who spoke highly of Henry and how he was a man of his word, always quick to volunteer when the people or organizations in the community needed help.

Brady sat there with his guilt growing greater with every person that spoke. The minister asked Brady if he wanted to speak, but he declined, fearing he wouldn't be able to without breaking down. The service seemed to go on forever, and when it finally ended, the organist played "Amazing Grace," as the pall bearers, including Brady carried the casket out to the waiting hearse.

The snow on the streets was melting and water was glistening in the bright sun as the slow procession of cars moved through Colby from the Methodist Church to the Beulah cemetery a few blocks away. Once there, the minister said a few last words as the wind blew lightly and birds were chirping somewhere in the distance. Brady could barely hold his head up he felt do disgusted with himself and guilty for what had happened.

He exchanged glances with Ashley's mom and dad. After everything was done and the casket was lowered into the ground, they came up to him and offered their condolences. It pained him tremendously to see them, but he hugged Ashley's mom tightly. The cars slowly dispersed out of the cemetery, and Brady walked with his mom back to the car provided by the funeral home. Their feet were muddy from the melting snow. Once inside the car, Brady broke down again in his mom's arms. She looked at him with deep worry.

"Brady, you're going to have to forgive yourself. This wasn't your fault," she said.

"Yes. It was," he said.

In Los Angeles, Ashley wasn't feeling much better. She had talked to her mom about the funeral and she felt terrible. She also felt guilt in association with Henry's death. She felt guilt for abandoning Brady. Her mom told her how absolutely broken up he was at the funeral. Ashley felt sick about it.

Compounding her bad feeling was the fact that she called Michael's office the day before and was told that he wouldn't be back to the office for two weeks. She wondered if she had been used and discarded. She kept telling herself that he was a busy and married man and that he had a reputation and obligations to keep that didn't include her. He would get back to her on his time, and she would have to live with that.

Things were getting obsessive regarding her relationship with Efrain. He had come over two times since that night at the hotel and they had headboard thumping sex. The night before he had been over and she saw the way he was looking at her after sex. Ashley could see that he was getting completely obsessed to the point of being crazy and it scared her. He was obviously the jealous type and probably dangerous. She kept reminding him that it was she who should be jealous, because he was the married one. Ashley wondered what had become of her morals - here she was carrying on with *two* married men.

She decided that she would have to break it off with Efrain before things got out of control. Efrain was somebody she turned to in a moment of weakness, and now he was a potential liability to her.

Efrain was a loose cannon who could derail any progress she was making.

She went to Jeremy Bone's acting class and continued to work on scenes, but she had a superior attitude, knowing that she might be moving to Dina Solomon's class. Jeremy Bone was drama queen himself and his theatrics were starting to irritate Ashley. It was kind of cute at first, but now was getting grating. Michael had promised to get her into Dina Solomon's class. She was supposed to wait for the call. She wondered if she should be proactive and make the call herself, using Michael's name. She decided against that.

She just had to sit tight and wait until after the New Year. Then everything would start happening for her. She decided she would break it off with Efrain later in the day. She got into her workout clothes and hurried off to the gym. She would do some intense cardio and blow off the steam and guilt and worry that plagued her. Chloe was supposed to meet her at the gym.

Brady went home with his mother and called his boss back in LA to find out if there was any work coming up. The boss told him there was nothing coming up for a couple of weeks. Brady thought about it and realized he couldn't wait to get out of town. He didn't want to spend one more minute in Colby. Several of his parent's friends and his uncles and aunts were gathered with his mom in the kitchen having coffee and preparing an early supper. Brady joined them there and pulled his mother aside.

He looked at her a long moment. "Mom, I have to go. They need me in LA for a shoot New Year's Day," Brady said, lying.

She nodded sadly, knowing he was lying. She hugged him.

"Please, Brady. Take care of yourself. I realize that you have your own life to lead, but I worry about you. Especially now," Margaret said.

Brady promised her over and over that he would take care of himself and come back in the spring. He said his goodbyes to the rest of the family and Jerry offered to drive him back to Denver, but Brady decided he would rent a car instead. After a tearful goodbye to his mom, and everyone else, Jerry dropped Brady off at the rental car agency in Colby.

Brady rented a midsized Chevrolet and headed out of town. He stopped at a gas station and bought a twelve pack of Coors. He cracked one open as he pulled onto the highway. He took one last look at Colby, Kansas in his rear view mirror. He had cried all the tears he was going to cry. He was cried out. He felt a little bad about leaving his mom so abruptly, but she was in the good hands of family and friends. He felt a smidgen of guilt about what had happened with Kevin and wrecking his mom's car, but he rationalized that. He had been through a lot. He had lost a lot, and whatever he had to do to cope with that, is what he had to do. Fuck em' all. He got onto the open highway of I-70 and took a long drink of beer, feeling better.

He tried to call Crystal but her phone only rang once and then a message played that said that her voicemail was full. Brady was momentarily irritated, because he wanted her to pick him up at LAX, and then he realized that she probably wasn't capable.

Ashley met Chloe at Balley's on Santa Monica Boulevard. The gym in LA is another place to see and be seen. The stretch of Santa Monica Boulevard known as Boy's Town has a row of the top gym franchises, which are all bustling with beautiful, buff people busy working on their perfect physiques. Ashley was already on a treadmill when Chloe showed up looking flustered and anxious. Ashley kept moving on the treadmill and Chloe climbed onto a treadmill right next to hers. There were dozens of people all around them moving in unison to grating loud pop music that was piped through the speakers. A row of televisions were perched in front of them displaying various trash television shows.

"You look stressed," Ashley said to Chloe.

Chloe smiled, trying to shake it off. She was still wowed in the presence of Ashley, though she did not want it to be obvious.

"Well, I just came from an AA meeting. I had to admit that I had broken my sobriety. I was doing so well," Chloe said. Ashley kept moving, didn't know what to say, and felt a little guilty for not being more supportive.

"Jillian is in a bad way," Chloe said. "That guy that she was seeing dumped her and won't return her calls. I've never seen her so broken up."

Ashley thought about Michael Levin and wondered if the same thing hadn't happened to her. "She's a strong woman," Ashley said.

"I don't know. I'm worried about her. She was supposed to go to Kraven with him tomorrow night, and now she has nowhere to go. I've never seen her this desperate," Chloe said.

"People put too much importance on these stupid holidays," Ashley said.

"She's saying some pretty crazy stuff. I'm afraid of what she might do," Chloe said.

Ashley realized that she wasn't really listening to Chloe and didn't give a shit about Jillian. Ashley was only thinking about how she was going to break it off with Efrain. He was somebody who was a complete secret in her life. She had told nobody about him. She wondered if she should confess the whole thing to Chloe, and then decided against it.

Every time she looked at Chloe she thought of that night in Palm Springs when they were sixty-nining, and she knew that was all Chloe was thinking about too. She was convinced that Chloe was itching to do it again, but Ashley wasn't so inclined. It was fun at the time though. Ashley looked over at Chloe and revealed a mysterious smile. Chloe was caught off guard, was suddenly self conscious, but smiled. That little smile from Ashley had made her day. She picked up the pace on the treadmill as the music kept blasting.

Jillian was lying in bed in her apartment completely despondent. It was after 3pm and she had not been out of bed yet. All of the shades were drawn and clothes were scattered everywhere. A magnum bottle of Pinot Noir was half empty beside the bed. Jillian sat up and took a swig out of it. She was naked and she could see herself in the mirror across the room. She looked old, pale, her breasts were sagging and her arms were flabby. All that she could see were her flaws and they seemed to be magnified 1000 times in that mirror. She threw the wine bottle at the mirror and smashed it. Red wine splattered everywhere like blood. "Fucking asshole," Jillian said to herself.

She opened a drawer on the nightstand beside her bed and she picked out the .38 cartridges that she had unloaded from the gun and put in there. She rolled the five bullets in her hand.

Brady arrived at LAX around 9pm. He was comfortably numb. He had drank the twelve pack of Coors on the way to Denver, had more drinks at the airport, and more on the plane. He stumbled through the airport among throngs of people arriving and departing for New Year's Eve. He tried to call Crystal again, and once again got the "voicemail is full," message. He stepped out onto the curb and looked for a cab.

The taxi got him up to the Hollywood Hills in record time. He paid the cab driver and stepped out onto Crystal's driveway. The dogs were barking inside. The house looked eerie. The shades were drawn and the blue light from a television flickered inside. Brady watched as the taxi backed out of the driveway. The garage door was open and Crystal's

Range Rover was parked next to the big Silverado in the garage. Brady suddenly got a bad feeling about the whole situation. The dogs continued barking. He was just sober enough to be scared.

He stepped through the garage and opened the door that led into the kitchen. "Crystal," he called out. He immediately smelled dog shit and the dogs came running into the kitchen barking and snarling. They saw that it was him and backed down, wagging their tails and happy to see him. He petted them and proceeded cautiously into the house. He could hear the television playing loudly in the living room. It sounded like a lot of empty irritating noise. A rerun of the Jerry Springer show was on.

He stepped into the living room and saw two big piles of dog shit on the floor. The dogs were moving with him and then he saw Crystal lying on the couch. The room was pretty dark except for the flickering light of the television. "Crystal," Brady called out. He stood there a moment watching her. She didn't move, and didn't seem to be breathing. The smell of dog shit was overwhelming, but another smell, like vomit invaded Brady's nostrils. "Crystal," he said again, gripped with fear.

He switched on a lamp and he looked at her from a distance. She was lying on her back on the sofa. He could see what looked like vomit caked around her open mouth. He stepped closer to her. The smell was horrendous. She was not breathing. Her eyes were closed and dried vomit was caked out of her mouth. Brady's heart started pounding as he realized that she was dead. He had never seen a dead body before.

Not even his dad. He wasn't allowed to see him. He saw a wine bottle sitting beside the sofa and a mirror with a smattering of cocaine was on top of the coffee table. Next to it was her phone.

Brady looked at her for a long moment. The dogs were whining and licking his hands. His mind was racing. What should he do – call the police? Leave? He sat down in a chair and the dogs continued licking him and whining. He picked up the mirror and formed a line of cocaine, and then slowly snorted it. He wondered how long she had been lying there dead.

He was sad, but couldn't muster a tear for her. It was what she wanted he supposed. It was what she had been trying to accomplish for years. He sat there a moment and felt the cocaine rushing through his bloodstream. He stood and walked out to the pool in the back. He stared at the lights of Hollywood in the distance and wondered if Ashley was out there somewhere. He picked up a cigarette from a pack lying there and lit it. He decided he would call 911 after he cleaned up the house a bit.

After the gym Ashley and Chloe went to dinner at a little Mexican fusion restaurant on Robertson, across from the Log Cabin where Chloe went to AA meetings. Ashley didn't want to be alone and she was contemplating how she was going to blow Efrain off. Chloe had invited her to an AA meeting after dinner and Ashley said she would go to support her. Ashley didn't guess that she had any problem at all with alcohol and drugs, despite the few recent incidences. Ashley actually blamed Jillian, Chloe, Owen, and even Brady for those. Ashley, on her own, could take alcohol or leave it. Chloe kept talking about AA and sobriety and Ashley let it go in one ear and out the other. Then she decided she would tell Chloe about the Efrain situation.

"I have kind of a bad situation, going on," Ashley said, interrupting Chloe.

Chloe looked at her a moment. "What is it? You're back with your ex again?"

"No. Someone else. A married man. A cop," Ashley said.

Chloe seemed a little shocked, though she tried not to show it.

"How long has this been going on?" Chloe asked.

"Since Christmas," Ashley said. "It's getting out of control and I need to cut it off."

"So do it. Cut it off now," Chloe said.

"I'm afraid of what he might do. He's getting pretty obsessed….he's a cop. He had this guy from my acting class run out of town," Ashley said.

"Oh, my God. What are we going to do with you?" Chloe said.

"Can I stay at your place tonight?" Ashley asked

Chloe laid her hand on Ashley's. "Of course you can. We'll figure this out," Chloe said, then leaned over and hugged her. Ashley held onto her tightly for a moment and was glad to be with her.

The waiter came with the check and Chloe paid it. They walked across the street where a motley looking group of people were gathered smoking cigarettes, waiting to get into the AA meeting at the Log Cabin.

Brady covered Crystal with a sheet and spent a couple of hours cleaning the place. He cleaned up the dog shit and removed all traces of drugs and empty bottles. He put the dogs in their kennel and called 911 and reported that he had come home to a dead body. He sat in the back smoking another cigarette and waiting for the police and paramedics. He finally heard them pull into the driveway after about a half hour.

He talked to a couple officers from LAPD and told them how he found her when he got back from Kansas. They looked at him like he was a criminal. He showed them his airline ticket to prove he just got back. The paramedics quickly determined that Crystal was in fact, dead. They put her onto a stretcher and wheeled her out.

"Do you live here?" one of the cops asked Brady.

"Yeah," Brady said.

"We'll be in touch if we have any more questions," the cop said. The cop scribbled down his phone number.

Brady nodded and they all left. He stood and watched the paramedic van drive up the driveway carrying Crystal's body to the LA County morgue. Brady wondered what he should do. He didn't know if Crystal had any relatives he should call, or if she was making house payments, or if he should leave. He decided he would stay until someone told him otherwise.

He let the dogs out of their kennel and he went into the bedroom and he could still smell Crystal's perfume on the sheets and he got a very sick, eerie feeling in the pit of his stomach. He looked at a picture of her where she was smiling and for a moment felt like he might cry, but he didn't. He decided he would sleep in the guest bedroom. He was very tired. He lay down and could hear sirens off in the distance. What a week it had been. The dogs came in and settled at the foot of the bed. Brady drifted off to sleep before he could count to 10.

Ashley sat in the crowded and raucous AA meeting with Chloe. The room was filled with tattooed hipsters, aging punks, homeless surfers, and D-list celebrities. Many of the men kept staring at Ashley and everyone wanted to meet her as Chloe introduced her. Everyone wanted to know if she was an alcoholic too and she politely told them that no, she was only there to support Chloe.

Ashley listened to their stories about shooting heroin and selling babies and she pitied them. Poor people. She couldn't even understand what Chloe was doing going to AA. Chloe had a great career, a brand new BMW, and a condo in West Hollywood. The meeting seemed to go on forever and Ashley had three missed calls from Efrain during that time. Ashley had told him the day before that they could get together when he got off work. Ashley watched her phone lighting up in her purse for a fourth time with Efrain's number on it and it really rattled her. Everyone was clapping about something in the AA meeting. Why were they always clapping Ashley wondered?

After the meeting Ashley followed Chloe in her car back to Chloe's place. She did not want to be at her place while Efrain was looking for her. Chloe told Ashley just to ignore his calls and that he would get the message. Ashley wasn't so sure about that. She stopped on the street next to Ashley's condo and listened to a string of voice mails that Efrain had left.

"Hey Ashley. This is Efrain. I'll be getting off early tonight, around 10:30. Can't wait to see you, baby. Let's hook up! Late..." the first voice mail said.

"Hi Ashley. Where are you, girl? I'm trying to get a hold of you. Call me back," the second voicemail said.

"Hi Ashley, it's 10:45 and I'm sitting here with my fuckin' dick in my hand. Call me back," the third voice mail said.

"Where the fuck are you? I thought we were going to get together tonight? I got off early. Fuck!" the forth voice mail said.

"You must be with that Jew Fucking agent. I get it. Have a nice life, whore!" the fifth voice mail said.

Ashley started to delete the voicemails, and then she decided she might need them. Chloe waited by the front door for her. Ashley got out of her car and went inside the condo with Chloe.

It was the first time Ashley had been to Chloe's condo and she was impressed by how well it was decorated. It was on the tenth floor and it had a little view of Century City and West LA.

Ashley told Chloe about the voice mails and Chloe told her to get a restraining order in the morning. Ashley thought about it and realized that she couldn't get restraining orders on every man she came in contact with. Ashley really felt like she needed a drink or a pill or something. She was really freaked out by the voice mails.

"I hate to ask you, I know you are trying to stop, but do you have anything in here to drink at all, or maybe one of the those pills? I'm kind of freaked out by those calls. I don't think I'll be able to sleep," Ashley said.

Chloe looked at her a moment, "Sure." She disappeared and then returned a moment later with a pill and a glass of water.

"Take this, it will relax you," Chloe said.

Ashley took the pill and swallowed it with water. Chloe was watching her with bedroom eyes. Ashley smiled. "I put out a new toothbrush for you in the guest bathroom, and there are clean towels in there if you want to take a shower in the morning. I'm going to bed now. You can stay up and watch television or whatever," Chloe said.

"Sure," Ashley said. Chloe came to her and lightly kissed her on the cheek and hugged her.

"Good night," Chloe said and then she walked out of the room leaving Ashley to stare out the window at the lights of West LA. Ashley finished her water and felt the warm feeling she had always felt when she took pills. The feeling that everything was going to be alright. She shut the light off and walked into Chloe's bedroom.

Chloe was lying in her bed reading. She was wearing a sheer slip. Ashley stripped all of her clothes off and stood in front of Chloe in all of her glorious nakedness.

"Can I sleep with you?" Ashley asked.

Chloe set her book aside. Ashley climbed into the bed beside her and kissed her on the lips. Chloe looked at her a moment, gasped, and then the two women started making out.

Efrain was parked in his own car, in his civilian clothes on Ashley's street. He was surveiling her apartment building. A few people came and went into the building. His mind was racing. Where was she? He had to remind himself that he was married with a newborn at home and why was he so obsessed with this white girl? He should just go home to his wife and forget about it. Forget about it for good. He had his good time with her and if it was now over that was probably a good thing. She would just end up costing him his marriage, his family, and probably his career.

It was the best sex he had ever had, though. The girl was perfect in every way. Flawless.

He couldn't think of one thing he would change about her. It was no wonder that every man in town was probably after her. He had done some checking and found out who had rented the hotel room at the Peninsula – Michael Levin. Efrain decided he would do some more checking on this Levin character tomorrow. Maybe dig up some dirt. Maybe he would roust the guy, put the fear of God into him.

Efrain looked at his watch – it was 1:45 AM. He had been sitting on Ashley's street for over three hours. He thought he should just cut his losses and leave now, but he couldn't do that. He decided he would go into the courtyard and see if she was in her apartment. Maybe she was there with someone. He didn't know what he would do if she was, but he had to know. He was capable of killing someone, he knew that. He had killed men in Iraq and he enjoyed it. Hajis, they called them. He had killed three Hajis that he knew about, and probably more in collateral damage. He remembered blowing the first guy's head off within about fifty yards. He had seen the man's frightened eyes just as he pulled the trigger. The guy was lying on the street in Bagdad with his brains scattered all over.

Efrain experienced a rush from that like no other. He remembered that he felt like passing out shortly after that, but on the subsequent kills he had felt almost nothing. He remembered laughing and posing for pictures with the dead men. They all did that over there. He could kill some fucker easily and probably get away with it. He was a cop, and he knew how to cover evidence.

Efrain decided that he would just check on Ashley's apartment, and then he would go home and try to forget about her. Here he was thinking about murdering someone over this fucking white girl. He got out of the car and walked over to Ashley's building. He was armed, carrying a revolver under his jacket. The security gate was locked, but Efrain easily jumped over it. He moved into the courtyard, walking along the dark hedges. He saw the window of Ashley's apartment and it was dark. He stood in front of it. It was completely dark and he tried to peer into the window. Maybe something had happened to her. Maybe she had gotten into an accident or something. Maybe he was jumping to conclusions.

Efrain could hear laughter coming from another apartment, like maybe someone was having a small party. Larry, the apartment manager stepped out of his apartment smoking a cigarette and he saw Efrain standing in front of Ashley's building. Can I help you?" Larry said.

Efrain didn't say anything and quickly walked out of the courtyard. Larry watched him, a little unnerved by the dark presence.

Efrain returned back to Montebello to his wife and crawled into bed beside her. She sensed a dark presence as well and she touched him, but he seemed to be laying there in anger. She wondered what was wrong with him, but didn't dare ask.

Nineteen

Brady woke up in the guest bedroom in Crystal's house. It took him several moments to remember where he was, and few moments more to remember the events of the day before. He was horrified. He suddenly remembered coming home to Crystal being dead, and the police and everything. He had thought it was a bad dream. The dogs were lying next to the bed. He had been hammered out of his mind. He barely remembered driving to Denver or the plane trip. He didn't remember returning the rental car at all. Brady shot out of bed and he felt nauseous. He went into the bathroom and puked. He washed his mouth out for several minutes and washed his face. He went into the living room to face reality. He looked at the couch and the remnants of vomit on it. The room still smelled of death. Brady quickly opened the large sliding glass door to the pool area to let some air inside.

The dogs followed him and stayed on his heals wanting to be fed. The first thing Brady did was struggle to slide the couch out of the house and then left it on the back patio.

He saw Crystal's cell phone on the coffee table and the battery was dead. He looked for the charger, finally found it and plugged the phone in. Once it had power he would check for phone numbers of relatives to call. He didn't know if Crystal had parents alive, or children, or anything. She never really talked about it to him. Brady fed the dogs and wondered what he was going to do. He couldn't just stay in the house, could he? He thought that Crystal owned it outright, but what bills needed to be paid. He saw a pile of mail on the kitchen counter and he started looking through it. An electric bill was due for $348. Several of Crystal's credit card bills were underneath it. He found a bank statement and opened it.

The balance of Crystal's checking account was $11,975.46. He saw other mail there from Smith Barney, and Merrill Lynch. Brady figured that Crystal had no will or surviving relatives. Who would get that money? He thought about his own father. Did he have a will? Brady then thought about his poor mother and how he had just abandoned her and a sharp pain went through his heart.

He looked in the refrigerator and there was no beer. He opened a bottle of Kendall Jackson chardonnay. There were at least five bottles of wine in the fridge and very little food. As he was opening the wine he saw Derek's Denali pull into the driveway. Derek must have the gate code. Brady didn't like that guy and didn't even really know who he was. The hair on the back of Brady's neck stood up as Derek killed his engine and got out of the SUV. The dogs were barking. Brady decided to meet Derek outside and he walked out of the house with the dogs following. The dogs knew Derek and ran to greet him. He petted them and then looked up at Brady.

"Where's Crystal?" Derek said, not smiling.

"Um, when's the last time you talked to her?" Brady asked.

"Two or three days ago. I keep calling and her voicemail is full. Where is she?" Derek asked.

Brady stood there, afraid to tell him, but finally did," I got back from Kansas last night....When I got here....she was dead."

"Dead?" Derek said.

"Yeah. Dead. I think she may have od'd. She'd been dead for a couple of days, I think. I called the police. I didn't know what else to do," Brady said.

"Where is she now?" Derek asked.

"I don't really know where they took her," Brady said.

"What did you tell the cops?" Derek asked.

"I didn't tell them anything. I didn't know anything," Brady said.

"Don't tell them anything about me. Got it?" Derek said on his way back to his vehicle.

"Sure. I won't," Brady said following him. "I don't know what to do. Who should I call? Did she have any relatives?"

Derek jumped into his SUV without saying another word and quickly backed out of the driveway. Brady could hear him speeding away down the canyon. Brady turned and walked back into the house with the dogs on his heals. He was more confused than before.

Ashley woke up sleeping next to Chloe. Chloe was clinging onto her. They were both naked. Ashley crawled out of bed and slipped into the bathroom to pee. She thought about what she had done with Chloe again and decided that it was no big deal. She had to shed herself of her Midwestern, middle class morality. It would not serve her here. She needed to be at Chloe's house last night to be safe, and she did feel safe there. She wiped herself, flushed the toilet and then returned to the bedroom to get her clothes. She had to be at the club at 1pm to prepare for New Year's Eve. She walked back into the bedroom and Chloe was now awake and smiling at her from the bed.

"Good morning, beautiful," Chloe said.

"Good morning," Ashley said, irritated by the "beautiful" comment, but she tried not to show it.

"I've gotta' run. I have to be at the club at one to get ready for tonight," Ashley said.

"Will you be ok? At home, I mean?" Chloe said.

"Oh yeah, sure. Thanks so much for letting me stay last night," Ashley said.

"Any time. You want to stay for a couple of weeks, no problem," Chloe said.

Chloe climbed out of bed, naked. "Oh, you don't have to get up," Ashley said.

"Hang on a minute," Chloe said. She disappeared into the bathroom and came out a minute later with a bottle of pills. She handed the bottle to Ashley.

"Take these. I don't want them in the house. Just be careful with them. They're highly addictive," Chloe chuckled.

Ashley stared at the pills a moment. "Thanks," she said.

She hugged Chloe, who was still naked and Chloe kissed her on the lips and held on to her a moment too long.

"Ok, see you tonight," Ashley said hurrying out. Chloe looked at her go, and then returned to bed.

Ashley hurried home to her apartment only a few blocks away. Nothing seemed to be out of place, but she was a little freaked out returning. She felt like she was going to have to move. She needed to get a fresh start somewhere. Just when she had got her apartment decorated the way she wanted it, she would have to leave. Efrain had left another message at 6:45 am and she didn't want to listen to it. She took a quick shower, ate a banana and some yogurt, and then spent a solid hour picking out something to wear. She finally decided on a sleek dress that Jillian had given her. She spent another half hour applying her makeup. She looked at the clock and it was 12:50. Luckily the club was within walking distance. She put on some sandals, but grabbed a pair of high heels to take with her. She thought about it a moment, before heading out of her apartment, then she took out the pill bottle and took one of the pills.

She walked out of her apartment and ran into Larry, the apartment manager.

"Happy New Year, Ashley!" Larry said.

"Happy New Year," Ashley said, trying to get past him.

"Is everything ok?" Larry said, taking a long look at her.

"Yes, I'm just running late to work," she said.

"Oh, well don't let me stop you," Larry said, stepping out of the way. She hurried off.

Ashley climbed up the hill on Palm Avenue heading toward Sunset. She was carrying her high heels and her purse. She was startled by the sound of a police siren that was just switched on for a second. She looked up and saw Efrain in his squad car driving slowly up Palm Avenue. Efrain rolled the passenger side window down.

"You scared the shit out of me! Don't do that!" Ashley said from the sidewalk.

"I've been trying to get a hold of you. You ok?" Efrain said. He was wearing dark sunglasses.

"I got the nice messages," Ashley said and continued walking.

"Where you been, girl?," Efrain said rolling in the police car slowly up the street as she was walking. She finally stopped and looked at him.

"Don't you have better things to be doing with that police car? It's none of your business where I've been. Just go back to your wife and kid and leave me the fuck alone!" Ashley said, emboldened by the pill that had just hit her system.

Efrain looked at her a moment, yelled something like "fuckin' slut," then sped away and turned right onto Sunset. Ashley crossed the street and hurried to the club, arriving at 1:02 pm.

Jean Pierre was already at the club directing the busboys who were filling balloons and putting up decorations. Ashley was a little flustered from the encounter with Efrain, but she hugged Jean Pierre and acted like everything was just fine. Kurt was stocking the bar, and he waved at Ashley as he went for another ice bucket. She waved back at him. The pill was pummeling her system and seemed to be coming onto her in waves. She suddenly felt very fucked up, and hoped it wasn't noticeable. Jean Pierre told her to get on the phone and start confirming reservations. She looked down the list of reservations and had a hard time focusing. She decided right then and there that this would be her last holiday working at the club. She picked up the phone.

"Hi, this is Ashley at Kraven. Just calling to confirm your reservation for tonight..."

Chloe went to a noon AA meeting at the Log Cabin, where she raised her hand and "shared" about how blessed her life was and that she had nine days sobriety since her last relapse. Everyone clapped. Chloe was still beaming from the sexual encounter with Ashley. As other people shared their experiences, Chloe pretended to be listening, but she wasn't. She was thinking about Ashley and couldn't wait to see her again. She looked to see if anyone was watching and she secretly smelled her fingers. She had worked hard seducing Ashley and it was finally paying off. She would come out of the closet if she was with Ashley. She would show the whole world that she was in love with a woman. Ashley wasn't just any women – she was the hottest, most desirable women Chloe had ever laid eyes on, and she was every bit as desirable in bed as Chloe ever imagined. She would even marry Ashley if she had the chance. Gay marriage was now legal in Massachusetts. They could go to Boston and get married, or maybe Martha's Vineyard. She would even invite her family to the wedding.

Chloe snapped out of it and realized she was getting ahead of herself. She suddenly felt guilty about giving Ashley the pills. Those were Schedule II narcotics, normally prescribed to terminal cancer patients and Chloe could be charged with a felony and certainly fired for giving them to her. Worse than that, it was manipulative. What was her real motive for giving the pills to Ashley? Chloe was troubled by it. What if Ashley overdosed on the pills? Chloe would never forgive herself for it, and that would just be her luck.

Chloe looked at the people around her in the AA meeting and knew that they would hate her if they knew she had given the pills to someone. A wave of anxiety overcame Chloe and she suddenly thought of Jillian, who had never called her back. They were supposed to go to Kraven for dinner and New Year's Eve. Chloe looked at her phone. No messages or missed calls from Jillian. The meeting was ending and everybody stood up to hold hands for the prayer. Someone said to pray for those still suffering, and Chloe prayed for Jillian as they recited the Lord's Prayer. As everybody was filing out of the meeting, Chloe decided she would drive straight over to Jillian's place and check on her.

Ashley had called through half the page of reservations. Only one cancellation. She noticed Chuck Alexander's name for a party of two. She called him and he confirmed after a few moments of flirtaceous banter. She noticed Chloe's name for a party of two and she wondered who Chloe's second person was. She came to the name, Ranger, and realized that was the code name for Jack Wrangler. A party of 8. What an asshole, Ashley thought, but also Michael Levin's number one client. Ashley decided that she would have to warm up to him somehow, get on his good side. She called the number.

"Hi, this is Ashley from Kraven. I'm just calling to confirm your reservation tonight? A gruff voice on the other end confirmed the reservation. Ashley assumed it was someone from Wrangler's entourage. Jean Pierre joined her at the hostess stand and put his arm around her, a little too tight for comfort and his hand rested on one breast. He smelled like he had been bathing in Givenchy cologne and his breath smelled like Chardonnay.

"How is it going, my love?" Jean Pierre said. He noticed the reservation for Ranger.

"That is Jack Wrangler's party. I don't need to tell you they are VIP's. Put them in the Godfather booth," Jean Pierre said. He looked into Ashley's eyes.

"I wish I had some of the drugs you are doing," he said laughing. Ashley didn't say anything, but seemed nervous. Jean Pierre continued looking at her.

"What has happened to my angel? The girl that was the picture of innocence when she arrived to me?" Jean Pierre said.

Ashley wiggled away from him, half smiling and picked up the phone to dial another number.

"This town, this town," Jean Pierre said, walking away.

Ashley wondered what his comment had meant. Had she changed that much? She guessed that she had, but she thought in a good way. She was tougher, stronger, more aware of what was going on and what it would take to achieve her goals. If that was a loss of innocence, then so be it. She was glad she was no longer the naïve Pollyanna from Kansas that could be pushed around and exploited. She thought of Efrain and how done she was with him. He was another small man who was trying to possess her. No man was ever going to possess her. She would be the one doing the possessing.

She took a pill from her purse and held it in her hand. When Jean Pierre walked by she took his hand and placed the pill into his. He looked at the pill and smiled at her. Then he popped it into his mouth and walked away grinning like a cat that had just swallowed a canary.

They had started playing the music in the club, some hard driving electronic stuff. Ashley swayed to the music and felt very warm and comfortable and surreal. This was going to be the best year of her life.

Brady felt on edge being at the house, but he also didn't want to leave it. He knew that there was a security system with cameras in the den, and that it had been unhooked. He monkied with the security monitor until he got it working. There were four camera views, including the front gate, in front of the garage, underneath the deck at the bottom of the property, and overlooking the front door. Brady poured himself another glass of Kendall Jackson, lit a cigarette and sat there watching the security cameras.

He would stop drinking tomorrow, and the drugs, and smoking. He would start going to the gym again and eating right and strengthening himself physically and mentally. He would apply himself to his job and become the best wrangler in the history of Hollywood. He would pay the electric bill and stay at Crystal's until someone told him otherwise. He didn't think Derek would be back out of fear of the police.

It was New Year's Eve., but Brady would stay right there in the house and wait it out. He had a bad feeling about leaving the house that night and was convinced that something bad would happen if he did. All of the bad omens had already visited him: The loss of Ashley, the death of his father, and now the death of Crystal. An incredible sadness engulfed him as he thought about what a lonely death she had. She had probably just died in her sleep, and hoped he would be so lucky. The police said that they would be in touch, and he wondered when they would. They had seemed so matter of fact about the whole ordeal and Brady figured they must see this kind of thing all the time. Brady watched the security cameras. There was no movement.

As night approached, it started to get hectic in the club. People started arriving all at once and Ashley and Jean Pierre were scrambling trying to get them all seated. Many of the people were not happy with their tables and threw a fit and Ashley just had to ignore them. Everyone was the "best customer ever," and "don't you know who I am?" Ashley took another pill and just smiled at the people who were complaining, set the menus down, and walked away as they continued complaining. Didn't they know who *she* was.

She got back to the hostess stand and Chuck Alexander was waiting with an Asian girl who looked like some kind of model or dancer. She was wearing an evening gown that was slit down to her belly button in the front and it exposed most of her large fake breasts. Chuck acted like Ashley was his best friend.

"Hey, Ashley, this is Keiko," Chuck said. Keiko had a perpetual red lipstick smile like a blow up doll and she shook Ashley's hand. Chuck slipped Ashley a $100 bill and Ashley sat them in one of the best booths. Kurt waved at Chuck from behind the bar. The music was blasting and people had to scream to hear each other as waiters were rushing around with bottles of champagne. Jean Pierre was blasted out of his mind from the pill and white wine. People could hear him laughing above the music as he greeted them at their tables. People were stacked up in front of the hostess stand waiting be seated and they stared at Ashley like Dodo birds. Jack Wrangler's Mafioso looking body guard pushed through the crowd to Ashley.

"Wrangler and his group are ready to come in," the guy said to Ashley. Ashley nodded, "bring them in," she said.

After a moment, the guy returned leading Jack Wrangler and his entourage of bimbos and degenerates. Ashley lead them to the "Godfather's booth," as everyone in the place was staring at them. Jack Wrangler didn't say anything to Ashley or even seem to notice her. The girls that were with him looked like whores and they all appeared to be on coke. Ashley started to return to the hostess booth when the body guard stopped her and slipped a $100 bill into her hand. "This is from Wrangler," the guy said. Ashley nodded and glanced at Jack Wrangler who was now smiling at her. She smiled back. A charge shot through her body as she walked back to the crowd of people waiting to be seated. Jack Wrangler had just smiled at her.

She spotted Chloe and Jillian standing among the waiting crowd. Jillian looked terrible. She looked fucked up out of her mind on something, and was pale and sloppily dressed. Not her usual self at all. Chloe was with her and seemed very chipper when she saw Ashley. Ashley waved them through, to the chagrin of the other people waiting. Jillian attempted a dopey smile at Ashley, and Chloe hugged and kissed her. Ashley led them to a booth that was directly across from Chuck Alexander's booth, where the Japanese bimbo was all over him.

Ashley noticed what she had done after they were already seated and by then it was too late. Jillian was shooting daggers with her eyes toward Alexander and his dates and he loved every moment of it.

"Do you want a different table?" Chloe asked Jillian. "No, fuck that fat son of a bitch, "Jillian said, not taking her eyes off of him and his date. Jillian's purse was open beside her and the handgun with the pink grips was on top of all the other contents.

It took a good two hours to get everyone seated, as the waiters were rushing around serving the five courses $200 per person dinner. Cocktails were $18, bottles of Dom were $375, Sodas were $12, no free refills. Kraven was going to make money on New Year's Eve. If you had to ask you couldn't afford it. The dance floor started heating up around 10pm. The DJ started cranking the tunes and swarms of people crowded onto the dance floor. A couple of the girls Jack Wrangler brought were dirty dancing and making a spectacle of themselves. Wardrobe malfunctions were the rule, not the exception, as tits and ass were falling out all over the place. Man after man kept approaching the hostess stand and hitting on Ashley. She just smiled and politely rebuked them. She was now drinking champagne and bobbing to the music. Jack Wrangler's body guard, Tony approached the hostess stand.

"Hey, we haven't met. I'm Tony. I work for Wrangler. I also work for Michael Levin," Tony said.

Ashley perked up upon hearing Michael Levin's name. "Hi, nice to meet you," she said taking Tony's hand.

"Mr. Levin sends his regards. He says he'll call you when he gets back to town in a couple of weeks," Tony said.

"Oh, thanks. Thanks for that," Ashley said, playing it very cool.

"Hey, if you're not busy, Mr. Wrangler was wondering if you could join him for a drink?" Tony said. Ashley looked around, could see Jean Pierre sitting at someone's booth deep in conversation. She looked toward the Godfather booth and nodded. Tony led her back to the booth and she squeezed in next to Jack Wrangler. His female guests were out on the dance floor. Wrangler smiled at Ashley and held out his hand.

"Hi, Jack Wrangler. Nice to finally meet you. Mike told me so much about you," Wrangler said. Ashley's mind was racing.

"Well, I don't know exactly what that means, but thanks," she said. Wrangler stared at her. His eyes were glazed over with the effects of some drug, or combination of drugs. He poured her a $75 glass of champagne. He looked like a sleazy gangster. Those were the parts he usually played and Ashley couldn't decide if he was in or out of character. Tony stood nearby watching the crowd. Ashley could see Chloe looking at her from across the room.

"Mike said you are an actress. Said you are studying with Jeremy Bone. That's cool. I worked with the faggot for a minute when I first fell off the turnip truck," Wrangler said laughing at his own joke.

"Don't worry, honey. We're gonna' get you into Dina's class. In the big leagues. Do you wanna' play for the majors, babe?" Wrangler said, patting the top of her hand.

"Yes, I do," Ashley said nodding with complete confidence. Her eyes were also pinned from the heavy drugs in her system.

"What are you doing later?" Wrangler asked.

"I don't know. I have a couple of options after the club closes," Ashley said, playing coy.

"We're having a little party over at the Chateau. You know, the Chateau Marmont?" Wrangler said. Ashley nodded. Wrangler's female guests finished a dance and stumbled back to the table. One of the girls shot Ashley a dirty look.

"Oh, hey this is Ashley," Wrangler said. "Ashley, this is Briana," he said and the two girls nodded at each other.

Across the room Chloe was trying to get a look at Wrangler's table, wondering what Ashley was doing over there. The curiosity was killing her. Was Ashley not going to stay with her again? Chloe drank two large bottles of Evian, and the waiter had gone for another one. Jillian sat there almost comatose sipping on a Manhattan. She couldn't keep her eyes off Chuck Alexander and his "date". It was almost more than she could handle.

"That fucking chink cunt is younger than the fat prick's daughter," Jillian yelled above the music.

"Don't say that word! What is wrong with you?" Chloe said.

"What word? Chink or cunt?" Jillian yelled. The dance floor was going crazy. Chuck Alexander got up and started dancing with Keiko. About the same time, Ashley got up and began dancing with Jack Wrangler. Chloe couldn't believe her eyes. Jillian was seething with anger watching Chuck try to dance with the much younger woman.

Ashley got onto the dance floor and lost all inhibitions. She began dirty dancing with Jack Wrangler and everyone in the place watched them. She could see Jean Pierre laughing, seated in a booth. Flashes from cameras kept going off along with strobe lights and the thumping beat of electronic music; it was one hour until the New Year countdown. Chuck Alexander was out of breath and holding his heart as he stepped off the dance floor to catch his breath and watch Ashley. Keiko continued dancing with another woman. Chuck walked past Chloe and Jillian's table. He looked at Jillian and laughed.

"Looks like you're having a ball!" he said and continued toward the bar laughing.

"Fucking cocksucker!" Jillian said standing. Chloe wasn't paying attention, was fixated on Ashley's dirty dancing. Spectators clapped to the beat.

Jillian stumbled along the side of the dance floor in pursuit of Chuck who was making his way to the bar. He finally got to the bar and was talking to Kurt who was sweating his ass off slinging drinks. Jillian could see the two men laughing about something. Chuck turned and pointed at her. Kurt started laughing. The music was almost deafening as the strobe lights flashed.

Jillian brought the nickel plated revolver out of her purse, pointed and fired. The first bullet struck a large bottle of Grey Goose just behind Kurt's head. The second shot struck the wooden frame that ran along the top of the bar just next to Chuck. Kurt went down behind the bar and Chuck jumped onto a bar stool and scrambled over the top of it, aided by a fresh shot of adrenalin. Jillian kept shooting, hitting the mirror and several bottles behind the bar. The music kept playing and everyone was screaming. Jillian leapt up on top of the bar like a panther and took two more shots at Chuck and Kurt who were scrambling for cover behind the bar. She missed them both times but broken bottles were spilling booze all over them. The music abruptly stopped and the lights came on.

People were screaming. Jillian was standing on top of the bar and she pointed the gun right at Chuck's head. "Don't do it!" he screamed. She pulled the trigger but the gun just clicked and clicked, out of bullets. She kept snapping the trigger when one of the bouncers ran over and swept her off the bar. One of her designer shoes fell off and stood upright on the middle of the bar as the big bouncer carried Jillian kicking and screaming out the front door.

As the smoke cleared, people rushed out of the club. It was utter chaos. Among those leaving were Tony, Jack Wrangler and his crew. Jean Pierre was screaming at the top of his lungs, "Everybody relax! It's over! It's over!" Ashley was covered with sweat and surging with adrenalin as she watched the surreal scene unfold. Chloe ran up to her and threw her arms around her. "Are you ok? Are you ok?" Chloe kept asking. Ashley just nodded, her ears still ringing from the gunshots.

Chuck Alexander and Kurt slowly emerged from behind the bar and were quickly surrounded by bouncers. Keiko was crying hysterically. Chuck was completely soaked with crème de menthe.

Ashley couldn't help but to start laughing. Chloe looked at her like she was crazy.

"I'd better go see what happened to Jillian," Chloe said, moving out of the club. Waiters were running around trying to close the checks. The sound of sirens approaching came through the open door front door as the patrons spilled out.

Brady was sitting outside by the pool in the Hollywood Hills. He had moved the security monitor out to the back patio and was watching it with one eye as fireworks lit up the sky across Hollywood and the LA basin. He could hear what sounded like a succession of gunshots and sirens were screaming from the city below. The dogs started howling in unison. Brady drank another sip of wine and thought of that old Bob Seger song, "Hollywood Nights." He thought about how surreal his life had gotten since arriving here and he wondered if he would ever return to some semblance of reality. Tomorrow he would, he guessed, but tonight he would just enjoy what looked and sounded like the encroaching apocalypse. Happy New Year, motherfuckers.

Jean Pierre was furious because many people rushed out of the restaurant without paying their bills. The waiters and staff were running around like chickens with their heads cut off. Several cops were already on the scene and were talking to Chuck Alexander and Kurt. Keiko was standing nearby, a nervous wreck. Jean Pierre was with Ashley at the hostess stand and they were looking at the reservations trying to figure out who left without paying. Everyone except the staff and the immediate witnesses were ordered out of the restaurant by the police.

"Call this one! Call them right now. Fucking shits left without paying a $1,200 bill!" Jean Pierre screamed at Ashley. She looked like she might start crying. She picked up the phone and started dialing. As she did that, more cops started filing in, including Efrain. He stood near the door watching Ashley. She saw him, but didn't react.

"This is Ashley at Kraven. Jean Pierre asked me to call you, because you left without paying your bill. Please call back at 310-555-2367, so we can get a credit card number. Thanks," Ashley said and hung up. Efrain slowly approached her.

"Are you ok?" Efrain asked.

"I'm fine," Ashley said coldly. She picked up the phone again to dial another number. Efrain hung by the hostess stand until another officer approached.

"Efrain, get outside and take statements from the doorman," the officer said.

Efrain reluctantly went outside, to Ashley's relief. Ashley spent the next hour and a half dialing people and trying to get their credit card numbers. Some of the people refused and said they weren't paying. The club should have had better security; their New Year's Eve was ruined, etc. At 1:48, Jean Pierre finally let Ashley go. She was frazzled when she walked out of the club. Several people, including paparazzi were on the sidewalk and someone took a picture of her as she exited. Tony was leaning on a black Escalade that was parked on the curb. He dropped his cigarette into the gutter upon seeing Ashley.

"Ashley, Wrangler asked me to come and get you. Take you over the Chateau," he said.

She looked at him for a long moment.

"He said he invited you earlier," Tony said.

Ashley was thinking that she was exhausted, that it was a night from hell and she should just cut her losses and go home, but here she was standing on Sunset Boulevard and a major movie star was inviting her over to his hotel room. Wasn't this what she had always dreamed about? Wasn't this the moment that all the aspiring actresses in LA were hoping for, and most never got the chance? Jack Wrangler, the $12 million movie star was requesting her presence at the Chateau Marmont on New Year's Eve. The Chateau Marmont that had all kinds of history from John Belushi dying there and who knows what else.

Rob Neighbors

Ashley nodded. Tony opened the door for her and she climbed into the Escalade.

Tony pulled out into the traffic of Sunset Boulevard and just started going when the flashing lights of a police car came on behind the Escalade. Tony glanced into his rearview mirror.

"What the fuck is this," he said, pulling over. "Sorry," he said to Ashley.

Ashley sat there nervous and cold. The cop shined a spotlight into the rear view mirror and after a long moment, Efrain approached the driver side window. He glanced in and saw Ashley.

"License and registration, please," Efrain said.

"Why did you pull me over?" Tony asked.

"License and registration, please," Efrain repeated.

"What is this? Do you have any idea who you are fucking with, pal?" Tony said.

Efrain's gun came up in Tony's face. "Get out of the fucking car!" Efrain shouted. Ashley almost screamed but didn't. She braced herself.

Efrain opened the door and yanked Tony out of the car, holding his gun to his head. He handcuffed him quickly and roughly started patting him down. He found Tony's gun and yanked it out of its holster.

"I've got a permit for that, pal. You are so fucking done," Tony snarled. Efrain yanked Tony away from the Escalade and shoved him down onto the curb. "You fuckin' punk. You are finished as a cop!" Tony said.

Efrain walked back up to the window and looked in at Ashley.

"You are crazy. What is wrong with you?" Ashley said very low.

He looked at her a long moment, then tossed Tony's gun onto the front seat of the Escalade. He leaned down and undid the handcuffs from Tony, then shoved him toward the car.

"Get out of here," Efrain said.

"I'm going to have your badge, motherfucker," Tony mumbled getting back into the car. Efrain got back into his car and sped away down Sunset. Ashley was shaking.

"Do you know that cop?" Tony asked.

Ashley nodded. Tony looked at her a moment, then returned his gun to its holster, put the vehicle into drive and pulled onto Sunset. Three minutes later they were pulling into the parking garage of the Chateau Marmont. Ashley pulled herself together and checked her makeup in the vanity mirror.

Tony escorted Ashley inside and up an elevator to one of the top floors. He knocked on the door of Room 59 and one of Wrangler's flunkies opened it. They walked into a large suite. Several people were inside the room as music was playing. The bimbos were there and a few guys. Everyone was drinking, and there was a plate with a pile of cocaine lying out on the table. A bartender stood behind a portable bar in the corner. All eyes were upon Ashley as she entered with Tony. Wrangler, who was sitting near the window talking to some guy, saw Ashley and his eyes lit up. He quickly stood.

"Ashley, glad you could make it. That was a fucking trip over there, huh?"

Ashley walked toward him and just fell into his arms like he was her long lost love. She just buried her head into his chest. He held her tightly and everyone was looking at them. He grabbed two glasses of champagne from the bar and walked her out onto the balcony. They looked at the lights of the Sunset Strip and the traffic crawling way below. Wrangler lit a cigarette and looked at Ashley. She shivered from the cold and he took his jacket off and put it over her shoulders.

"You doing ok? I mean it was intense and all, but nobody got hurt," Wrangler said, laughing. She took his cigarette from him and took a drag, then gave it back.

"It's all just a little bit overwhelming," Ashley said, leaning into him. He smiled at her and raised his glass to toast.

"Well, happy New Year! It's going to be a great fucking year!" Wrangler said, as they toasted. Wrangler kissed her movie star style just after that. After they were done kissing, Ashley smiled at him. He kissed her again like it was love at first sight.

"You know this is the room Howard Hughes used to stay in," Wrangler said.

"Howard Hughes?" Ashley said, not really knowing who he was. Wrangler laughed.

"It don't matter. We're here now. That's all that fucking matters," he said.

She cracked a smile. She was shitting bricks inside with delight over what was happening, but she didn't want it to be so obvious. She felt really comfortable there with Jack Wrangler in that moment. He was her hero she decided, just like in the movies.

Shortly after that, Jack Wrangler kicked everybody out but Ashley. They drank champagne, Ashley did coke for the first with Jack Wrangler and they stayed up all night talking and laughing. They went back out onto the balcony and watched the sun come up as they smoked cigarettes. Wrangler was completely infatuated with her. He was at least 20 years older than Ashley. She smiled at him.

"What a night, huh?" Ashley said.

"Yeah, I can't believe I met you," Wrangler said.

"You mean that? Really?" Ashley said, looking vulnerable.

"Fucking A, I mean it," he said and he kissed her. They stood there awhile watching the sun rise, and then they went into the room and fell asleep in each other's arms on the bed with all of their clothes still on. Sunset Boulevard below them was strangely silent and empty on New Year's Day. A lone homeless man shuffled up the street and picked up a half full Heineken that was sitting on the sidewalk and drank it.

Twenty

Chloe sat in a small room in front of a large Plexiglas window at the Sheriff's station in West Hollywood. Jillian sat on the other side of the glass dressed in a dark blue jump suit. Her eyes were red and puffy from crying. She could barely hold her head up.

"Right now your bail is set at $500,000. I talked to a bail bondsman and I would have to come up with $50,000 cash. I don't have that kind of cash on hand, Jillian," Chloe said.

Jillian just hung her head, not saying anything.

"What were you thinking? You're in serious trouble, Jillian. They're saying two counts of attempted murder," Chloe said.

"I just wish I would have hit the two cocksuckers," Jillian said.

Chloe shook her head sadly. "I'm so sorry, Jillian. There is nothing I can do for you."

"That's ok. It's over for me now. I've accepted that," Jillian said, completely despondent.

"Good bye, Jillian," Chloe said.

Jillian nodded and stood. She knocked on the door behind her and after a moment a Sherriff's deputy opened the door. Jillian glanced back at Chloe one last time, and then walked back into the jail.

Chloe walked back out to her car and thought about her friend and her life. It was a New Year and time to turn a new chapter. Jillian never was much of a friend, and really was only out for herself. Chloe could have come up with the $50,000 cash for Jillian's bail, but why risk it? Would Jillian do the same for her if she had the money? Not in a million years Chloe guessed. Chloe tried to call Ashley, but her phone went straight to voice mail. Chloe drove out of the parking lot and turned on to Santa Monica Boulevard and drove towards Robertson and the Log Cabin.

Efrain showed up at the station early for his shift and was met by the union rep, Sergeant Morgan in the hallway. Morgan did not look happy. "Velasquez, we need to talk," Morgan said.

Efrain nodded, having no idea what the problem was. He followed Morgan into an empty interview room. Morgan turned and faced him, obviously angry.

"Did you pull over Anthony Spinelli last night on Sunset?"

Efrain didn't say anything. "Did you?" Morgan asked.

"Yeah," Efrain finally said.

"Do you have any fucking idea who he is?" Morgan asked.

Efrain just stood there and didn't say anything.

"He's a P.I. that works for some of the biggest names in this town. Last night he was working for Jack Wrangler. Wrangler donated $200,000 to the Police Protective League last year," Morgan said. Efrain just stood there, anger rising to his face, but he stuffed it down.

"They want you fucking fired. We're going to have you reassigned to Harbor Division instead," Morgan said.

"Harbor Division?" Efrain protested.

"Yes, fucking Harbor Division. Do you have a problem with that?" Morgan screamed.

Efrain's jaw was twitching with anger. "No sir," he finally said.

"Good, now get the fuck out of my sight," Morgan said.

Efrain turned and started out. "And one more thing, Velasquez," Sergeant Morgan said. Efrain stopped and looked at him.

"Stay away from the girl. If there is as much as one phone call, message, drive by, anything, and you'll be lucky to get a job busting shoplifters at Walmart in Pomona," Morgan said.

Efrain didn't say anything and walked out. Being transferred to the Harbor division was the same as being transferred to Siberia in his mind. He wished he had never laid eyes on Ashley.

Jack Wrangler was born Jack Amato in Brick, New Jersey. He had been a carpenter when he was younger and then at one point when he was out of work had drifted to New York to try acting. Everybody always told him how good looking he was. An agent convinced Jack to change his last name to Wrangler, so he wouldn't be typecast. Wrangler was typecast anyway, and got small parts playing Mafiosi. He was working as an extra in a big mob picture when the director noticed him. The rest was cinematic history as Wrangler went on to do hit movie after movie for that director for the next fifteen years. The director died and Jack became a whore. He had started out only doing one movie a year and now was doing anything and everything for money because he had gotten greedy. The producers that hired him didn't care if Jack was a whore because they needed his name to get their films financed.

When Ashley awoke, Jack Wrangler was on the phone with somebody making arrangements to fly to New York. An advertiser was arranging for a private jet for him. He smiled and winked at Ashley as she saw that she was awake and looking at him. He cupped the phone.

"Wanna' go to New York this afternoon?" Wrangler asked.

Ashley stared at him a moment in disbelief. "Sure, I guess," she finally said. She got up and went into the bathroom as Wrangler continued his phone conversation. She saw that Chloe had called her. As she was peeing she dialed Chloe. Chloe told her about Jillian and her bail amount and what she was charged with. Ashley told Chloe about the night with Jack Wrangler, and the incident with Efrain, and then casually mentioned that she was going to New York with Jack.

"I'm really happy for you," Chloe said, almost at a loss for words. Ashley sat on the pot, smiling to herself and wondering what the folks in Kansas would say if they could see her now.

That morning Wrangler ordered breakfast from room service with champagne. They ate a little, drank champagne and then had sex afterward. Jack Wrangler was built from constant personal training sections and body sculpting by plastic surgeons. Viagra kept his 46 year old cock stiff and coming back again and again for more. Every man seemed to have some "thing" that they got off on and Wrangler's seemed to be eating her pussy and licking her ass. He couldn't get enough of it. He nearly wore Ashley out as they fucked and sucked until almost an hour before the car came to pick them up for the airport. Ashley wanted to stop by her place and pick up some winter clothes, but Wrangler told her they would buy new ones in New York. They left from the Burbank Airport on a Gulfstream G-650 that was owned by a large beer company Jack was doing a campaign for. He normally didn't do advertising, but this was for a Super Bowl commercial. He was to be paid $2.5 million for a day's work.

They drank Crystal champagne on the plane and Ashley joined the mile high club as she had sex with Jack at 35,000 feet, probably flying over Kansas, which caused Ashley to orgasm even harder. The flight crew waited in the front of the plane for the antics to subside.

Once in New York, they checked into the Refinery Hotel on 38th Street. Ashley's head was spinning. She had never been to New York City and there was so much to take in. Jack arranged for them to see an off Broadway show starring Jessica Lange. As they were entering the theater, a photographer took a close shot of Ashley holding Jack Wrangler's hand. It was common knowledge that Wrangler had been married five times previously, and romantically linked to several actresses. Everywhere they went in New York, tongues were wagging – "Who was that stunning blonde with Jack Wrangler?" The pair of love birds ended their night having a few cocktails at the Mulberry Street Bar in Little Italy laughing it up with Wrangler's known mafia associate friends. He had met them when preparing for one of his films. Wrangler never had to pay for anything, as everyone fought to pick up his tab.

Everywhere they went, Wrangler introduced Ashley as his "girl," and people rolled out the red carpet for them. Ashley thought that he was being a little presumptuous. But she went with it, it felt good, and she knew she had to go on this ride to get where she was going. She wondered if Jack Wrangler had talked to Michael Levin and what Michael had told him. She only knew that so far Wrangler was being the perfect gentleman, wining, dining, and opening every door for her. She knew that her dad was a fan of Jack Wrangler's movies and she wondered what her dad would think of this. She wondered what Brady would think of this. She thought of Efrain, and Tony's threat to him. She hoped that Efrain wouldn't lose his job as a result of his involvement with her. Efrain was a good fuck, she would give him that.

At 4am, Ashley and Jack Wrangler finally returned to their hotel room and they both collapsed exhausted. The events of the previous days were spinning inside Ashley's head along with $500 a bottle champagne. Ashley took one of the pills Chloe had given her to help her sleep. She gave one to Wrangler too and he happily took it. She thought of that song, "Life in the Fast Lane," by the Eagles.

The entire next week was more of the same. During the day they would go to lunches that would last for hours. Ashley met writers, directors, and actors she had heard about and seen in movies as she was growing up. Everyone treated her great and Jack would introduce her as an actress. They drank Barolo and Nero d'avola and ate delicacies at the best restaurants in Manhattan. Jack fancied himself an aficionado of fine Italian wines. Afterward they would go back to the hotel and have sex, take a nap, and then get up for dinner and then usually to the Mulberry Street Bar.

At times, Ashley felt like she was just arm candy to Jack, because he talked and laughed with his mafia buddies and pretty much ignored her at the bar. She would sit and talk to the mafia girlfriends whom she had nothing in common with, and she was a little disgusted by all of them, though fascinated. She was almost out of birth control pills and she knew she had to get some more as soon as she returned to LA, because she felt like Jack Wrangler was purposely trying to get her pregnant.

She felt a little bit like a hostage and she casually asked him when they were going back, and he just said, "What, you're not having a good time?" Ashley still had some of the pills that Chloe had given her and was taking them daily. She hid them from Jack, because he liked them too, and she only had a few left. They helped her cope with whatever frustration she might be feeling. She had talked to her mom a couple of times, but was hesitant to tell her where she was and who she was with. Ashley didn't know why she was keeping it a secret. Chloe had called a couple of times, but Ashley only talked to her briefly and told her only the good stuff.

Jack took her shopping and bought her a whole winter wardrobe to wear around New York. She called Jean Pierre and told him she was out of town and couldn't come into work, and he said that was ok because the club was slow after New Year's, but to get back ASAP. Jack told her not to worry about her job, because he was going to get her signed with his agency and get her working right away as an actress.

Jack had a temper and was abusive toward his assistants, drivers, hotel staff, and restaurant staff. He acted either aloof toward people, or outwardly hostile. One night they returned from Mulberry Street to the hotel and Jack was very drunk. He couldn't find the hotel key so they returned to the front desk to get one. An obviously gay male at the front desk was talking to some other customers when Jack arrived at the desk with Ashley in tow. Jack didn't feel like the desk attendant gave him the proper respect as he chatted with the other customers while Jack waited. When the other people walked away, Jack approached the desk.

"Didn't you see me standing here, cocksucker?" Jack said.

The desk attendant was stunned by Jack's hostility.

"I'm sorry Mr. Wrangler, I had to finish up with those people..."

Jack cut him off, "I don't give a fuck about those fat fucking pieces of shit! Get me a new fucking room key, pillow biter," Jack said, and with that he slapped the guy.

"Jack, what's wrong with you!" Ashley screamed and she pushed herself between Jack and the desk.

"Fuckin' faggot don't treat me right," Jack said.

"Just go back to the room. I'll get the key!" Ashley said.

The poor desk attendant was holding his face searching for the key. Jack was staring down the desk attendant who was rightfully angry. "What are you lookin' at, motherfucker?" Jack said.

Ashley pushed Jack away. "Go!" she said.

Jack reluctantly stumbled off toward the elevater. Ashley looked at the desk attendant.

"I'm so sorry. I don't know what got into him. He's drunk…" she said.

"He's an abusive asshole. What are you doing with him? You can do a lot better, missy. I hope he has a good lawyer." the guy said shoving a new key card at her.

Ashley caught up to Jack in the elevator and convinced him to pay the guy $500 to keep his mouth shut. Jack only wanted to pay him $300, but Ashley finally got $500 out of him and took it back to the desk attendant. She convinced the guy to forget about it. When Ashley returned to the room Jack was passed out on the sofa with all of his clothes on.

The words of the desk attendant were ringing in her ears *"He is an abusive asshole. What are you doing with him?"* She remembered how he had acted that first night she had seen him come into the club. She was often embarrassed being with him because he was so rude to people. She would say something to him about it, but it just went in one ear and out the other. He had yet to act that way to her, but she knew it was probably coming if she crossed him in any way. Ashley just wished she could be back in her own apartment, but she knew she would have to tolerate this a while longer. Until she got what she needed out of Jack.

She thought of Jillian sitting in jail and it pained her to think she was acting in a similar way to her. Using a man to get what she wanted. Is this what all the female actors had to do to make it? Ashley wondered. One night, one of Jack's mafia buddies slipped him a gram of coke and they went back to the hotel and snorted it. Jack was also taking Viagra, and wanted to keep fucking all night. He wanted Ashley to submit to anal sex. Even though she didn't want to, she let him do it and it was painful, and she felt violated.

The next morning she could barely look at him, but he was happy and oblivious to her anger and announced that they were finally going home that afternoon. Ashley thought that she would not let herself be controlled by this man once they got to LA. Then she remembered that he could make things happen for her, so she guessed she would have to tolerate him awhile longer. Her rectum hurt from the night before, so she took two of the pills Chloe had given her and washed them down with a beer from the mini bar. She was pretty much out of it on the flight home, and luckily Jack didn't try to have sex with her.

Brady cleaned up his act in the first week of the New Year. He hauled the couch that Crystal had died on down to Hollywood and dumped it in an alley. He cleaned the house from top to bottom and it needed it. He scrubbed the baseboards and the walls and he rented a carpet shampooer and did the carpets. He took all of the booze and marijuana from the house and put it in a box and set that on Hollywood Boulevard. The homeless man who found it thought he had died and gone to heaven. Brady went on daily runs in the canyon and plotted a six mile course, pushing himself a little harder each day. He bought a bunch of fruits and vegetables and used the juicer that was in the house, making himself healthy protein shakes. His boss told him they would be back to work within a week.

He waited every day for news of Crystal, but none came. No news from the coroner's office, or the police. No visitors or phone calls to her phone. He would stare at the numbers in her phone and wondered if he should call people and tell them the news. He guessed that maybe Derek had told the people she knew. He thought that it was sad that nobody seemed to care. The dogs followed him everywhere and seemed to be depressed that she was gone. She loved those dogs. He decided to have a little memorial service for her. He put her picture on a little homemade alter out by the pool. He and the dogs sat there in front of the alter and then he said a few words for her. He sat there silently with the dogs listening to the wind blow and the birds and hoped that Crystal was finally at peace.

Brady guessed he would continue living in the house and driving the truck until someone came and told him not to. He paid the electric bill and paid the cable bill when it came. He watched the security screen now and then, but as the days went by he got less paranoid.

He talked to his mom nearly every day on the phone and she seemed to be adjusting to life without his father. He lied to her about his living situation and told her he was renting a room. He didn't want to explain the whole crazy situation to her. Brady noticed that he didn't think about Ashley as much and that was a good thing. He had heard no news about her. When he did start thinking about her, he would immediately get busy cleaning, or go on a run, or do 500 pushups. He was looking very lean, and felt good as all the alcohol and drugs detoxed out of his system.

One day he went down to the boulevard to get his hair cut. He drove through the alley where he had dumped the couch. It was still there and a couple of homeless guys were sitting on it drinking malt liquor out of paper bags. Brady considered the irony of that and wished he had burned the couch.

As Brady sat in the barber shop waiting to get his hair cut he thumbed through a People Magazine. He saw a picture of Jack Wrangler with Ashley walking into a New York theater. He stared at the photo a long moment. Adrenalin rushed into his system. It was clearly Ashley. They were holding hands and smiling. Jack Wrangler was wearing sunglasses at night and looked like a sleazy thug. The caption said, "Jack Wrangler on Broadway with unidentified woman." Every bit of hurt, anger, and rejection instantly rushed through Brady's body and he felt like he might puke. The barber called him to get into the chair, but Brady stumbled out of the barber shop with the magazine.

Brady went straight to a bar, Boardner's, around the corner and ordered a shot of tequila and a beer. Only a couple of Hollywood heavily tattooed degenerates were sitting in there at 10:30 in the morning. The tattooed female bartender could see that Brady was upset, but didn't press the issue and served the drinks as ordered. Brady stared at the photo and let the alcohol hit him. It didn't ease the pain one iota, and Brady ordered another round. Brady just sat there and stared at the picture of Ashley with Jack Wrangler in the magazine. Metallica's "Nothing Else Matters," was playing on the juke box, and the degenerates were laughing. Their stupid stoned voices grated on Brady's already exposed nerves and he felt like beating their heads in, but he just sat there silently brooding. Brady chugged the new shot and beer down and ordered another round.

A couple of hours later, Brady was driving recklessly down the alley in the big Silverado. He stopped next to the couch in the alley. The homeless guys were gone, but some of their blankets remained. Brady threw the blankets aside and then he retrieved a gas can from the back of the truck. He doused the couch with gasoline, threw the People magazine on top, and then lit it on fire. He roared away up the alley in the truck as the sofa burst into flames.

When Ashley and Jack Wrangler returned to LA, Ashley just wanted to get back to her apartment on Palm Avenue and get back to her normal life. Wrangler had other plans for her. He wanted to take her to his place in Malibu. She now really felt like she was being held hostage. She didn't outwardly protest. She just pouted on the car ride back to Malibu. Wrangler didn't notice because he was on the phone to his accountant the entire trip. They finally arrived to his palatial gated estate on Point Dume. The car stopped in front of a huge marble fountain that Jack had imported from Italy. Ashley stared at the fountain, thought it was beyond ostentatious, but that didn't come out of her mouth. "Wow, that's incredible," Ashley said.

Wrangler stared at the fountain, which was his pride and joy. "You like it? I had it brought over from Florence. I dropped two hundred and fifty grand on it," he said.

The driver unloaded the bags from the car. "Want me to take them in?" The driver asked.

"No, that's good," Wrangler said, done with the driver.

The driver got into his car and drove away without so much as a thank you from Wrangler. Ashley noticed this. She was really beginning to despise Jack Wrangler, but she guessed she had better tolerate it a bit longer.

She and Jack Wrangler pulled their own bags into the huge mansion and were met at the door by Felecia, the maid, who took the bags.

The house was ostentatious by Liberace's standards. A sweeping Marble foyer served as the entrance with and gold circular staircase that spiraled up to the second floor. A huge picture window in the back opened up to a view of the Santa Monica Bay and Paradise Cove. Ashley walked toward the window and stared out at the ocean. So, this is where you end up when you have arrived, thought Ashley.

"Want a drink, Ash?" Wrangler asked.

"Sure," she said, knowing it was a bad idea. She also knew it would make this experience more bearable. Wrangler ordered Felecia to make them some Plymouth gin and tonics.

They got the drinks, and Wrangler took Ashley back to his den, where the walls were covered with pictures of him: He with various other celebrities, with the president, various ex girlfriends, and supermodels. Ashley gazed at the photos and wondered if the other women felt the same way about Jack Wrangler as she did. She wondered if they got what they wanted out of him. Wrangler pointed to the various photos and told a story about each one. He was very full of himself, Ashley thought. He was a fucking prick, Ashley thought. The drink went down her esophagus and hit her stomach and soon a warm feeling was spreading throughout her body.

Jack Wrangler sat on a leather love seat and Ashley sat on his lap and wrapped her arms around him. She kissed him. "Thanks for a great trip," Ashley said. Wrangler smiled, and was putty in her hands.

"Did you have a good time, baby?" Wrangler asked, as he was running his hands all over her body.

"Yes, it was unforgettable. The greatest New Year of my life," Ashley said.

"It's only gonna' get better from here, Ash. Tomorrow we're gonna' get you in Dina's class, and get you some new pictures and get Michael going on you, so you can start working," Wrangler said.

That was just what Ashley wanted to hear. She kissed Wrangler again and then started unzipping his pants and shirt. Within moments she had his pants undone and his cock, half hard and all the way in her mouth.

Felecia walked in with a tray of appetizers and stopped short. This was nothing new to her.

"Just set them over there, Felecia," Wrangler said waving her away. She sat the appetizer tray down on a table and walked out as Ashley gave Wrangler one of the top ten blow jobs of his life.

Brady picked up a hooker, Naomi, on Sunset and brought her up to the house. They smoked crack together out by the pool. She looked around the place like she was casing it. This wasn't the first house in the hills that she had been to.

Brady told her about Crystal. That she had died, and the hooker tried to act like she cared. Really, they both were just waiting for the next turn at the crack pipe.

"Smokin' the devil's dick, that what we be doing," the hooker said laughing as Brady took another hit. Brady exhaled the white smoke from his lungs and it drifted above the swimming pool and then dissipated over the Los Angles basin. Brady wondered if crack smoke contributed to air pollution in Los Angeles. The dogs were growling and rough housing with each other nearby. Naomi was clearly afraid of them.

"My ex girlfriend is fucking Jack Wrangler, "Brady said.

"Jack Wrangler, the movie star?" Naomi asked.

Brady nodded; the crack was surging through his brain and out of his fingertips and toes. He watched her take another hit and couldn't wait for his turn again. He didn't say anything else.

After they ran out of crack, Brady drove her back down to the boulevard and dropped her off. Brady turned onto Sunset, not knowing where he was going, but not ready to go home.

Twenty One

The following weeks were a whirlwind for Ashley. She signed with the agent, Michael Levin. She sat in the office with Levin and Jack Wrangler and felt embarrassed by their prior encounter. Levin didn't seem the least bit bothered by it. He was clearly in the pocket of Jack Wrangler. When Wrangler said jump, Levin asked how high. There was a little twinkle in Michael Levin's eye when he hugged Ashley as they left. Ashley knew that Wrangler was leaving for Europe in a week to do a movie and she couldn't wait. She just wanted to go back to her apartment. She had a whole new expensive wardrobe at this point that Wrangler had bought her and she doubted she would ever wear anything she had at home again.

Chloe had called her a few times. Jeremy Bone had called her a couple of times, wondering why she hadn't showed up for class. She didn't call them back. It occurred to her how people in Kansas never did that. People in Kansas wouldn't dream of not returning someone's phone call. People in Los Angeles didn't return phone calls as a statement. It spoke volumes when you didn't return someone's phone call. It meant that you were too busy, too important, too occupied to take a minute and return a call. It meant that those people were no longer of use to you.

In Ashley's case, she didn't return the calls because she was ashamed of herself. She couldn't tell Jeremy Bone the truth that she was going to Dina's class, because Dina was considered the pinnacle of acting instructors in Los Angles and to be in the A-list, you had to study with her. Ashley didn't want to return Chloe's calls because she knew that Chloe was sober and she didn't want to tell Chloe the truth: That she had allowed herself to be held hostage by Jack Wrangler at his Malibu mansion, and she was drinking nonstop with Wrangler and having sex with him several times a day. Not because she wanted to, but because she felt it was what she had to do. Anything it takes. She had made that vow to herself early on and she was doing *everything it took*. Ashley hadn't even talked to her mom much. When she did, it was all very superficial. She had yet to mention that she was "dating" Jack Wrangler. It would all come out soon enough, and then people would know why Ashley had no time or energy to return phone calls.

Ashley wondered if this was what it meant to sell your soul to the devil, and she looked over at Jack Wrangler sitting next to her in the car. They were on their way to a Beverly Hills designer to pick out Ashley's gown for the Golden Globes. She was going as Jack's date later that week. She looked at him as he talked on the phone to one of his mafia buddies in New York and wondered if he *was* the devil. He was pretty close to the devil. He was pretty close.

Brady had gone through an initial binge on drugs, hookers, and other debaucherous behavior upon hearing that Ashley was dating Jack Wrangler. The whole spiral of self destruction cumulated when Brady ended up at the gay bar, Rage, in West Hollywood and then participated in a meth fueled orgy in a sleazy Hollywood Boulevard motel with two gay males from the club.

Brady was horrified in the morning when he realized what he had done. He wondered if he had contracted AIDS and the thought terrified him to the core. He drove away from the motel so utterly disgusted with himself that he called Alcoholic's Anonymous later that afternoon from Crystal's house. They directed him to a meeting in West Hollywood at the log cabin, where Brady stood up crying and shaking and admitted that he was an alcoholic. Chloe was there with her new girlfriend and she clapped for the newcomer and thought that she recognized him from somewhere.

Ashley got to see firsthand what all the glitz and glamour was about when she attended the Golden Globes with Jack. She was dressed in a $10,000 Christian Dior gown. She drank Champagne in the back of a stretch limo on their way to the Beverly Hilton Hotel where the Globes were held. Jack was nominated as best actor for a movie, Lethal Consequences, he had done last year playing a mafia hit man. They crawled down Santa Monica behind a procession of limousines headed for the same place. Ashley looked out the window and saw Palm Avenue as they passed by it and she wondered if her plants were dead inside her apartment.

Jack Wrangler took call after call from people who were wishing him luck. Ashley could tell that Jack was nervous and really wanted the award, though he kept telling people, "it was no big fucking deal." She knew that he wanted it and not only that, expected it. Ashley decided at the last minute, just before they arrived to the red carpet to call her mother. She told her mom to turn on the television to the Golden Globes and watch for her on the red carpet. Her mom was confused, but excited and promised she would watch for her. Adrenalin started pumping through Ashley's veins as they got closer.

They finally arrived at the hotel and someone opened the door. They climbed out to a cavalcade of camera flashes. Ashley stepped onto the red Carpet and Jack took her hand and the lights and camera flashes were blinding as they stepped onto the red carpet.

Ashley's mom rushed into the living room where Jim Duncan was sitting, drinking a Coors and watching a National Geographic special on television.

"Change the channel to the Golden Globe Awards. Ashley is going to be on the red carpet," Ginny said.

Jim frowned. "What?"

Ginny grabbed the remote out of his hand and started flipping through the channels until she landed on the Golden Globes. A wide shot showed the Beverly Hilton Hotel with a long line of limos lined up on the street waiting to make their way into the hotel. It cut to the glamorous shots of the stars walking up to the camera, and being interviewed by an over bubbly hostess.

"I hate this crap," Jim said.

"Oh shush," Ginny said, anxiously watching for Ashley.

A moment later they saw Ashley walking up the red carpet in the fantastic green gown holding hands with Jack Wrangler, who was wearing his signature Way Farers.

"There she is! There's Ashley!" Ginny shrieked.

Jim sat up in his chair leaning into the television in awe.

"I'll be damned," Jim said. Ashley was smiling broadly and flashes were going off all around her. The bubbly hostess pushed her microphone in Wrangler's face.

"Any thoughts, Jack, on the outcome of your nominated category?" the hostess asked.

Wrangler looked into the camera with a crooked smile. "May the best man win." Ashley and Wrangler disappeared off screen.

Jim was still sitting up, electrified. Their phone started ringing immediately. Ginny answered it. "Yes, we just saw her. I'm speechless," Ginny said into the phone.

Ashley's face made close ups many times during the broadcast. Jack Wrangler kept drinking throughout the ceremony and won his category, B*est Actor in a Motion Picture, Drama.* He made a sarcastic remark during his acceptance speech. "Let's hope the Academy gets it this year," he said without one ounce of humility.

Jillian was sat inside the Sybil Brand correctional facility for women, dressed in her jail house blues. She was playing cards with a group of convicts at a table and the Golden Globes was on television. She suddenly spotted Ashley on the television screen and she took notice. She dropped her cards and walked away from the table and stood in front of the television. A small smile rose on her face, as Jack Wrangler came back to the table and hugged Ashley.

After the awards show, Ashley accompanied Jack to a grueling two hour press conference, where the winners were grilled about their awards from reporters with the various media outlets on hand. The cameras never stopped flashing. Jack was drunk and wearing his sunglasses and shooting around his usual thuggish witticisms that everyone laughed way too hard at. Many people were looking at Ashley and she realized she had to remain "on" with a big white and wide smile on her face at all times. Everyone seemed to want to know who she was. She did look smashing in that green velvet gown, and some man told her she looked better than any woman in attendance.

After that they got into their limo and went to a party hosted by HBO at a restaurant on Third Street. Ashley started to feel claustrophobic and awkward as Jack mingled and everyone congratulated him and wanted to get pictures with him. Flashes from cameras were constant. Ashley didn't know anybody, and the other women were not exactly welcoming her with open arms. In fact, she detected a sense of contempt coming her way from many of the women in the room.

She saw several stars she idolized growing up, and several up and comers and they all gathered to kiss Jack's ring. A young English actress who had won another category stepped up to take a picture with Jack. He put his arm around her and at one point Ashley noticed him touch the girl's ass. Hot blood ran up into Ashley's face. What a pig, she thought. A drunken boorish, pig. To add insult to injury, Jack Wrangler kissed the actress on the lips after the picture was taken. They stood there a few moments staring into each other's eyes and going gaga for each other while Ashley looked like Cinderella alone at the ball.

Ashley just wanted to leave at that moment. She wanted to break away and just walk back to her apartment. She wanted to get away from all of the sickness, phoniness, and false adoration. These people were making movies and you would think they had just cured poverty and cancer all at once the way they were behaving.

Ashley listened to the cruel laughter and the catty chatter coming from every direction and she felt as if she would suffocate. She wanted out of there immediately. Jack Wrangler made his way back over to her. He could see that something was bothering her.

"What's wrong, Ash?" he asked.

"I want to leave," Ashley said.

"We just fuckin' got here. What's wrong, babe?" Jack said.

"I just want to go back to my own apartment. I'm done with all this," Ashley said.

Jack tried to put his arms around her, but she broke away from him and pushed through the crowd with him chasing after her.

"Ashley! What's wrong, babe?" he kept saying.

She broke outside of the party and was immediately photographed by at least twenty photographers. She started walking quickly down the street that was cordoned off and blocked for the event. The night was cold for Los Angeles and she could see her breath as she kept walking. Jack Wrangler did not follow her, but she could hear him yelling her name.

Helicopters were circling the area, and she could see spotlights sweeping the sky in the distance. Her phone was blowing up with calls from Jack Wrangler, his assistant, and Tony Spinelli. She ignored the calls and walked the back streets ten blocks to Palm Avenue and up the hill to her apartment. She was freezing in the gown but got energized and sober on her way home.

Ashley arrived at her apartment, which she hadn't seen for weeks. She locked and bolted the door behind her. She turned off her phone and stripped out of the $10,000 Christian Dior evening gown and collapsed onto her own bed. Thoughts raced through her mind about how she had been to the ball she had always wanted to attend, but wasn't sure if she liked what she had seen. She also realized that she had manufactured the fight with Jack because she just wanted to come home to her own apartment and that he would probably just want her more as a result. She drifted off into a deep sleep.

Twenty Two

The day after the Golden Globes, Jack sent a dozen red roses to Ashley's apartment, and left a bunch of messages. Tony Spinelli finally caught her outside of her apartment and begged her to go back to Jack. She finally relented and that afternoon she moved out to Jack's Point Dume compound. He was leaving for Europe to do a film, but had convinced her to stay at and "take care" of his place while he was gone.

In the weeks that followed, things moved into high gear. Ashley started working privately with acting guru, Dina Solomon. Michael's agency hired a top Beverly Hills PR firm to make Ashley the hottest commodity unknown actress in Hollywood. Her picture, profile, and interviews were in nearly every magazine. The agency was suddenly flooded with offers and scripts for Ashley.

Michael Levin and Jack both pressured her to do an Indie project by a hot new writer/director called "Cat and Mouse." She would play a kidnap victim who was abducted by a serial killer. Her character is then raped and sodomized for weeks, until she finally psychologically outsmarts her captor. Ashley did not want to do the project, thought it was exploitational, and knew she would have to do several nude rape scenes. Michael and Jack convinced her that it would be controversial and jumpstart her career. Maybe even get her some nominations for next year's awards.

She met with the writer/director for lunch at the Chateau Marmont. He was a typical chubby film geek and could barely speak he was so intimidated by her beauty. She signed the ink to do the picture in early February. She was to be paid $50,000 for the part, plus a piece of the back end. She talked to her mom back in Kansas daily. She had yet to talk to her dad, but her mom had told her that he smiled briefly when he had seen her on television. That made Ashley feel better.

Brady got his act together and was going to AA meetings at the Log Cabin daily. He was working with an AA sponsor who had him doing a bunch of step work on his relationship with Ashley. Brady was taking that one day at a time, just like he was taking his sobriety one day at a time. He continued living at Crystal's house in the hills and paid the electric bills. He knew the day would probably come that he would have to leave. Possession was 99 percent of the law he had heard. He was working a lot, and was out on movie and TV sets daily supplying the various exotic animals. One day he came home and all of the electronic gear and the Range Rover were gone from Crystal's house. Brady guessed that Derek had done it. He knew the gate code. He probably had a key. Brady didn't report it to the police.

Brady heard from his mom that the whole town of Colby was abuzz with gossip about Ashley. He tried to not let it bother him. He tried to stay in a place of gratitude and acceptance.

Chloe was also going to the Log Cabin daily, and was a rising star in Alcoholics Anonymous. She was elected secretary of the noon meeting at the Log Cabin. She planned on going back to school and getting a degree in addiction counseling. She had finally come out as gay to her family and everyone else. It didn't end up being much of a big deal, and Chloe felt very relieved. She had a new girlfriend, a cute little Japanese girl she had met at the cabin. She visited Jillian once a week at the jail, and put money "on the books" for her. Jillian had accepted a plea deal and was waiting to start serving a two year sentence at a state prison for women in Kern County.

One day Brady was dispatched to a movie set at Raleigh Studios in Manhattan Beach. He had to take a Rottweiler down there to be in a scene. The movie being shot was "Cat and Mouse."

Brady parked the truck and was directed by a production assistant to take the dog to a sound stage across the lot. As Brady walked the dog over there on a leash he noticed a trailer that had the name "Ashley Duncan," in big letters on the door.

A shot of adrenalin jolted him as he stood there staring at her name. He remembered that she had a restraining order against him. He hadn't seen her in months. He wondered if she was going to have him arrested or thrown off the set. He remembered reading somewhere that she had signed to do this movie, but he had forgotten about it when he left for the set with the dog.

He continued on and as he rounded the corner of the trailer he ran right into Ashley. She was wearing a long kimono and was smoking a cigarette on the side of the trailer. She froze upon seeing him and the dog, and he froze too.

"Hi Ashley." He said.

"Hi," she said staring at him. A faint smile formed on her face.

"I forgot that you were working on this. I have to deliver this dog," Brady said, almost stammering.

She looked at him a long moment. "It's ok," she said.

She approached the dog leaning down to get a better look. "Can I pet him?" she asked.

"Sure," Brady said.

Ashley started petting the dog. She looked tired and sad. Brady detected that she was high by her glassy and pinned eyes. She kneeled in front of the dog and let him lick her face.

"He's a sweetheart! What's his name?" She asked.

"Bandit," Brady said.

"Bandit? Bandit, huh," she said sadly and she kept petting and hugging the dog as Brady stood there. Ashley took another drag off of her cigarette and then threw it away.

"You started smoking?" Brady said.

"Yeah. Everybody does it," she said. "How have you been?"

"Good. Good. I'm working a lot. Living in the Hollywood Hills. Things are good," Brady said.

"I'm happy for you. You look good," Ashley said. She noticed the tattoo on his arm and she lifted his arm to get a better look. She noticed her initials in the center of the tornado and a wry smile came to her face. She let go of his arm.

Brady suddenly felt on pins and needles. They stared at each other a moment and Ashley's gaze went back to the dog.

"So, you're really doing it. You are really doing this thing!" Brady said, trying to seem excited for her. Ashley lit another cigarette and Brady could see that her hands were shaking.

"Yeah. Things happened kind of fast. My mom's coming out here to visit next month. Dad's not coming. He won't leave the farm, you know how that goes," Ashley said.

The second AD, a grubby bearded hipster with an ear piece on came walking up.

"Oh, there's the dog we were waiting for," the AD said. "Five minutes, Ash," the AD said, and then walked away.

"Well, it was nice seeing you," Brady said. "Say hello to your mom for me."

"Yeah, I will," Ashley said. She leaned into him and hugged him tightly. Her hair smelled like cigarette smoke. She felt frail. She finally let go of him and backed away petting the dog.

"I'd better get ready. It was really nice seeing you," Ashley said.

"Take care of yourself," Brady said.

"You too. Bye bandit!" she waved as she backed away. She took another drag off of her cigarette and tossed it before disappearing into her trailer.

Brady continued on with Bandit, his heart was fluttering.

Rob Neighbors

Acknowledgements

Putting a book together is a lot of work and I could not have done it on my own. I would like to thank Don Potter, a fellow writer, for his constant encouragement as I was writing the first draft, and it was he who pushed me to go for 80,000 words.

I would like to thank Nia Campbell for line editing the book. She had many great comments and suggestions and I used most of them. I would also like to thank some of my test readers, who read the first draft and offered comments.

Jessica Chortkoff was the photographer for the front cover art, and Arune Villiers was the model. Also, I wish to thank Rand Chortkoff for letting me use his house for the photo shoot.

I would like to thank Amy Pierce for her invaluable consulting services on this book. She helped me throughout the whole book layout process and offered excellent ideas and constructive criticism. She also did some of the photo editing and the back cover design. Her attention to detail is something that I lack, and I always need another eye on the ball.

Finally, I would like to thank my kids, Willie, and Pia, my parents, Bud and Nancy Cranford, and Tom and Lynette Neighbors for being supportive of me, even during the darkest times. Those days are over now.

Made in the USA
San Bernardino, CA
06 April 2015